TRADING INTO SHADOW

TRADING INTO SHADOW

THE MAGIC BELOW PARIS™ BOOK ONE

C. M. SIMPSON

MICHAEL ANDERLE

DISRUPTIVE IMAGINATION

LMBPN Publishing
PMB 196, 2540 South Maryland Pkwy
Las Vegas, NV 89109

First US edition, March 2019
Version 1.02, September 2020
eBook ISBP 978-1-64202-144-8
Print ISBN 978-1-64202-192-9

TRADING INTO SHADOW TEAM

Thanks to our Beta Readers

Kelly ODonnell, Rachel Heise, Mary Morris , Sarah Weir

Thanks to our JIT Readers

Nicole Emens
Diane L. Smith
Jackey Hankard-Brodie
Daniel Weigert
Dorothy Lloyd
Larry Omans
Misty Roa
Angel LaVey
Charles Tillman
John Ashmore

Editor

SkyHunter Editing Team

DEDICATION

This is for all those who believed in me enough that, eventually, I had the courage to believe in myself.

Thank you.
—C.M. Simpson

To Family, Friends and
Those Who Love
to Read.
May We All Enjoy Grace
to Live the Life We Are
Called.

— Michael

SHADOW MONSTER AMBUSH

Marchant ran through the caverns, fleeing shadows that reached through the dark. She ran from their flaming eyes, and grasping claws, trying to get out of the range of limbs that stretched and flowed like molasses through the cracks of the Irth. It wasn't long before she'd put some distance between herself and the shadow monsters, but still, she ran. A little distance was never going to be enough.

Marsh towed a frightened pack mule—ridden by the two children she'd managed to grab and toss aboard—along the trail of glow rods. They were meant to mark the safe zone, forming a barrier the shadow monsters could not cross. Trouble was, the damned things stalked the line of light, and if any of the glows went out? Well, that was what caravan guards were for—if you could afford to hire them.

Or if your boss wasn't too tight-fisted and hired light, or stuck you with a caravan and no guards of your own. You'da thought he'd take better care of the goods he needed her to deliver, even if he didn't give two gems' worth of a damn about her. Well, she'd be saying something about that when she got back to Kerrenin's Ledge. *If she got back...*

Screams rang out behind her as she fled the battle, the rest of the caravan proper strung out in her wake. She wondered how many of the guards would survive, and how many had already died. They'd stepped in to fill the path between the sudden black of a section of dead glows and the leading mules just as the monsters had struck. It soon became clear they were outmatched, and the caravan's mage would have had no time to repair the trail and drive them back.

Obeying the orders to run, the rest of the caravan had turned back toward the safety of the last waystation. Having paid the least to join it, Marchant and her mule had been assigned the last position in line—the most dangerous place in any traveling party. Even the families looking to settle in the caverns around Ruins Hall had paid more, but Marsh hadn't thought twice about scooping up their kids and giving them a ride out of danger, when she'd taken the lead.

Their parents were following a little way behind, having had to round up their other children. They were trying to control two mules apiece, not an easy feat when the beasts were panicking. Marsh kept moving, the rest of the caravan trailing behind her. She even thought they'd make the waystation— right up until the glows on either side of the path went out.

She'd barely had time to register the loss of light before the mule brayed in terror and dropped to its knees, pulling the lead tight in her hand. Marsh ducked and felt the air move above her, but she didn't stop. She spun and snagged the kids before they fell or became shadow fodder, then picked a gap where the shadows seemed lighter and bolted toward it.

They'd passed a side tunnel leading into the gods knew where. Its only importance was that it sat just off the main trail and the caravan hadn't avoided it, so maybe the shadows didn't come from there. Maybe it led somewhere they didn't like to go.

She pushed aside the idea that anything that frightened shadow monsters into avoiding a place should frighten her as well. The glows frightened them, and she wasn't afraid of those. Struggling to carry both children beyond the path, Marchant let her eyes adjust to the dark. If she was lucky, the mule's thrashing and bellowing would distract the shadows long enough for them to get away.

Marsh didn't want to think about what was happening to those still on the path as they made it to the tunnel wall. Stopping long enough to set the bigger child on his feet, she tucked his little sister under her arm more securely, grabbed the boy's hand, and hurried quickly around an outcropping of rock, seeking to put anything she could between her and the chaos at her back.

If their luck held, the monsters would go after the easy prey on the path before seeking any stragglers who made it into the dark. A quick glance showed her that the markers farther up the trail were still alight. She didn't want to count on them staying that way, though, so she headed for the junction, leaving the glow behind her.

They reached the side passage, glad of the darkness

wrapping around them like a cloak. The ground was rougher here, not worn smooth by the passage of thousands of hooves and feet, and Marchant slowed.

"Don't stop," the boy whispered, his eyes flashing white, his voice too loud in the dark. "Please don't stop."

He bolted past her, dragging her forward as he wound around boulders and stalagmites, his breathing fast and panicked. Under her arm, the little girl hung, as silent as a sack of shrooms but ten times heavier. For a minute Marsh worried that she might be carrying a dead weight, but there wasn't any time to check.

The way the boy was running, the shadow monsters had to be hot on their heels. She almost looked back but couldn't risk taking the chance. If the monsters *were* behind them, the last thing she needed was to fall. The only trouble was that not knowing how much of a lead she had meant she didn't know how much faster she needed to go —and the ground was growing more uneven by the second.

Soon it wouldn't matter how far behind them the monsters were; they were going to have to slow down. Even as Marchant thought it, the boy suddenly pulled her sideways, ducking between two stalagmites and wriggling his way into a crevice barely wide enough to take them.

Stopping just in front of it, Marchant dropped his hand so she could shift the girl from under her arm to across her chest, then she squeezed into the gap after him. Why she should didn't even cross her mind. She was just running on instinct, the same as he was—and he seemed to know the way.

Stupid, she thought, feeling rock scrape and catch at her pack and clothes. *Stupid, stupid, stupid.*

But it was done, and there was no going back.

She almost got stuck a few feet in, but the boy grabbed her by the pack's shoulder straps and pulled her free. This time, when she noticed them, his eyes looked almost black, but the impression faded as he dragged her to one side of the crevice, then tried to push the closest large rock in front of the entrance.

"You're sure?"

It was a dumb question, but Marsh asked it anyway. The boy gave her a look that told her just how dumb it was and put his weight behind the boulder. If she didn't intervene, the kid was going to do himself an injury.

"Here, let me."

She set the girl on the ground beside her, ignoring her whimper even as it relieved her mind, and slithered back against the wall. Putting her hands on the rock beside the boy's, Marsh helped him push it across the floor into the narrow gap, then they filled the space above it with smaller rocks and wedged pebbles around its base.

"Let's hope we don't need to go through there to get back," Marsh said, and he glared at her.

"We're not going back," he countered and looked around the cavern they'd crawled into.

Marsh followed his gaze—and gasped when something wrapped itself around her leg. Her hand dropped to her sword as she looked down. Two large blue eyes looked back at her, and the grip on her leg eased.

"Up," the little girl demanded, stretching out her hands. "Up."

Taking a shaky breath, Marchant lifted the child.

"You're heavy, you know," she grumbled, but the child merely wrapped her hands around Marsh's neck and clung tight.

Marsh sighed.

"Fine!"

She surveyed the cavern, noting the presence of glow moss in shiny gold patches on its walls and several of the upright pillars. After the darkness they'd run through, it was almost blindingly bright, and Marsh found she needed to adjust her eyes. Like so many of the spaces in the caverns, this one was manmade.

Marsh eyed the soaring pillars. Their edges were too square to have resulted from a stalagmite and a stalactite meeting, and they had the dull finish of ancient concrete in any case. The cavern walls were far too straight to be natural formations as well, even with the holes left by fallen rubble. The whole thing made her pause. She stretched out a hand and grabbed the boy by the shoulder.

"Wait."

He hesitated, briefly looking back at her over his shoulder, before turning to stare at the cavern. Marsh kept her hand on him and searched her memory for any mention of these ruins, but there was none. She couldn't even be sure the side tunnel had been explored, let alone the crack she'd crawled into.

Running her mind back over the path she'd taken, Marsh tried to work out where she was—and exactly how she was going to get down to Ruins Hall. In spite of losing the mule and everything it had been carrying, she still had one delivery to make. She hadn't entrusted everything to the pack saddles—and Kearick, her boss had been especially anxious that this package made it to its destination.

Well, she could do that.

Turning what she thought she knew of the caverns through her mind, Marchant tried to solve the problem from two angles. She could try heading up to the surface to work her way through the canyons of the ancient city's ruins. That thing was vast, stretching as far as the eye could see from the watchtowers above Kerrenin's Ledge.

Or she could try to work her way through the tunnels until she could get back to the main trail. It would probably be as easy as going up to the surface, given that the ruins would block her view of the hills. Most likely safer, too. People came back from the Underneath, not so much from the surface lands.

That made the decision easy. After all, she had two other lives to think of, not just her own.

"This way," she said, setting out across the glow moss cavern, and ignoring the expression on the boy's face. She could do without having to explain herself to a ten-year-old.

He stared at her for a moment, then trotted after her. Either he agreed with her decision, or he wanted to go wherever she was taking his sister. Marchant didn't care which; she just kept walking. Stepping over the pointed caps and bulbous mounds of fungi, she headed for the far side of the cavern, and then followed the broad, flat-ceilinged corridor farther into the complex.

This one led to an even wider space, one with small chambers around its edges. Marchant imagined that the Ancients had once lit all these spaces, but now they crouched in the dark, and she had no way of knowing what lay within. Surveying the area before her, she noted the two ledges tiered above the first, running up to a sweeping overhang that ringed the cavern. There were three wide corridors leading off from the center of each wall, and more overhangs draped in glow moss, lichen and stalactites.

The size of it gave her pause, and she wondered just how high the walls of the chasm ran. From the looks of it, it might even lead to the surface. A tug on her sleeve interrupted her thoughts, and she looked down. Before she could utter a word, the boy laid a finger across his lips, his eyes wide with alarm.

Marchant nodded and raised her finger to her mouth to show she understood.

No talking.

The boy didn't move, but regarded her carefully, his eyes wide as a schrobuck's caught in a search lamp. Marsh waited for him to explain, feeling his little sister's arms tightening around her neck. When the kid gave her a swift nod and pulled her around a corner and through a narrow gap, Marsh followed without a sound.

In the small chamber beyond, she was surprised to see the child drop into a swift crouch and turn to face the door. She took a breath, meaning to ask him what was going on, but he raised his finger again, the whites of his eyes flashing in the dark. Marsh lowered his sister to the ground and turned to face the gap.

A sharp tug on her leg made her look down as the boy signaled her to crouch beside him. Frowning, she glanced back to the gap but obeyed, starting when she heard the sudden rush of claws and muffled barks from the hall beyond, and again when the girl wriggled between them.

The three of them stayed that way for some time, barely breathing as they listened to the pack foraging in the main cavern. Panicked rustles and squeaks would be followed by an excited yap, and then a whistling squeal. The sounds kept on for what seemed like forever, and then suddenly ceased. The boy laid a hand on Marchant's knee.

"What…" she began, but he shook his head.

Frowning with impatience, Marsh pushed to her feet. It didn't matter how scared the kid was; they had to get going.

"We don't have time—"

She choked on her words when a huffing cough echoed through the hall and down the corridor—a hoshkat!

Frenzied barking greeted the sound, and claws rushed and scrabbled again. Marsh imagined the pack scattering in a dozen different directions, each animal desperate to get as far from the big feline as it could. The kat screamed in reply, the echoes of its cry rebounding through the complex. The little girl gave a squeak of fright, and her brother clapped his hand across her mouth.

2

KIDS, KATS, AND KRYPTHUNDS

Marsh stood, and crept closer to the gap leading out of their hiding place. Looking back, she surveyed the room and saw the faint outline of what might be a hidden door at the rear. There wasn't any other obvious way out. Peering up the corridor, she strained her eyes trying to look through the black, but she couldn't see the kat. The barking stopped, and a shadow crossed the reflected light of the glow moss.

Marsh backed quietly away, touching the boy's shoulder as she passed. He'd wrapped his arm around his sister and was holding her tight, his focus torn between Marsh and keeping an eye on the entrance. With his free hand, he searched the floor for loose stones—like that would do him any good.

One hit from a piece of rock and the hoshkat would be on him like a fly on manure, but with far worse consequences. A rock to the head was only going to piss it off. Marsh hurried over to the outline and pulled her dagger, running the short blade along it until she found a groove. It didn't take long to work out that they didn't have time to free the door from the frame.

She moved slowly back to where the boy and his sister were crouched. He looked at her, his eyes holding the question he was afraid to ask.

Marchant shook her head.

There was no other exit.

The hoshkat's distinctive cough came, again, followed by a loud snuffling as it scented the air. Marsh wrapped her arm around the two children and gave them a brief hug, then stood and set herself squarely between them and the door. There was no way in the Shadow's Dark she was going to be able to save them, but she had to try. She drew her short sword and settled into readiness. Maybe she could keep the big beast busy long enough for them to sneak out of the room past it. Maybe...

Sudden movement exploded in the corridor, followed by a yelp of fright and the frantic scrabble of claws. A small, dark form shot through the gap in the wall and bolted toward them, looking over its shoulder as it came. It fled past Marsh, who had to choose between trying to hit it or dealing with the hoshkat that was sure to follow.

Their only hope was that the kat wouldn't be able to fit through the gap, or... Marsh grabbed hold of her whirling thoughts. She knew the kat would fit. A full-grown hoshkat could go where most adult humans went, especially a slightly-smaller-than-average-one like her. She would just have to face it, and either hope she could beat it or that something intervened.

The kat sniffed the air again, then rubble shifted beneath

its weight. The shadows deepened beyond the gap as the hoshkat's large form blocked the light. Her eyes caught the slightly lighter shadows of the clear space above its back.

"Shadow's Heart," she whispered.

The damn thing really *was* going to fit.

Even as she thought it, the cat lowered its head, a growl rumbling from its throat as it stalked into the chamber. Marsh did not doubt that she had its attention. Its gaze was fixed firmly on her face as its growl stroked her skin. She shuddered and readied her blade. Behind her, the girl whimpered and was hushed, and claws skittered on stone, then fell silent.

Marsh took a slow, deep breath and looked into the hoshkat's azure eyes.

"It's time you left," she told it, and its lips curled back from its teeth.

A second growl echoed through the chamber and the big beast crouched.

Marsh wrapped her free hand around the sword hilt so that she had a two-handed grip and faced the kat. She figured she only had one chance, and she was going to need all the strength she had.

"You're making a really bad choice," she told the kat, staring into its eyes and really wishing she didn't have to kill it—or die trying. "You really are."

"Don't!" the boy cried—and Marsh's world changed.

She fell, although her feet were firmly anchored to the ground. Yet she fell, and the hoshkat rose to meet her, swallowing her with its eyes until their thoughts met and mingled. Marsh snarled at it as she prepared for its strike, her voice echoing in the chamber. The kat lifted its lips, assessing her with a steady gaze.

"We're both going to die because of this," Marsh told it, drawing the sword hilt close to her shoulder and preparing to meet the kat's leap.

"No!"

Somewhere in another world where her body mirrored the actions of her mental self, Marsh heard the boy shout in angry denial.

"Sorry, kid."

Her lips moved, her voice soft in the stillness surrounding them, but Marchant's attention didn't shift. She couldn't let it. She would have one chance, like the kat, but it was the kat who had to choose which way this meeting went. It could die, or it could live. It only had to turn away.

If it turned, she would let it go. If it didn't pursue them through the caverns, she would let it go, and it would live to continue its hunt and feed its cubs. If it turned, she would not strike.

Marsh tried to picture what that would look like—her, standing, sword poised to meet its leap, while it turned back along its own length, trusting its strength and ferocity to be enough for her to let it depart. That was what she hoped for—the great beast moving back through the gap and out into the many-tiered cavern to hunt to its heart's content, but not her and the children. A truce between them.

She could imagine the alternative, too: the kat leaping to the attack and her stepping into the sweep of its paws and the gape of its jaws so that she could drive the blade deep into its chest or stomach. What followed…

Marsh swallowed hard against the fear in her throat. The blade would be trapped, and the kat would go into a frenzy. She wouldn't be able to let go, or it would take the children next. She stared at the beast opposite , willing it to leave her and her own cubs be.

The kat hissed and Marsh snapped free of its eyes, landing in her own skin more completely than before. She bent her knees, preparing to take the impact of its leap, but she didn't try to strike.

"Leave us alone," Marsh whispered. "Leave us—and live. My word for your life, your word for ours."

It made no sense to speak to the kat. The beasts were known for their ruthless cunning and their ability to kill, but their private lives were a mystery. How she'd known it had kits was beyond her. She locked eyes with it, but this time she didn't fall into its gaze.

The kat's lips rippled, a soft hiss gliding between them, and it glanced back to the chamber's entrance before returning its attention to her face. Marsh froze, hardly daring to breathe. The kat shifted its eyes to her blade as though noting that it hadn't moved and then it slowly uncoiled, pulling out of its crouch and extending its forepaws.

Marsh still didn't move, hardly able to believe her eyes as the big beast stretched in front of her, its eyes both wary and mocking as though daring her to attack. Marsh resisted the urge to strike, as well as the one that told her to shake her head. The boss might call her all kinds of stupid, but that wasn't one of them. She stayed as still as the walls around them as the kat gave a languid yawn before coming out of its stretch to curl back along its own length as she had imagined.

Marsh held her breath.

She was still holding it when the last of the kat disappeared. The gap in the wall was an empty patch against the darkness, although it was hard to tell if the kat was really gone or waiting just outside. The longer she stood there, the more Marsh became aware of the sounds traveling through the dark, including the distant cough as the hoshkat resumed hunting through the hall beyond.

The cough broke through her fear and Marsh slowly lowered the sword. It surprised her to find that the chamber was darker than she remembered. She turned, looking for the children, and saw only shadow, ink-black and thick as paint. Raising the sword, she thought about poking the darkness and then decided against it.

As effective as it would be, she didn't want to risk poking holes in either of the children—which reminded her that she didn't know either of their names. Until she'd grabbed them in the attack, there'd been no need, and their parents had discouraged them from talking to the other members of the caravan.

"Kids?" she asked, reluctant to take the single pace that would take her into the thick black.

And the shadow dropped away.

It was replaced by a slowly brightening glow. The light shuddered unsteadily as the boy held it in his cupped hands, his lips moving as though he were whispering it into existence. Beside him, his sister crouched, her eyes as wide as saucers—as if what her brother was doing was more impressive than the creature that had just left.

When the glow steadied, the boy huffed out a quick breath and pushed up onto one knee, setting the glow on top of the boulder beside him. His face looked drawn and pale in the light, and he wobbled unsteadily as he got to his feet. Marchant tossed a quick glance back toward the entrance and then focused on the boy.

"Are you okay?" she asked. It was his sister who answered.

"It always makes him tired."

"What does?"

"Playing with the shadows and the light. Mama gets so cross."

Marsh realized what she had seen.

"You called the shadows?" she asked as the boy sagged against the rock.

He nodded, and Marsh indicated the glow.

"And you made that."

This time it was more a statement of fact than a question. After all, she had watched it grow in his hands. Again he nodded. Marsh looked at the girl.

"Can you do the same thing?" she demanded.

The child stood and wound her hand around her brother's, ducking her head and looking up at Marsh through her fringe.

"Well?" Marsh insisted, and the child shook her head, pressing into the boy's side.

Before she could ask anything else, the boy spoke.

"Where are we going?"

"Ruins Hall," Marsh said and looked around the chamber. "Just as soon as I can remember the way."

"And the kat?"

"She won't come after us."

That got his attention.

"How do you know?"

Marsh shrugged.

"I just know."

His frown got deeper.

"How?"

Marsh frowned. It was a good question. In the end, she just shrugged and made a show of looking around the room.

"What do you think about staying here for the night?"

This time the boy didn't answer. He just plopped back down on the floor.

"They took our parents," he said.

For a moment Marsh thought he might say more, but then one of the nearby rocks stirred, its movement catching her eye. Marsh dropped her hand to the hilt of her sword and took a step toward it, but the little girl gave a horrified shriek and dropped down beside the rock, wrapping her arms around it.

As soon as she had, the "rock" shuddered, becoming a fluffy ball of black and gray fluff with striations of khaki and brown. A pointed snout and two pricked ears became apparent, and Marchant stared as the krypthund puppy turned its head and washed the little girl's face. The child looked at it adoringly, her blue eyes shifting to a glowing green. The pup froze, staring into her face as though mesmerized.

The boy looked across at her.

"Aisha, no!" he muttered. Marsh was sure that was supposed to come out as a shout.

Aisha glared at her brother, pursing her lips as she hung onto the dog.

"He is *my* puppy," she said in a tone that brooked no argument. "*All* mine!"

The fluffball wriggled closer.

Marchant looked from one to the other of them.

"What just happened?"

The boy shrugged.

"Don't know, but Dad said we should never look in a wild beast's eyes or we might lose our ability to think like a human."

Marchant's eyebrows lifted as the boy continued.

"He said I had to be careful because I had magic." His voice crumbled around the edges. "We were moving so we could be near the shadow mages." Marchant didn't know what to say when he added, "We were moving because of me."

Marsh heard the tears and searched frantically for something to head them off. In the end, it wasn't much.

"We need to eat," she said, unslinging her pack and setting it on the ground in front of them.

The boy watched her, eyes dull and face still drawn. Whatever he'd done, it seemed to have sapped him of all his energy. Marchant dug into her pack and pulled out a loaf of travel bread, and Aisha stepped cautiously closer. Her expression was still wary, but her eyes were on the bread. The pup was not so shy.

It watched as Marsh tore off a piece of bread and held it

out to the boy, panting slightly as he took it and held it in his lap. When Marsh did the same for the girl, the pup lunged forward, nipping the bread from Marsh's hands and turning away from them to wolf it down, its small jaws ripping and crunching through the crust.

"Hey!"

Aisha was not impressed, but Marsh grabbed her before she could try to get it back.

"I have some more."

When the little girl was nibbling her bread, Marsh took a small piece for herself, realizing she had another problem. There were three of them, not counting the hund. She only carried a couple of days' supplies in her pack, and the water canteen would need filling. She was going to have to get them to Ruins Hall quickly—or ask the boy to conjure up some more bread.

She wondered if he could.

3

A PATH THROUGH THE DARK

Marchant woke stiff, her eyes adjusting as she glanced around the chamber. The soft light of the glow made it easy to notice things she hadn't registered the night before—like the lockers lining one wall, the darker brown of a creeping mass of moss, and the water stain in one corner.

At least it was a stain and not an actual pool.

Marsh stood, checking on the children, who were curled under her blanket. She was sore from spending a night on the floor, and bone-achingly tired from the previous day's run and pushing the rubble across the gap leading into their refuge.

She was surprised to see the krypthund puppy curled up under Aisha's arm, but not surprised to see its gleaming eyes watching her as she stretched.

"Don't you have a home to go to?" she asked it, but it didn't respond except to raise its head and watch as she crossed to the nearest locker.

It was probably a waste of time, but Kearick would kick

her tail if she told him she'd seen them and not looked inside.

The first one was full of nothing but dust and black-furred moss, and the second had more of the same. It was as she went to open the third one that the puppy started to growl.

Marsh glanced at him.

"What? It's not like anyone cares."

But he wormed his way out from under the blanket, letting Aisha's arm drop to the floor as he trotted toward her. Marsh shook her head and laid her hand on the locker's door—and the pup gave a sharp bark and bounded over, sinking his sharp little teeth into her trouser leg and pulling.

Marsh let go of the latch and took a step in the direction the hund was yanking. The tips of her fingers snagged as she moved away, and it lifted a little, but she ignored it, following the determined tugs on her ankle.

"Okay, *fine*. Okay. I'll leave the lockers alone!"

At least she could tell Kearick she'd opened a couple and they'd been empty.

The pup had woken the children up with its growling, and they were staring at her in sleepy confusion. Aisha was pouting, as though it was Marsh's fault that the dog had left her. Suddenly the pout turned to wide-eyed alarm and she scrambled to her feet, climbing onto the boulder holding the glow with a shrill squeal of fear.

At the same time, the pup let go of Marchant's leg and bounced past her.

Marsh turned, both to see what it was doing and to see what had put the look of fear on Aisha's face. It didn't help that the boy had picked up the blanket and the pack and stepped up onto a piece of rubble of his own. What in the Shadows....

Oh.

The slender form of a cave viper had emerged from the locker's partially opened door. Its head and the first foot of its rough-scaled body were heading in her direction—or they had been until the pup had leapt between them. Marsh was just in time to see the pup bounce once to the left, feint forward, and then pounce.

The snake reared, and the pup's small jaws closed over its neck.

"Scruffknuckle!"

"Aisha!"

The cries were all the warning Marchant got, but she was still able to grab Aisha as the girl rushed by. She pulled the youngster back, relieved when the boy got a firm grip on his sister and freed Marsh up to help the dog.

Because he needed help. He might be doing something he'd seen his parents do, but he was nowhere near big enough to deal with the viper on his own. It hissed angrily as its body looped and coiled, trying to pull free of the pup's jaws. The pup growled in response, shaking his head from side to side.

Marsh brought her foot down on the snake's curling body before pulling the broad-bladed dagger at her belt. She only hoped the pup could keep its grip a couple of seconds longer. Scruff growled louder, pulling so that the snake stretched taut between Marsh's boot and his bite. It was all Marsh needed. She slashed the dagger down, severing the snake's body, and then kicked the remains into the gleaming, brown moss.

Scruff continued to growl and jerk his head back and forth, refusing to let go of the viper until it had stopped hissing and moving. And then he trotted over to the edge of the moss, and, with a flick of his head, threw those remains into the patch as well. He danced away quickly, yapping and snarling at the brown mass, before trotting over to Aisha.

"You are a *good* boy!" the little girl crooned, kneeling in front of him and tangling her fingers through the thick fur of his neck. "Bon puppy. *Tres, tres bon*! Yes, you are."

"You better come away," the boy said, and Marsh glanced at him.

He waved his hand toward the moss.

"It's not safe."

Not safe? How would he know? Marsh hadn't seen that kind of moss before, so it was unlikely the kid had. She glanced down at it—and then backed quickly away as a fringe of inch-long tendrils sprouted around the snake's carcass, lengthening as they curled around it and pulled it deeper into the spongy surface. A faint fizzing sound reached her ears as a light brown froth bubbled up around the body.

She backed off another couple of steps, surprised to see more tendrils sprouting around the edges of the brown mass—and mildly alarmed when they grew to a hand-length long and stroked curiously over the bare floor closest them.

"What *is* that?"

"Unfriendly?"

As the boy scrambled off the rock, Marsh noticed the color had returned to his cheeks and that his face looked less gaunt.

"We saving the bread for tonight?"

Marsh knew what he was asking. He wanted to know how much they had left, and as much as she didn't want to tell him, he had a right to know. Ten was old enough, right?

"Yes," she said, and would have left it at that if he hadn't pushed for more.

"So, when do we have to get to Ruins Hall by?" he asked, and his eyes darted to his sister.

Marsh understood; he wanted to know how many days' food they had left, but he didn't want to worry Aisha. That was good, because she didn't want to worry the child either.

"Three days at the most," she told him and wondered how in all the Shades she was going to manage it.

"Do you know the way?"

The question gave her pause. Truth? She didn't know the way. Did she think she could work it out? Sure. Well, maybe. It depended on how far these ruins went before they turned back into tunnels. Outside of Ruins Hall, this was her first experience with what the Ancients had left behind—and she didn't quite know what to make of it. What she did know was that she needed to get back out into the corridor if she was going to try to match up the maps in her head with the direction they'd traveled in.

"I can figure it out."

The boy stared at her, demanding an explanation, and Marsh gave an exasperated sigh.

"Look..." She paused. "What *is* your name, anyway."

"Well, it's not 'anyway,'" the boy snapped back, "but thanks for asking. It's about time you bothered. I'm Tamlin. She's Aisha."

Aisha was horrified.

"Tams! That's rude!"

"Yeah, well, it's not like she bothered to ask."

They were both right, but Marsh narrowed her eyes at them.

"I could just leave your asses right here!" The threat popped out before she realized she'd said it and she glared, daring them to protest her cussing.

Aisha put her hand on her hip and cocked her head.

"You're rude, too."

Tamlin let go of her arm and scooped up the glow

"Come on, Aysh. It's not like we haven't heard it before."

The little girl favored Marsh with one more glare before turning to follow her brother. Together, they started clearing the rocks away from the crack, leaving Marchant to collect her pack. The sight of Scruff earnestly pawing away the smaller stones beside Aisha made her smile, and she stooped to push the largest chunk of rubble out of the way.

"Ruins Hall, right?" she asked and slipped through the gap into the corridor beyond.

"Three days," Tamlin reminded her.

Leaning against the tunnel wall, she closed her eyes, and wondered if the boy would ever let up.

Twenty heartbeats later, she discovered he probably wouldn't.

"You can't work it out, can you?" he accused, sounding as snarky as anyone she'd ever crossed.

Marsh opened her eyes.

"I'd have better luck if you'd shut your mouth and let me concentrate."

Aisha stamped her foot and turned her back on the pair of them, the pup watching her every move.

"Well, we can't go back the way we came," the boy told her. "The trail won't be fixed, and the shadows will be waiting."

Like he was the expert!

Marsh bit back the retort that rose to her lips.

"I know that. Just let me sort it through. If you're quiet, it won't take long."

"Mmhmmm."

With another glare, Marsh closed her eyes. She had the lay of the tunnel now, and how it linked to the main chamber not ten yards away. She even thought she'd worked out how the crevice and the tunnel beyond connected in relation to the trail. What she didn't know was exactly how far they'd run before turning into it. She hadn't been paying attention to that.

And that was part of what was making it so difficult. She needed to figure out if they had to return to the tiered chamber or if they could follow this corridor. With luck, it would meet another cavern that might lead back to the trail or circle around to one of the caverns off Ruins Hall. She thought she almost had it when Tamlin spoke again, jolting the picture right out of her head.

"We can't stand here all day," he grumbled. "If the hoshkat has kits to feed, it'll be back—and I don't think last night's trick is going to work again."

Marchant wasn't so sure. They'd made a bargain, and

the kat had kept her end of it—so far. The boy had a point, though. Maybe she *didn't* want to go back through the main chamber. It would be better if she didn't tempt the shadows. That didn't mean she liked his nagging!

She opened her mouth to say as much when Aisha's light footsteps caught her ear. She realized the girl had wandered past her to where a fall of rubble had exposed the natural cavern wall. As she turned to see what the little brat was doing, the girl scrambled to the top of the rubble pile and looked back at them.

"We go this way," she said, and jumped to stand on top of another piece of rubble. "This way."

"Aisha! Wait!" Tamlin was after her like a slime bat on a pickled egg.

Marsh hurried after the pair of them. She couldn't run, but with her longer stride, it didn't take much time to catch up. Like most of her people, she was narrowly built but wiry and strong, and able to pick out details in the dark if she had to—and like most of her people, she preferred to live by the light of the glow stones or luminescent lichens or the end-of-day twilight in the surface world. What she didn't let on was that she could adjust to the brighter light of full day, just like her parents had. She was different enough as it was.

It had been something of a bone of contention between her and her uncle. He'd always wanted her to help him with the waystation or go out and take over her parents' steading, and she'd always refused. He'd harped on the fact that her mom and dad had always said she didn't mind the full sun as a baby, and she'd always managed to avoid having to prove it still wasn't a bother.

She didn't want to dwell on the surface world. That had been her parents' dream, but they'd vanished before she could join them and share it. Now Marsh preferred the caverns and the secret places, and the idea of treading where the Ancients had dug and uncovering their secrets. It was why she was working for Kearick.

The dealer had promised to find her a mentor among the seekers, as he called the retrieval specialists who brought him artifacts—*after* she'd served as a messenger for him, of course. Fair was fair, he'd said, and he wouldn't recommend her until she'd worked with him a while. Marsh had agreed, and her uncle had almost had a fit.

"But you could be a trader!" he'd protested, "Or a trail guide…or run Downslopes!"

Downslopes had been her parents' holding, and Marsh was having none of it.

"Let Gabe do it. He loves the surface," Marsh had told him, and stormed out.

She hadn't been back, either, always finding an excuse to take the next run or go over maps of the trade route and the tunnels connecting to it in Kearick's library. It had been six months since they had spoken. Marsh sighed, pushing the memories away as she reached the pile of rubble and had to concentrate.

"Took you long enough!" Tamlin sniped, and Marsh wondered if she'd get away with giving him a clip under the ear. Would there be angry relatives to answer to when she got them to Ruins Hall?

If she got them to Ruins Hall.

She gazed after Aisha.

"Why this way?" she called, scrambling over the tumbled concrete blocks and fallen steel.

She was more curious about how Aisha had known it was the right way to go rather than why she'd chosen it. It was the way she would have picked if Tamlin had given her another few heartbeats to think about it.

Aisha didn't quite give her the answer she was looking for.

"'Cos," Aisha told her and moved quickly along the corridor until they came to another open area.

"Aysh…" Marchant started, and let her voice trail away. "Whoa."

A million lights danced on the cavern floor, and the drip and splash of water echoed around them. Colors arced over their heads and rippled under painted stars that mirrored the sky in the surface world. They made Marsh's head spin, even as she resisted the urge to stare. It reminded her of something she'd seen in a book, and she wished she had more time to explore it. This *was* why she'd become a seeker, after all.

Before she could do more than register the amazing sight before her, Aisha had stepped smartly to the right and started moving along a tight ledge until she reached a long narrow cavern with tall square pillars and vaulted ceilings. The little girl moved quickly, then stopped and crouched in the shadow, reaching for Tamlin's hand as he came to a halt beside her. Before he could speak, she raised her finger to her lips and waved for Marsh to join them. Scruffy sat on the floor just in front of her, ears pricked and eyes alert.

For a minute Marchant wondered where the pup's

parents were, but Aisha reached up to pull her head close to Tamlin's and her own.

"Tamlin has to make the shadows," she whispered. "And we has to be very quiet. I'll 'splain later."

She looked at Marsh, letting go of Scruffknuckle's neck to wind her arms around Marsh's shoulders.

"Up."

She put her finger against Marsh's lips while Tamlin increased the darkness around them, then they'd crept along the edge of the pool and away from it into the dark.

4

VOICES IN THE DARK

That night, they set up camp in a hollow gouged into the side of a long natural tunnel. By then it was Tamlin leading them, his voice firm and his directions sure as they came to each junction. He'd stop every time, closing his eyes as though communing with the shadows. It was clear that he didn't realize closing his eyes didn't stop Marsh from noticing the faint white glow when he opened them, again.

Marchant made sure the two children and the pup were settled at the back of the hollow and took her place at the front. Despite its ragged edges and low entrance, she was worried that something might come by and see them, so she had Tamlin cover the glow.

"We'll camp dark tonight," she said, handing out the bread and including Scruffknuckle in the feeding.

Giving him water was harder. In the end, she poured water into the bowl she usually ate from. Aisha reached out and patted her knee.

"Scruffknuckle says thank you," she told Marchant, and

took her turn sipping from the canteen as the pup lapped noisily beside her.

Marsh wasn't going to ask her how she knew what the pup was saying. If she hadn't seen the way Aisha's eyes had flashed when looking at him that morning, she might have thought the child was just giving her own thanks instead of the pup's. After all, she didn't have to let the dog travel with them.

Uh huh, and just how do you think you would stop him?

There was no answer for that, so Marsh looked out into the tunnel dark, letting her eyes adjust until she could make out the lighter walls and patches of shadow where they were pitted by hollows or cracks.

"How did you know which way to go, today?" she asked, and this time her question included both of them.

They both looked at her, but it was Aisha who answered first.

"I asked the rocks," she replied like it was the most natural thing in the world, and Tamlin stared at her.

"But you can't talk to the rocks," he said, and Aisha had scowled at him.

"Can so, too!"

Marchant watched Tamlin open his mouth to argue and then change his mind. Instead of challenging his sister, he asked a question.

"When did you try it?"

A mischievous smile crossed the girl's face as she replied.

"Hide and seek." She sounded so pleased with herself that Marsh had to suppress a laugh.

Tamlin was outraged.

"You little cheater!"

Aisha's smile faded.

"Am not!" Then she added, "*You* call the shadows!"

Tamlin poked his sister.

"So?"

"Cheater!"

Aisha poked him back. Before Marsh had time to intervene, the two of them were poking and tickling and giggling like a pair of mad things and the krypthund had taken refuge behind her feet. Their happy madness was, however, short-lived.

The hund suddenly turned so he sat with his back against Marchant's ankles, his muzzle facing out toward the tunnel. His movement caught the children's attention and they stopped rolling around on the floor, their giggling abruptly ceasing. Then the pup gave a sudden sharp yap and circled around Marsh to rub against Tamlin and Aisha's faces. Aisha got it first.

"Ssshhh!" she said, holding her finger up in front of her mouth and rolling off her stomach into a crouch.

Tamlin didn't argue. Instead, he mimicked her movements even as Marsh ducked so she could see past the overhang concealing the hollow's entrance. The hund came to stand beside her, dabbing her cheek with his tongue before turning his attention to the tunnel beyond. Uncomfortable with the gap in front of them, Marsh tipped her pack onto its side and set it carefully across the open space, leaving just enough room to peer past it.

The dull stone-colored cloth would blend with the

tunnel walls and help conceal the existence of the hollow—
or so she hoped. Not long after that, they heard voices.

"I tell you, it sounded like children laughing."

"And what would you know about that? One look at
your face and they always cry!"

"A bit like you and the ladies!"

"Oh, shut up."

"At least, I have a wife and—"

They heard a dull thump, followed by an indignant
"Ow!"

"We've heard all about your wife and your kids and
how you're ever such a lucky man, yadda, yadda-de-yadda,
but I still think you're hearing things. You've been away so
long you've got your children on your mind."

"Ssshhh! This is where it'll be."

The third voice came as a surprise, and Marsh
wondered just how many *were* out there. Behind her, the
children sat as still as stones and didn't make a noise. Even
the pup stayed uncannily frozen.

Marsh listened in the darkness as the sound of booted
feet walking down the tunnel became audible. The footsteps approached cautiously, but their tread was heavy, as
though stealth was not something that came naturally. For
a moment, Marsh thought about going out to meet them,
to see if they would help get her and the kids back to Ruins
Hall—and then it crossed her mind that they were far from
any trail she knew, and there were raiders afoot.

Maybe it would be better if they stayed out of sight, at
least until she could be sure whoever was out there was
safe to approach. She held her breath, listening for any sign
that they'd been discovered.

"You're both out of your tiny little minds," the third voice said. "What would a bunch of children be doing this far from the settlement?"

"You never know," the second voice replied. "Children are known to wander."

"Mine don't."

"And yet here we are."

"I tell you I heard something."

"Told you to watch them mushrooms."

"Didn't touch the mushrooms," came the protest, which was met by laughter.

"What if it's a trap?" That third voice sounded closer, and Marsh was able to make out the rough edges of its words and the hoarseness of the throat that made them.

"What, kids?" Voice Two didn't believe him, but the third voice wasn't perturbed.

"Nah, the sound of kids. All sorts of things in these tunnels. Who's to say one of them hasn't learned to mimic kids to draw folk out where it can eat them?"

The footsteps stopped as though he'd mentioned something from a shared nightmare and Marsh held her breath.

Suddenly one of the men gave a startled oath.

"The shadows!" he exclaimed, and Marsh held her breath. "The shadows are moving."

Boots crunched over rubble as the men outside moved nervously, and then another of them whispered, "What was that?" Marsh heard steel rasp as swords were drawn.

"Back to camp," the first voice said, and the boots moved as one, debris crunching underfoot and pebbles rattling as they were knocked aside.

"Easy," the third voice cautioned. "Keep your eyes on the dark."

It sounded closer than it had been, and Scruff rose to his feet. Quick as she could, Marsh lashed out and wrapped her hand around his muzzle, willing him to be quiet, but it did no good. A growl leaked out, and all movement in the tunnel stopped.

"Did you hear that?"

"*Oui.* Back it up slowly. We'll be safer in camp."

Marsh let go of Scruff's nose and he growled again, sounding much bigger and fiercer because the hollow magnified his voice. This time the footsteps did not falter. They might even have picked up speed.

"Steady…"

Together, they listened as the men moved away, not relaxing until Scruffknuckle huffed a sigh of relief and settled to the floor. When she was sure she wouldn't be heard, Marsh turned to Tamlin.

"Was that you?" she asked. The boy was sitting with his back against the wall instead of crouching.

He nodded, then leaned his head against the wall and closed his eyes.

"He needs to eat," Aisha said. "He always needs to eat when he calls the shadows."

Marsh reached for her pack, but Tamlin waved a hand.

"Not this time, Aysh. I'll be fine." But Marsh could hear the weakness in his voice, and she knew his sister was right.

"You heard the men," she said. "There's a settlement not far from here. We can spare the bread."

If they couldn't, she would go without until the following evening.

She didn't tell him that, just pulled a third of the loaf she'd set aside for the next night's meal from the pack and passed it to Aisha. As she did, Scruff lifted his head; it was a race to beat the pup to what remained.

"Oh, no, you don't," Marsh told him, stuffing the loaf farther into the pack and pulling the top closed. "We'll need that tomorrow."

The dog nudged the bag and whined, but after Marsh pushed him away from the top of it, he settled back to the floor. When she was sure he'd given up his fight, Marsh tipped the pack back on its side, this time with the top close to where she was sitting, and the base closest the pup. Somehow, she doubted he'd eat his way through the package Kearick wanted her to deliver, and she'd notice if he tried to get at it through the top.

Satisfied the bread would be safe, she settled down, leaning on the pack. The children curled up under the blanket she'd pulled out earlier. It didn't take Scruf-fknuckle long to make his way over to where they were lying and worm his way between them. His contented sigh made her smile, and she stared at nothing until sleep over-came her.

It was still early when she woke, and it was quiet. Remembering the voices and footsteps she'd heard the night before, Marsh shifted the pack carefully away from the opening to their camp and listened to the silence in the corridor beyond. She started when she heard a scrape behind her, relaxing as Tamlin settled beside her.

"Feeling okay?" she asked.

"Still tired," he said. "You think that settlement is far away?"

"Way they were talking last night," Marsh answered, "I thought it was pretty close."

"Think you can find your own way in?"

"I was just going to follow the tunnel," Marsh told him, and he sighed.

"There's at least one more turn," he said, "and you should know it's not Ruins Hall, but somewhere outside it. Maybe a waystation for explorers."

"Seekers?"

"Yes. Them too."

"How do you do it?"

She felt him shift, his clothing rustling against the stone, and glanced toward him.

"I ask the shadows."

"Like Aisha asks the rocks?"

"Sort of."

It would be a useful skill, but Marsh had never shown any talent for magic. Tamlin didn't know that, though.

"I could teach you." Marsh stared at him and he continued, "It's like you talking to the hoshkat."

She felt her eyes widen. Now, why in all the Shades did he think she'd done that? She'd just been hoping the kat would see the implications of how she'd been standing. The rest had been wishful thinking. Tamlin studied her face, and his eyes grew wide with surprise.

"You didn't know you were really talking to the kat?" he asked, his voice rising in pitch. "Truly?"

"What makes you think I did?"

"You talked about it having kits. Only way you would

have known was if you'd been inside its head. I heard what you said. You gave it your word for its life and asked its word for ours. Hoshkats never end a hunt without a kill, but this one left. You talked to it."

"But I can't use magic," Marsh protested. "I've tried. I just can't."

"Look," Tamlin replied, "there are stories that say anyone can use the magic—and I can't speak to the shadows today. I don't have enough energy to do it right. I'm tired, and you need your hands free in case we need your sword. You don't need to be carrying me, which is what will happen if I use any more magic before I have a proper meal. We *need* you to try."

"Why can't Aisha do it?"

"Because she's too little," Tamlin told her, "and she's heavy. You don't want to be carrying her any more than you want to be carrying me."

Marsh looked back out into the corridor as she thought about it. He was right about her not wanting to carry either of them, and right about her sword arm, too. But the location of the nearest settlement wasn't the only thing she needed.

"Can the shadows tell me where those men are?"

"The ones from last night?"

"*Oui.* I don't want them catching up with us and real-izing it was you and Aysh they heard last night."

"Just ask."

"How?"

"How did you ask the kat?"

"I didn't think I had. I was just wishing very hard."

He pressed his lips together and frowned.

"I don't do it that way," he explained. "I picture what I'm looking for and ask the shadows to help me find it. For the settlement, I think of all the people I'm trying to find, and it feels like I'm being pulled toward them."

Marsh wondered what would happen if there were two tunnels that would take him where he wanted to go but decided not to complicate matters.

"Give me a minute," she said. "I'll need to practice. Why don't you and Aisha share the last of the bread with Scruff?"

"What about you? You're going to need to eat when you're done."

Would she? Marsh didn't remember feeling particularly hungry when she'd finished talking to the kat.

Of course, that could be because she'd felt too relieved at being allowed to live, which was not something she wanted to think about.

"I'll be fine. You go eat," she said, and Tamlin didn't need to be told twice. He slithered back into the hollow, dragging her pack around until he could undo the top.

Marsh watched as he pulled out the bread, smiling as the pup bounded out from under the blankets and had to be pushed away. In the end, Aisha wrapped her arms around its neck until Tamlin was ready to give it its share, and then she let it go so she could take hers. Once they'd settled to their meals, Marsh closed her eyes.

Talk to the shadows, right?

Well, first she was going to have to find herself some shadows. That shouldn't be too hard, given that she was surrounded by them. Taking a deep breath, she thought about the shadows, about how they were everywhere and touched everything, how they might feel against her skin, and how everything the shadows knew, she could know— because they were connected.

They were connected.

All she had to do was pull the knowledge through them. The men from last night had been drawn from their camp by the sound of the children laughing, so they weren't too far away. The same shadows that touched her would be touching them, somewhere in the caverns.

"Where?" she whispered, the word coming out on a single breath. "Where?"

She thought of the direction the footsteps had taken, of where the voice had been when it said "Easy" and then "Steady" and searched the shadows in that direction.

"Show me where," she requested, and opened her eyes so she could slip out and stand straight in the shadows along the tunnel walls.

"Where?" she repeated, stretching a hand out into the dark and feeling the threads that ran through the shadows and connected everything they touched.

There!

It was as though the shadow vibrated under her fingers and all she had to do was follow it.

5

EXPLORATION AND INTRODUCTIONS

Marchant found it easy to draw on the thread of shadow, pulling in the information it was connected to. The men had camped not very far from where she, Tamlin, and Aisha had emerged from the last tunnel. Back then, they'd been relieved to find a broader path to travel down, and Marsh had held secret hopes that Ruins Hall wasn't far away. Tamlin's guidance had taken them away from where the men had set themselves up, a hundred yards down a side tunnel that branched off the main corridor in the opposite direction from the one they'd taken.

She continued to think about where the men were, asking what their camp looked like and discovering that they'd been lucky enough to find a small self-contained grotto with water seeping through the wall at one end and pooling in a deep hollow. When she pulled the information back, she realized the campsite was empty.

Where were the men?

The thread could not answer that, so Marsh stopped

pulling on it. It had given her what it knew, but it couldn't give her what it didn't have. She let it go.

"Where are they?" she asked, whispering to the shadows, her voice a soft echo in her ears.

It was hard to relax, not opening her eyes to make sure they weren't already creeping up on her and the kids, but she managed it. Taking a deep breath, Marsh re-focused on the shadows, feeling the glide of them over her skin, the touch of their fingers on her face.

"Show me where they've gone," she said, wanting their reassurance that the strangers she'd heard outside the hollow were well and truly gone. Dropping into the patois of her parents, she tried again. "*S'il vous plaît. Montre moi.*"

Please. Show me.

As if the words could open doors, she knew where the men had gone. Not far, but farther than their camp, and not alone. The shadows showed them in the company of others. How many was not relevant; it was not a question she'd asked. Where? Well, heading away down the side tunnel—and at a lot slower pace than they'd moved the night before.

Marsh watched them go, without seeing them. She felt their presences fade farther along the strands that linked them through the dark—and she breathed a sigh of relief.

"*Merci,*" she whispered, then switched back to Traders' Common. "Now, show me the town. Show me Ruins Hall."

At first, the shadows responded, different threads tweaking against her skin, but when she mentioned Ruins Hall, all pressure stopped, as though "town" and "Ruins Hall" were two different things. Marsh paused.

"The town, then," she said, clarifying when several different threads responded at once. "The *nearest* town."

Well, that was easier. A single thread maintained its pressure, and Marsh reached out to draw the knowledge through it. She felt like a fisherman taking knowledge from the dark; chasing something specific, but not knowing exactly what would come back on the line.

The town was there. It was small, and she wondered how many people were in it. Another line in the shadows wound around the first, bringing her the answer. Not many—and nowhere near as many as those who traveled with the men from the night before. For a minute, Marsh thought about taking the children back down the tunnel so they could join the men and whoever was with them, but she didn't like the fact they were so far away from Ruins Hall and using routes that led to nowhere she could think of.

That thought made her pause, and she stopped to consider it.

Perhaps she'd forgotten one of the four towns Kearick had business in?

Slowly letting the shadows slip from her mind, Marsh went over the routes she'd traveled and the ones she'd memorized, and the answer was still no. The men were moving along paths she didn't know; paths that didn't exist on any of Kearick's maps and didn't lead to any of the four towns that made up her world.

It left her feeling strangely unsettled.

Why were there so many traveling with them, then? Where had all the people come from, and where were they going? She opened her eyes, and fatigue rolled over her like a wave.

"What the f—" She cut the word short as she heard movement behind her and remembered the kids and the dog.

"What?" she asked, trying to hide the tiredness behind that one curt word.

She looked down to see Aisha standing beside her, her small arm holding up the last of the loaf of bread. Behind her came the skitter of claws and a frustrated whimper as Scruff tried to join them.

"You need ta eat." The girl eyed her doubtfully. "And maybe to sit down."

Marsh took the bread as Tamlin gave a short cry of frustration and Scruff shot out from under the overhang in a flurry of paws and fur. He barreled past them in a blur before skidding to a halt and coming back to look up at Marsh. He eyed her chunk of bread and gave a small, whining wuff.

Marsh laughed at him.

"I think I'll stand while I eat this," she told Aisha, watching the pup.

The pup did not return her gaze but kept his large golden eyes fixed firmly on her food.

"Not a hope in all the shadows," Marsh told him and took a large bite.

The pup gave a grumbling wuff and continued to sit, watching, until all the bread was gone.

More sounds came from under the ledge and then Tamlin emerged, dragging her pack.

"So," he said. "We going? You know the way, right?"

Marsh glanced at him as Aisha handed her the water flask.

"*Oui*," Marsh said, taking a long swallow and capping the flask before she pushed off the wall.

She was still tired, far more tired than she should have been from the past two days' walking. When she reached out to take the pack from him, he shook his head.

"Nah. You look like you might fall over. I'll carry it."

Much as she wanted to, Marsh didn't argue. The kid had a point. She not only looked like she might fall over, she felt like it. Tamlin narrowed his eyes.

"We could go later," he said, but Marsh shook her head.

"It's not that far," she told him, hoping she'd judged the shadows right.

"You sure you remember the way?"

Marsh reached out and ruffled his hair.

"I remember the way. It's part of what I do as a courier. The shadows showed me where to go, just like a map, and I remember."

She didn't add that this was a really good thing, because she wasn't going to be asking the shadows any questions until she'd slept—and maybe not even then. Tamlin didn't ask her anything else, and Marsh reached out to take Aisha's hand. The three of them headed down the tunnel away from the hollow and the much larger company of people moving through the dark.

Marsh wanted to ask someone about that, but the kids weren't that someone. For one thing, they probably wouldn't know, and, for another, she didn't want to worry them. They might know more about talking to the shadows and the rocks and whatever, but they were still just kids. *She* was supposed to be looking after *them*, not the other way around.

Marsh led them along the tunnel, relieved when it opened into a much larger cavern. The walls rose around them to a ceiling that vanished into the dark, and Marsh wondered if they'd crossed into another portion of the ruins or just found one of the many giant spaces that existed below the surface. The tumbled boulders and stones that had littered the passage gave way to much larger rocks, and then the more angular shapes that answered her question.

This was another of the great spaces left behind by the ancients, but one in which stalagmites and stalactites grew and descended as the natural world slowly reclaimed the ground. Marsh took a deep breath, drawing in the slightly musty odor of fungi, and the earthier scent of cattle and mules. Water, too.

She took another breath, savoring the clean, slightly sharp smell of fresh water, and kept moving forward. All she wanted to do was sleep, and that wasn't possible until she was sure the children were safe. She kept walking, relieved when the tumble of rubble and debris gave way to the faintest thread of a path that led to a much wider trail.

Looking both ways along the trail, Marsh saw that one end of it vanished into a squared off entrance in the tunnel wall, while the other rounded a pillar of stone. Both sides of the trail were lined by glows, and she felt the tension ease inside her. Glows. Not many, but enough that the shadow monsters would be deterred.

Marsh turned away from the cavern exit, hoping to find the settlement just around the pillar. She was disappointed, but not by much. The walls of a waystation formed a square outline against the lighter cavern walls beyond. Well before it, though, there stood the much lower and simpler outlines of a stone farmhouse.

"We'll stop there," Marsh said. "See if I can pay for a night of sleep."

"You look like you need two nights," Tamlin offered, and Aisha giggled.

"Lots of nights," the girl added, "lots and lots and lots and lots."

"Thanks for that, kid," Marsh told her, but her voice creaked with tiredness and her body ached, so she didn't argue. She just hoped the farmers wouldn't think she was sick and turn her away.

Even as she thought it, something big bounded out of the main building, baying as it came toward them.

"Great," Marsh muttered as a familiar ball of fur bounded past her on a collision course, yapping fiercely.

"Scruffknuckle!" Aisha cried, tearing her hand free of Marsh's grasp and racing after the pup.

"Aysh!" Tamlin took off after his sister.

"Well, Shadow's Heart," Marsh muttered, but couldn't find the energy to pursue any of them.

Instead, she made herself keep moving as fast as she could lift her feet without losing her balance. She figured once she hit the ground, she wouldn't be getting up again. Ahead of her, Tamlin managed to grab his sister and hold onto her despite her best efforts to grab the pup. Scruffknuckle, for his part, had planted himself firmly between Aisha and the bigger dog and was barking as fiercely as any puppy.

The farm dog had stopped and was staring at him, and then, as Marsh watched, it closed the distance between them, stretched out a paw, and set it squarely between the pup's shoulder blades. Scruff twisted beneath it, snapping at the big dog's ankle, as it pressed him to the cavern floor.

Scruff yelped and Aisha shrieked, and the dog raised its head and looked at the girl. Seeing that neither she nor the boy was trying to move toward him, he looked past them to where Marsh was walking up the drive. He didn't move, ignoring the squirming puppy beneath his paw and both children as he waited for Marsh to reach him.

"Hey, pup," Marsh greeted him as she approached. "We mean no harm. We just need somewhere to sleep."

She didn't stop, and he growled.

"Give it a break, dog," she said, sounding as tired as she felt. "Why don't you go tell someone we're here and do something useful for a change."

"Hey!" Tamlin exclaimed when Marsh kept moving.

She didn't go straight at the dog but altered her course to steer around him.

"Hey," the boy repeated, and realized one important thing: He'd had a go at her for not asking his name, but he'd done exactly the same thing. He didn't know what to call her.

"Yell if he doesn't let you past," Marsh told him, but she didn't stop walking.

She didn't dare stop. If she did, she just might not get started again, and she didn't want to spend the night on the path. The big dog rumbled at her as she went past, but it still had Scruff under its paw. If it wanted to do anything to stop her, it was going to have to let the puppy go—and

Scruffknuckle was growling like a demon and trying to twist free.

"Come on, kids," Marsh called, but softer than she'd intended.

She yawned.

Behind her, she could hear Tamlin talking to Aisha, trying to convince her that Scruffknuckle would be all right and she only had to do what Marsh told her. Marsh had almost reached the porch before the dog let go of the pup. By that time, Tamlin had dragged his sister around the bigger dog and was trying to convince her that Scruff was going to be okay.

"No, he's not!" Aisha wailed, the shrill treble tones bouncing off the ceiling and around the cavern.

The farm dog raised his head at the sound, looking nervously toward the ceiling and around at the cavern. It looked to Marsh like he was searching for another danger. He took his foot off the pup and trotted after her, passing Tamlin and Aisha like they didn't matter. When he got to her, he stretched up and grabbed her hand in his mouth.

Marsh almost stopped, but his teeth didn't break her skin as he pulled her in the direction of the porch. It made her suddenly nervous about what Aisha's cry might have woken in the cavern dark. Now she did stop, looking at the pillars and shroom groves growing along the edges of the road. She tried to pull her hand from the dog's mouth, turning to go back to the children.

"Gotta get the kids," she told the dog, but he tightened his jaws, so she tried looking over her shoulder as she moved with him.

"Run!" she cried, her gaze passing over Scruff as she looked back.

She was relieved to see that Scruff was already on his feet and shaking the cavern dust from his fur. Tamlin towed his sister into a run and Marsh stumbled. She snapped her attention back to the front and focused on following the big hound up the steps to the porch and to the door. As soon as they'd crossed the porch's stone floor, he dropped her hand and nudged the door, whining.

When Marsh didn't react quickly enough, he nudged it, again and then pawed at it.

"Okay, keep your furry britches on! This had better be unlocked."

Marsh put one hand on the dog's head and grabbed the door handle. To her surprise, it turned without difficulty and the door opened.

"Allo?" she called. "Anyone home? Allo?"

Only silence greeted her, and she hesitated. The dog, however, had no doubts. He pushed past her, and then turned in the small entry hall beyond, whining anxiously. Tamlin and Aisha arrived and Marsh ushered them in, following on their heels. She was about to close the door behind them when Aisha broke free of Tamlin's grip and ducked past Marchant's legs.

"Scruffknuckle!" she shouted. "You come here. Wight. *NOW!*"

She had a good set of lungs on her—Marsh would give her that—and the pup obviously got the message. He flinched at her "Now," gave the dark one more defiant growl, and scampered for the door. If Marsh hadn't been watching for it, she might have missed the way the knee-high brown-nose toadstools shuddered at the base of the nearest pillar, or how a small cluster of blue button mushrooms shattered and smeared the pillar's side.

A darker shading of blue and brown passed over the pillar's surface and through the fungi. Marchant stared at it, completely missing when the path leading to the porch streaked in color. Movement shifted into form just as Tamlin slammed the door shut, then fought to get the heavy locking bar to slide into place.

"Help me!" he said, and his voice jerked Marchant out of her contemplation of the heavy stone portal.

Since when were doors made of solid stone? Who would…

"Hey! Hey, *you*!" Tamlin shouted, and she came back to reality and helped him slide the locking bar home.

"What were they?" she asked because she'd never seen that…those…*things* before.

"Joffra," Tamlin said, and he pulled the glow stone he'd made from his pocket, holding it up to light the house's interior. "We had them sometimes at the old farm in Dimanche."

His voice dropped to a whisper.

"They hunt in packs."

So Marsh had seen. She looked down at the farm dog.

"Still want to eat me?" she asked, remembering the way it had come bounding out from the farmhouse, hackles up and barking.

The dog gave her a look that bordered on disgust and walked through the door on the other side of the entry hall. Tamlin shook his head and laughed.

"He probably wants you to feed him."

He stopped and cocked his head to one side.

"I never asked you your name."

Marchant resisted the urge to accuse him of not caring. She was, after all, a good bit older than ten, and *someone* had to be the grown-up.

"Marchant," she said, "but most folks call me Marsh."

That wasn't exactly true, but her uncle called her Marsh, and so did her cousins, and she'd feel weird if these kids used her full name—especially since it looked like she'd be the only family they'd have for a while. She gave Aisha a stern glare.

"You need to stop chasing that puppy into every stupid problem it digs itself into," she said. She meant both Scruff trying to face down the farm dog and the girl running outside to call the pup back in.

The little girl looked her up and down and arched her eyebrow.

"You chase after *us*," she said and Marsh decided it would be better if she followed the dog.

She was in no mood to argue with someone who was barely out of diapers, especially when they might actually have a point. She *had* chased after them to stick them on the mule, and who knows how much farther she'd have gotten if she hadn't. Leaving the kids to decide whether they'd follow her, she headed through the door leading deeper into the house.

6

FARM STAY HOST

The dog had gone directly to the kitchen. He turned soulful eyes to Marsh as she followed him into the room.

"Couldn't let us get eaten by a pack of lizards, huh?" Marsh asked him. "What sort of a guard dog *are* you?"

He whined and scratched at one of the cupboard doors.

"And now you want me to feed you."

It wasn't a question, so Marsh opened the cupboard and found a bag holding cured meat mixed with solid balls of black and brown shrooms.

"I can't believe you actually like this stuff," she grumbled, looking around for a bowl.

It was sitting on the other side of the kitchen, near another door. This one had a locking bar, too. Marsh didn't bother opening it, just slid the bar across. By the time she got back with the bowl, the dog already had his head in the cupboard and was eating straight from the bag.

Marsh just looked at him and decided she was too tired to try pulling him out of it.

"Fine. Serve yourself, then! It's a good thing you're not *my* dog."

The pup arrived. He bounded into the kitchen and stopped, lifting his muzzle and scenting the air, before bouncing over to the farm dog and putting his paws on the side of the bag, bumping the larger dog's chin with the top of his head.

"You're game!" Marsh told him, as the big dog growled.

But the pup would not be deterred. He backed off from the bag and whined, and the big dog stopped eating and snarled. The pup sat and whined once more, but the farm dog turned back to the bag and resumed eating. Marsh laid a hand on Aisha's arm when the little girl went to intervene.

"Let them work it out," she said, in no mood to either break up a fight or clean up the mess that was sure to ensue.

The pup bounced forward again and the big dog growled again, a low rumble that rolled across the kitchen floor, and raised goosebumps on Marsh's arms. That was enough for Scruff. He sat back on his haunches and howled, and the big dog stopped, sighed, and pulled the bag out of the cupboard.

Marsh groaned as the animal upended the bag and sent shroom balls and jerky rolling across the floor.

"You're cleaning that up," she muttered, looking at Aisha.

The little girl pouted, but she didn't argue. She just changed the subject.

"I'm hungry," she said, and Marsh sighed just as loudly as the farm dog had.

"Give me a minute," she said, looking around the kitchen.

If this had been the waystation, she would have known exactly where she needed to go. But in a stranger's kitchen? She was just about to see what was behind the tall door in one corner when Aisha crossed to it.

"Can you cook?" the little girl asked, and Marsh wondered if the child was six or going on sixteen.

"*Mais oui*," she replied.

Of *course* she could cook. She didn't want to, but she could if she had to. Tamlin seemed to read her mind.

"*I'll* cook," he said, even though he didn't look big enough to lift a skillet.

"Mum makes us help when we hit ten," he explained. "I can do stew."

Aisha made a face and looked imploringly at Marsh.

"*Pleeease* cook."

Marsh shook her head and moved toward the door.

"I'm going to make sure the joffra can't get in," she said, figuring the kids would be fine with the two dogs. "Stay in here."

Just as she got to the door, another thought struck her, and she fixed Tamlin with a stern glare.

"And don't burn the place down."

She wanted to add that she was pretty sure the joffra would eat them roasted just as well as they would eat them raw, but she didn't have the energy—and she didn't want either of them working out she was lying. She wasn't going to lock the place down.

If it hadn't been locked down, they'd have been joffra food already.

She was going to see if the farmers were home and hiding, or well and truly gone.

Her footsteps echoed over the stone floor as she made her way slowly through the house. There were five other rooms on the ground floor: a dining room with a table large enough to seat a dozen men, sleeping quarters with two three-tier bunks, another room for just sitting and talking from the looks of it, a bathroom with three wash bays and three privies, and a laundry with clothes soaking in two large tubs and sitting in a basket by another door.

Figuring the door led outside, Marsh slid the locking bar in place. Maybe she hadn't been lying after all. She studied the room and then headed back the way she'd come.

The wash-bays in the bathroom were wet, and damp towels had been slung into a basket in one corner. The bunks in the other room had all been slept in, but two had covers that looked like they'd been hastily flung aside. The whole room smelt like a barracks. Whoever slept here hadn't been gone for long.

Marsh found a set of stairs leading up and followed them. The second floor was almost like the first but without a bathroom or laundry. It looked like the farmer and his family had made this their private domain, with slightly better-crafted furnishings in a master bedroom and two children's rooms. They were empty, but Marsh felt like she was intruding. Again, there were signs the house was occupied or had been occupied not long ago, but not a single person in sight.

A large office looked out over the cavern, clear rock covering two large windows that allowed a view. Leaning on the window ledge, Marsh caught sight of movement, her eyes drawn to the joffra exploring the grounds around the house, leaping onto boulders and raising their muzzles to scent the cavern air. The windows also gave a clear view of two orderly mushroom patches, both fenced in stone, and a field with a large closed building at one end.

As she stared at it, Marsh saw one of the darkened slots lighten as though a curtain had been lifted. Beyond it shone what could have been the dull yellow glow of a lantern, but she couldn't be sure. The curtain dropped, and the glow disappeared. Why would someone be hiding out in the barn?

Marsh decided that was a problem for another day. As far as she could tell, the house was deserted when there should be someone inside.

And the joffra couldn't get in.

With a sigh, she pushed off the ledge and made it back to the stairwell. As tempting as it was to collapse onto one of the beds up here, she couldn't—although how long she would be able to resist the fatigue dragging at her limbs was difficult to judge. All she wanted to do was sleep. She'd taken two steps down when she heard something behind her.

Marsh turned and saw nothing.

Taking another careful step down and away from the opening leading into the passage, Marsh held her breath. When she was far enough down that she couldn't be struck from around the corner, she stopped, listening in the dark, but the sound did not come again. After several heartbeats more, Marsh slowly made her way back to the kitchen.

There was no stew.

Instead, there were three plates with rough-cut sandwiches set on the kitchen table. The two dogs stretched out in front of the cold kitchen oven as though it would make a difference.

"What happened?" Marsh asked.

"Sandwiches were faster," Tamlin told her, his face daring her to make a fuss about it.

He cut a quick glance at his sister, but she returned a look of such fake innocence that neither he nor Marsh was comforted. Marsh decided sandwiches were enough and slid onto the bench on one side of the kitchen table.

"Good job," she said, lifting hers from the plate.

They ate in silence for a while, Marsh enjoying the thick slabs of meat and cheese between the round-top shroom bread. Back at Kerrenin's Ledge, they were experimenting with flour ground from grass seed, but she liked the earthier flavor of the shrooms. The cheese was a bitey dark orange, its nutty flavor a perfect complement to the richer smokiness of the meat. Both gave her a better idea of what was in the big building walling the open field.

"So..." Tamlin broke the silence and Marsh looked toward him. "Did you find anyone?"

And she sighed. She hadn't fooled him for a second.

"Might be in the other building," she admitted, and he frowned at her.

"What other building?"

"The big one on the other side of the pasture."

"The barn?"

Marsh shrugged. "*Oui*, if that is what it's called."

"How do you know?"

"I don't. *You* called it a barn."

Now it was Tamlin's turn to sigh. "No. How do you know there might be people there."

"Thought I saw a light."

"Well, they won't come out while the joffra are around."

Marsh rolled her eyes. "Tell me something I don't know," she snapped, realizing exhaustion was making her short-tempered. "Sorry. Need to sleep."

"Did you find beds?"

"There are some upstairs," Marsh told him and instantly regretted it.

Upstairs, where she had thought she'd heard a noise.

"There are some downstairs too," she hastily amended. "We could use those instead. They're closer to the bathroom."

But Tamlin had been watching her face, and he knew exactly what she was doing.

"What?" he asked. "What happened upstairs?"

Marsh took another bite of her sandwich, avoiding the question, but she knew Tamlin wasn't going to let it go. He mirrored her, eating his sandwich, matching her bite for bite and chew for chew, making a point of it. It made her remember that no one did annoying like a ten-year-old. No one... and then her gaze fell on Aisha. Well, almost no one.

"I thought I heard a sound," Marsh answered and felt her face heat as she blushed.

Now that she said it out loud, it sounded ridiculous.

"You didn't go see what it was?"

"I thought I was hearing things."

Which was partly...well, mostly... Well, almost true.

"You didn't check?"

Again with the sarcasm. Marsh glared at him.

"Tired."

Tamlin glared back.

"No excuse."

Marsh swallowed the last of her sandwich. The boy had a point, but she didn't think she could take on a determined kitten, let alone anything bigger.

"Let's hole up in the kitchen," she said. She thought he'd argue, but he didn't.

Instead, he studied her carefully before slipping off the bench with a nod and closing the kitchen door.

"I'll light the fire."

"Sure, kid. You do that," Marsh told him, but tiredness rolled over her in a dizzying wave and she closed her eyes.

It was meant to only be for a moment, but there was a skillet on the oven top and the smell of meat frying when she woke. Marsh opened her eyes all the way and realized she'd gone to sleep propped between the wall and the table. The kitchen was warm, and Tamlin looked up at her from beside the stove.

"Feeling better?" he asked and continued when she nodded. "Joffra are gone."

"How do you know?"

He waved a hand at the unbolted kitchen door.

"Dogs needed to go outside."

"And you just opened the door?"

"They wouldn't have gone if the joffra were still there—and they'd made enough of a mess."

He waved a hand and Marchant followed the gesture. Aisha was sitting in the middle of the spilled dog food, casting rebellious glances at her brother as she slowly picked it up piece by piece. Marsh pushed out of her chair and looked into the pan.

"Any eggs?"

Tamlin shrugged.

"Might be some out in the *barn*."

Hearing the stress on the last word, Marsh gave him a look. He was smirking but pretending to focus on the pan, so she decided to let it slide.

"Let me deal with whatever might be upstairs first."

She adjusted her sword and belt and unblocked the door.

"Nice idea," she said, pushing the box aside, then hesitating.

Tamlin glared at her when she looked back at him.

"I know," he grumbled, waving the spatula in her general direction. "Don't burn the place down."

Marsh was grinning as she went back into the corridor, drawing the door closed behind her. She let her grin fade as she tried to work out what to do next. First things first. She needed to check out the sound upstairs, although if it was a person who lived here, they'd probably be needing to visit the bathroom.

It reminded her that she needed to do the same, so she moved carefully in that direction, checking through each of the rooms on the way. As soon as she was sure each one was clear, she pulled the door closed and moved on to the next. It didn't take her long to go through the laundry and then head into the bathroom.

It was almost disappointing to find it empty, and she did what she needed before heading upstairs. This time she paused before she hit the top of the stairs, listening carefully before sliding around the corner. She thought about drawing her sword but decided against it. If someone was up here, they were doing their best to stay out of sight, and probably not planning on coming down until she and the kids had left.

Well, too bad, Marsh thought. *I need to know what happened.*

And that meant she needed to find whoever or whatever had made the sound the night before. She eased down the corridor, her head in constant motion as she kept glancing over her shoulder to keep an eye on the stretch of hall behind her, even as she tried to watch where she was going.

The office was empty, and nothing moved in the cavern beyond. Marchant was both pleased and very relieved to see that the glows still lit the trail leading out of the cavern. After checking under the desk and in the cupboards she left the room, closing the door behind her. She hoped whatever had made the sound had stayed hidden and not snuck down the stairs while she'd been in the office.

The first of the children's rooms yielded nothing, and the second one was just as empty. Both had a few toys made of stone and cloth and several small volumes of books on the shelves set between the beds. Marsh guessed there were about five children in all—or there had been before whatever had happened here. She figured farmers went for large families if these guys and Tamlin and Aisha's parents were anything to go by.

It made sense; there was a lot of work that needed to be done around a farm—and children were a lot cheaper than hiring labor. More loyal too, mostly.

That didn't matter, though. What was most important was that she find the source of last night's sound... and discover what had happened here. After that, she was going to head out to the barn to see who had been responsible for the lantern the night before.

Once she'd looked under the beds and in the closets, Marsh moved toward the last room on the floor. Her ears strained as she listened for any sound that would tell her she was not alone, but she didn't hear a thing. She felt like an intruder as she stepped cautiously over the threshold of the master bedroom. Leaving the door deliberately open behind her, she turned first toward the closet.

It was quite deep but easy to inspect. Not many clothes hung within.

And it was empty of life.

Marsh turned away, closing it behind her. As she came around to face the bed, she was sure she heard a sound, just the softest whisper of movement from somewhere across the room. She froze, and the sound faded. After a minute of waiting in the dark, Marsh took a step toward the bed.

No sound greeted her.

She took another step.

Still no sound.

She crouched parallel with the bed, and something desperately scampered away from her. Instead of trying to reach under the bed, Marsh bounded over it, catching hold of the small form emerging from the other side. It twisted and shouted in her grasp, but she didn't let go.

"Stop!" she said. "Stop! I'm not going to hurt you. Stop!"

The form didn't stop, trying to pull free with such force that it nearly succeeded. As it slipped from her fingers,

Marsh made a sudden lunge toward it, wrapping her arms around it and tumbling them both to the floor. The impact as they landed on the stone jarred through her, but the child she'd captured stopped moving.

For a moment, she thought she'd killed her.

"Are you all right?" she asked, shaking the kid. "Hey. You good?"

The person responded by punching her in the chest.

That might have hurt, except they were wrapped too close together and the kid didn't have enough space to get a good wind-up.

"Get off me! I'm not going anywhere with you! Get—"

Marsh cut her off before she could go any further.

"I'm not taking you anywhere! I just want to know what happened. Okay?"

When the girl stared at her, Marsh shook her just a little.

"Bon?"

"Not taking me away?"

Marsh shook her head.

"You're not one of them?"

Again, Marsh shook her head. The girl looked confused.

"Then why are you here?"

Marsh pushed herself up and onto her feet and reached down to offer the kid a hand. Warily, the girl took it.

"Long story," Marsh told her, helping her up. "You want breakfast?"

FEEDING TIME AT THE FARM

"Who's that?" Tamlin demanded when he saw the girl.

"Who d'you think?" the girl snapped back, crossing the kitchen like she owned the place and taking the spatula from his hand. "Fetch me the eggs."

Tamlin stared at her and she waved the spatula at him, pointing to a stone cupboard on the other side of the kitchen.

"The eggs!"

He looked at Marsh for an explanation, but Marsh only shrugged and indicated he should check the stone cupboard for eggs. It didn't take them long to be sitting around the table eating breakfast, the girl having won Aisha's friendship with the first bite.

"You cook better than Tams," the little girl said, and the older girl shrugged responding coolly.

"I'm thirteen," she said as though that was all the explanation needed.

Tamlin scowled and focused on his plate.

Marsh waited until they'd eaten before she asked, "What happened here?"

The girl raised her head and then stood, gathering the plates from the table. Lifting the kettle she'd set to boil on the stovetop, she filled the sink with hot water. Only then did she explain.

"They came yesterday, late in the day cycle," she said. "There were a half-dozen men, but three of them were mages and they commanded the shadow. Mama was putting away the laundry when she saw them coming, and she told me to hide. I wanted her to hide too, but she had to find Tory and Curt. I hid. I don't know what happened to them." The girl's words stuttered to a halt, and her fingers fumbled in the water. "I heard fighting, then everything went quiet."

She stopped until Tamlin and Aisha stirred restlessly at the table.

Marsh was going to tell them to be quiet, but the girl started at their movements and kept speaking.

"When Hugo started barking... Well, I thought they had come back, so I hid again."

She pulled another plate from the water and set it with the rest of the clean crockery.

"You know the rest."

Wiping her hands on her dress, she turned to face them.

"When you're done, wash your plates. I need to look after the animals." Before Marsh could call her back, she walked out the back door.

"Tamlin..." Marsh began. The boy finished the sentence for her.

"I know, wash the dishes and mind your sister. You'll

find us when you're done."

From the sound of it, he'd heard those words before, although not from her. There really wasn't a lot she could say.

"Thank you."

Marchant hurried out the door after the girl, catching up with her when she stopped to open the gate to the field. Neither of them said anything as they crossed to the barn.

"It's locked on the inside!" the girl exclaimed, and Marsh backed up a step to look the stone structure over.

One thing she had learned from talking to retrieval experts and other adventurers was that there were more ways than one into a building. It didn't take her long to spot the smaller door at the other end of the barn or to find that whoever had lit the lantern last night hadn't been as careful as they thought.

"This way," she said, pushing it open. "I saw a lamp in here last night. Maybe your mother was able to hide."

"Well, if she had, the animals would be fed," the girl retorted and picked up a bucket, which she filled from one of the feed bins in a small stone-lined chamber, "and they're not."

From the way she moved, Marsh could see she was determined to wrench some sense of normalcy from doing the daily chores. The thing was, Marsh didn't think they had time for it. The raiders could return, or the mages could come and remove the glows, or...

"We have to go," she said, grabbing the girl's wrist as she returned to refill the bucket.

The girl shook her head.

"Moutons need feeding."

"You can't stay here on your own."

"Have to. Someone's got to look after the farm."

Marsh was about to argue the point when Tamlin and Aisha arrived, Hugo and Scruffknuckle on their heels.

"Girl's got a point," Tamlin said, picking up a bucket and filling it. "Animals need feeding."

"Girl's got a name, too."

"Girl should introduce herself, then."

"Fine!" The girl finished slamming scoops of dried shroom into the bucket and shoved it against Tamlin's chest. "Eveline. Got it?"

"Sure thing, Ev," Tamlin teased, stepping swiftly out of arm's reach before taking the bucket farther into the barn.

Marsh registered the hungry animals' urgent bleating. It sounded like there were hundreds of sheep waiting to be fed. From the size of the barn, it couldn't be that many, but still…

"*Bon*. You three get them fed, and I will see if I can find who was staying here last night. Maybe they are still here."

The girl did not answer, just took the two extra buckets she had filled and hurried off to feed the animals. Marsh looked around, noting the ladder leading to the upper level, and wondered if that was where the chickens were kept. If it was, she'd better be quick, or Eveline would have her collecting the eggs—and she didn't want to spend any more time in the cavern than she had to.

She had to get the kids to Ruins Hall. She had to deliver Kearick's package, and she had to warn the caravans at the settlement that the glows were down and the trail to Kerrenin's Ledge was compromised. She *really* didn't have time for this!

Of course, she didn't have time to drag a farm girl kicking and screaming from her home either, which only meant she had to do things faster because Eveline was going with them whether she wanted to or not—and it would be easier if she wanted to. Keeping the need for haste firmly in her mind, Marsh reached the top of the ladder and looked around the loft, blinking against the sudden brightness of the single glow.

Eyes watering, it took her a couple of heartbeats to adjust to the glare. She'd forgotten that chickens needed more than the soft luminescence of glow moss or mushrooms in order to thrive. Once her eyes had adjusted, she looked around.

"Shadow's Heart, there must be a hundred chickens in here!" she murmured, wondering just what it was going to take to convince Eveline to leave.

She couldn't leave the girl here. Not alone.

Maybe she didn't have to.

Marsh turned slowly on the spot, taking in the laying roosts and the gate leading to the chicken run beyond. Someone had gone to a lot of work to make sure the birds stayed fed and happy. By the looks of it, the farm had started with the idea of keeping the waystation up the road well supplied.

The waystation! Marsh had forgotten about it. Now that she'd remembered it was there, she knew she had to at least walk through it to see if anyone else had managed to stay out of the raiders' reach.

"*Merde.*"

Taking a deep breath, she went to the gate leading to the chicken's enclosure. It opened to a small double-gated space, and she made sure to close the first gate before opening the next. The very last thing she wanted was to have to get a hundred chickens back into their pen—not that they'd want to leave in the first place.

After stepping through the second gate and securing it, Marsh let her gaze travel over the enclosure and gave a long, low whistle. Shrooms and lichens grew from every wall, interspersed by every kind of moss the creatures loved to eat. Boulders and rocks poked out of the floor, providing places for them to perch and more surfaces for their favorite foods. It was amazing that the floor hadn't collapsed under the weight.

Marsh recalled the angle of the ladder and noted which way the chicken run had been built, taking only a moment to realize that the enclosure had been carved from the cavern walls.

"*Very* nice!"

Moving swiftly around the well-appointed space, she didn't take long to confirm the chickens were the only ones in residence, or that they'd be fine without human care. Maybe convincing Eveline to leave wouldn't be as hard as she'd imagined. She wondered if the moutons had a similar space at the back of the barn, or if there was another level above the woolly creatures' pens.

She couldn't find a single door leading anywhere else, not in the length of the enclosure or in the egg collection area. There was no other way out that she could see.

Leaving the chickens to their clucking and scratching, Marsh left the enclosure, making very sure not to let any of the feathered monsters out with her. It wasn't that she was worried about what Eveline would say; she just didn't want to deal with another snot-nosed child today.

Unfortunately, the children had other ideas.

"I'm not going!" Eveline declared, not quite stamping her foot when Marsh told her she was returning to Ruins Hall with them. "Someone has to stay with the animals!"

Said with all the conviction of a thirteen-year-old, the statement had the finality of prophecy—and Marchant wasn't going to let it stand.

"I won't leave you here alone!"

But the girl wouldn't be moved.

"Then you're going to be here an awfully long time."

"Can't. I have business to attend."

"So do I."

That took the wind out of Marsh's sails. They'd made it out of the barn, the girl opening the doors to let the moutons into the field. To get back to the gate, they had to work their way through a herd of woolly bodies, every one of which seemed intent on getting as underfoot as possible. By the time they made it to the gates, Marsh had seen all the moutons she wanted to encounter for the rest of her life.

"At least come back with us so we can get help out here," she finally said. "They might not believe me, but they know you live here, right?"

Eveline nodded.

"So they're likely to come out if you ask."

Eveline's face went serious, but she still refused to commit.

"I'll think about it," she said, and Marsh decided to give her a little more time to consider the idea.

"Bon," she said. "I have to see if there's anyone left at the waystation. You coming? They'll need to see a familiar face."

Eveline gave a deep sigh.

"Fine."

Tamlin and Aisha followed them, Aisha keeping one small hand firmly entwined in Scruffknuckle's fur even though the pup whined to be allowed to chase after Hugo. The big farm dog bounded on ahead as though he knew where they were going. Marsh watched him closely, remembering the joffra from the night before and knowing he'd give the earliest warning they could hope for. She only hoped it wasn't when they were halfway between the station and the farm, because that would be bad.

She didn't have to worry.

Hugo led the way, bounding ahead to check the trail and the ground on either side and then bounding back to nudge Eveline's hand. He completely ignored Marchant, Tamlin, and Aisha, who were walking behind Eveline, except to occasionally come over and nudge Scruff.

Each time he did, the pup would look up at Aisha and whine pleadingly, and each time Aisha would fix the krypthund puppy with a firm stare.

"No," she'd say, and Hugo would bound away, the pup staring forlornly at his retreating form.

Marsh kept a close eye on Eveline. The Shadows knew the girl had experienced enough shocks to cripple someone older—and the same went for the other two—but none of them seemed to be reacting to what had happened. Tamlin and Aisha held hands, sure, but neither of them cried for their parents, and Ev didn't either. She kept walking, setting a fast pace toward the waystation's walls and not looking back.

When she raised a hand as though wiping her cheek, Marchant pretended not to notice. If the girl wanted to keep her tears a secret, who was she to break the illusion? She was glad when neither Tamlin nor his sister chose to comment, and gladder still when they reached the waystation's gates.

These were closed, but not barred or locked. The four of them put their hands on them and pushed, and the gates opened beneath their palms. Once they reached the other side, they all turned and pushed the gates closed again, lifting the locking bar in unison to drop it into place. The cavern might seem safe and quiet, but none of them had forgotten the raiders, and the joffra would not be far away.

Instead of splitting up, they stayed together, the children checking under beds and opening cupboards while Marsh led the way into every room and up or down every set of stairs. In less than a full turn of the hourglass, they had been through the station proper and found no one.

"We need to leave," Marsh said, and Eveline nodded.

"Can we stop at the farm first? I need to pack a few things."

Marsh wanted to tell her no, although she was glad the girl had decided to go with them. She wanted to get them out of the cavern and on the road long before the night cycle began and the joffra decided to check for stragglers. But she didn't. Instead, she nodded, accepting that they might have to spend one more night at the farmhouse. At least she could sleep in one of the beds.

The thought wasn't much comfort against the urgent restlessness she felt. The raiders had come and gone and left everything in its place. They hadn't touched a single item of value, from the money they'd found in the station master's office to the mules she and the children had fed and watered in the station's stables.

"We should let them loose," Marsh said, but Eveline had disagreed.

"We leave them out in the cavern," the girl had told her, "and the joffra will eat them inside a day. Just give them enough feed for me to get to Ruins Hall and back. I've got the merchants' names."

And she did.

Marsh had shown them how to work out which caravan had stopped the night of the raid, and how many travelers had arrived, and where their animals were kept. When they'd checked the rooms, the traders and travelers were gone, but their belongings were not. The whole scenario had reminded Marsh of the stories told about Downslopes and her parents' disappearance.

They'd set up the waystation a day's journey over the surface below Kerrenin's Ledge—and their station had been found in exactly the same condition as the one she'd just walked through. The memory sent a chill down Marsh's spine, and she'd been glad to push the waystation's gates closed behind them and wedge them shut with stones gathered from the edge of the path.

Eveline insisted on putting the moutons back in the barn as they passed the field. Of course, she did. As her chances of leaving that day diminished, Marsh helped the girl add extra feed to the animals' troughs and ensure the water pipes flowed freely. Hugo started getting restless as they left the field behind them, the barn securely locked and the moutons content.

Marchant looked around the cavern, noting that Hugo didn't stray far from them now, and how he returned to Eveline more often, whining every time he did so. Marsh figured the joffra were coming and they needed to hurry. She increased the pace, reaching out to grab Tamlin's hand when Aisha wouldn't give up her grip on Scruffknuckle's neck.

Eveline raced ahead and was waiting to secure the door behind them when they arrived. She was scolding Hugo as they entered.

"Get your big nose out of the feed sack, and keep it out of the pup's bowl."

The pup had a bowl? That was news to Marsh, but it was also a good idea.

"Go wash up!" the girl ordered before Marsh had a chance to speak. "We missed lunch, and the joffra are out. We're not going anywhere until day cycle."

Marchant wanted to ask her who'd died and put her in charge but pushed down the urge. It *was* Eveline's house, after all, and the Shadows knew some girls were very territorial. She'd encountered enough in Kerrenin's Ledge to know.

Marsh held up her hands in mock surrender and made a show of walking around the girl to get to the corridor leading to the washroom. Walking backward out of the kitchen wasn't her best move, however, as the sudden sharp blow to her skull made all too clear.

8

SHADOW-MAGE RAIDERS

Marchant woke with a start in a strange bunk with a splitting headache and a violent need to throw up. It took her a second to recognize the bunk room and that she was alone, but her location wasn't the most urgent of her concerns. Marsh threw back the covers and bolted for the bathroom. When she'd finished losing what was left in her stomach, she wasn't alone.

"I'm sorry for your discomfort."

The voice was new, and the source of it was the doorway. Marsh guessed that if the woman had meant her harm, she'd already be hurting. She shifted slightly, making sure her stomach had finished with her. When she was sure of it, she stood and crossed shakily to the closest wash bay, painfully aware of the woman watching her every step of the way.

"This your house?" Marsh asked, knowing what the answer must be.

"It's been my home since we settled here fifteen years ago."

Fifteen years—which meant Eveline had been born here.

"I was going to take your daughter to Ruins Hall for help."

"She told me."

The woman crossed the bathroom to stand by the wash bay's door.

"Let me help you to the kitchen," she said. "That was a good hit."

Marsh noticed she wasn't apologizing, and figured she shouldn't have to since she'd been defending her home and her daughter.

"Mama?" The new voice caught Marsh's attention; it sounded like its owner was on the edge of panic. "She's not in the bed, Mama."

"That's 'cos she's in here," the woman said, and a boy who looked no older than four came and clung to her trousers.

The woman turned to Marsh.

"I'm Fabrice. The children call me—"

"Fabby!" Aisha's voice had a panicked pitch, and both Fabrice and Marsh turned toward it. "Fabby! Fabby! She's gone!"

"It's all right, Aysh. I'm here," Marsh called as Fabrice answered, "She's in here, child. She's okay."

Aisha appeared in the doorway seconds later and raced over to wrap her arms around Marsh's legs. A familiar ball of fur bounded beside her and planted both forepaws on Marsh's other leg, whining excitedly as he licked every bit of her he could reach. Marsh's head spun as she tried to push the pair of them off her.

"I'm okay. Okay. Let go of me. Scruffknuckle, get down! Ouch!"

"Okay, that's enough." Fabrice might have done a better job of sounding stern if her voice hadn't been shaking with laughter. "Why don't you go and clear a space for her in the kitchen and tell Tams and Ev she needs a cup of tea?"

"*Bon.*" Aisha let go, bolting back out of the bathroom with Scruffknuckle hard on her heels, her shrill treble echoing down the hall. "Tams! Tams! She's awake!"

Marchant exchanged looks with Fabrice.

"Anyone would think I'd been out for a week," she said, starting to shake her head and stopping with a wince. "Just how hard did you hit me?"

"Hard enough to put you out for almost a full cycle," Fabrice admitted, her cheeks coloring. "I am truly sorry."

Marsh started to shake her head again and stopped. Instead, she accepted the woman's offer of help and let her steady her as she walked down the corridor.

"Don't be sorry. You were just protecting the children."

"It's just a shame I couldn't save my husband," Fabrice admitted. "I don't know how I'll run the place now. I was going to head up to the waystation and ask for help, but Eveline tells me it's deserted."

Her words made Marsh's insides turn cold. Deserted like her parents' waystation, nothing gone except the people. Fabrice continued, unaware of what Marsh was thinking.

"I've never seen the like," she said. "Or heard of it. Have you?"

Fortunately, they had reached the kitchen, so Marsh was saved from answering.

"Marsh!" Tamlin seemed relieved to see her.

Fabrice gave Marsh a sideways glance.

"He thought I'd killed you."

Tamlin's face colored.

"You went down like a wet sack, and then you were so still."

"I'm okay." Marsh tried to reassure him although she felt anything but.

She looked up as Eveline placed a mug in front of her.

"Here. Drink this," the girl ordered. "You'll feel better."

"*Merci*," Marsh said, not sure if she should thank Ev or tell her to take the murky brown brew away. "What is it?"

"Ferbchai. Good for healing."

Which meant it would taste terrible, Marsh thought, but she raised the cup to her lips and took a sip. The first taste wasn't too bad, so she took another, and then a third. Then she set the cup down, holding it fiercely with both hands as she bowed her head and fought to keep the brew in her stomach. Ferbchai. She'd heard of it but never had the misfortune to need it. Now that she did, she found it lived up to the legend.

After the first wave of nausea passed, she remembered the advice of all the caravan guards who'd ever been dosed with it.

"Best to get it all down and chase it with something stronger."

She hoped Fabrice had heard that advice too. If she hadn't, Marsh was sure as Shadows going to ask for something strong to chase it with. Her uncle would not have approved, but he'd never had to drink the stuff. If he had been, Marsh was sure he'd change his mind.

She raised the mug once more and stared at the brew. Across the table, Tamlin rolled his eyes.

"Don't be such a baby," he said. "Drink."

Marsh shot him a glare, then put the cup to her lips and slowly but surely drained it. When it was empty, she set it on the table in front of her. Whatever the kids were cooking smelled good, but her stomach was in no mood for it. Marsh folded her arms on the table, then rested her head on them and closed her eyes, listening to the movements of those around her.

She could hear Tamlin and Eveline tending the pot on the stove, while Aisha was sitting on the floor feeding the dogs pieces of kibble with the little boy and a girl around her own age. She was wondering who the little girl was when she felt the mug taken out from in front of her and a glass set in her hand.

"Drink that," Fabby told her. "It'll help with the taste of the chai."

Marsh raised her head and looked at the glass. It was made of rough-cut crystal, the kind usually used for water, but this one held something else. The liquid was a strong blue and semi-opaque.

"It's best not to breathe it in. Just let it get acquainted with your tongue first," Fabby advised as Marsh lifted the glass.

Eyeing the liquid warily, Marsh raised the glass to her lips, held her breath, and took a large sip, rolling the drink across her tongue and around her mouth. At the first taste, her stomach roiled, and Marsh swallowed cautiously, a little bit at a time, surprised when the rebellion subsided in her gut.

By the time Fabby placed a bowl of stew and a side of shroom bread in front of her, Marsh was thinking food might be a good idea. She was also slightly drunk.

"What cycle is it?" she asked after she'd finished most of the bowl and a slice of bread.

"Too late to leave," Fabby told her, anticipating what she was going to say next. "You can go in the morning once the chai has done its work."

Marsh frowned.

"What about you?"

"Me?" Fabby laughed. "I'm not going anywhere. I have a farm to run and a bunch of animals that need me. I'll get you to hire me some good hands and send them back out here."

Marsh started to shake her head but stopped when her stomach protested.

"What if they come back?" she asked. "They missed you this time, but next time…"

She let her words trail off, giving Fabrice time to put the picture together for herself. When the woman frowned and set her lips in a stubborn line, Marchant tried a different tack.

"Do you know why they came in the first place?" She waved her hand around at the kitchen. "I mean, they left everything behind. Everything they could have sold for a profit or used in future raiding, they just left. It doesn't make sense. Even the mules. Why would they leave mules behind?"

She paused as though mulling over the problem but only finding more questions.

"And supplies… You'd think, if they were taking people,

they'd be taking supplies as well. It's not like we encountered a whole bunch of... Oh."

She stopped. They had encountered a whole bunch of people in the tunnels...or rather, she'd sensed a whole bunch of people moving away. If they didn't need supplies, did that mean they'd killed everyone?

No, that didn't make any sense. If they'd wanted to kill everyone, they could have just done it and left the bodies right where they dropped. Besides, if they killed everyone, that meant her parents were...

Marchant shook her head and closed her eyes.

Nope. Her parents were alive. She knew it. So, if the raiders didn't need supplies then... Then, what?

"They were looking for anyone who could do magic."

Eveline's voice cut through her thoughts like a hot knife through butter and Marchant opened her eyes.

"What did you say?"

"She said they were looking for anyone who could do magic," Fabrice said, "but they took everyone they could find. I escaped because I was already preparing to hide."

She gestured at her children.

"I had to keep them safe. Patrik insisted it was the most important thing, so he made a place for us to hide."

"Out in the barn," Marsh said when she paused, and Fabrice nodded.

"There's a secret room behind the feed shed. No one's found it yet."

She shot Marsh a half-smile.

"We watched you feed the animals and check the chickens. I almost came out then, but the children were afraid. I figured we could meet you on our terms without compromising our hiding place."

Marsh remembered their meeting very well and couldn't stop her hand from rubbing gently at the lump on the back of her head.

"Then why did you hit me?"

"I was scared," Fabrice said. "I saw you in the doorway, and it was just too much after what I heard through the walls."

She looked at Eveline, who was doing the dishes.

"I had to be sure."

Marchant tried to understand that. After all, the woman had seen her with the children earlier. Why would she feel the need to hit her with a…

"What did you hit me with?"

Fabrice blushed.

"I was near the sink when I heard you returning. I just grabbed the first thing that came to hand."

"This," Eveline said, hefting the skillet she'd used to cook their breakfast in. Marchant winced.

That explained why she'd dropped like a stone. She was lucky the blow hadn't killed her. She shifted the conversation back to why the raiders had come.

"Tell me about them," she said, catching Fabrice's eye.

"Why do you need to know?"

"Because I think we saw them in the tunnels." She hesitated, then let her breath out in a soft sigh. "And because I think they may have taken my parents."

"Your parents?"

"They had a waystation on the Surface, Downslopes. It was found empty, just like the station up the road. Not a living soul. Just the animals and valuables left behind." She stopped. "I was a child, staying with my uncle while they set it up. I've always hoped they were alive, and now I just might have to go looking for them."

Fabrice's face brightened.

"Will you look for my Patrik too?"

Her request caught Marchant by surprise, and she almost backed away from the hope in the woman's eyes. Who was she to promise such things? But she knew she was going to try. Her parents, Fabrice's husband...

"And the children?" Fabrice pressed. "They took everyone who lived here. I was lucky to be able to take my youngest two and hide. For a long while, I thought I'd lost Eveline, too."

Her eyes filled with tears, but not a single one fell as she looked at her daughter with a shimmering gaze.

"They didn't search the laundry baskets," Eveline said, "and Raph dumped a load of dirty clothes on top of me before he went out to help Papa."

"Shadow's Heart be with him," Fabrice said.

"And Shadow's Hand," Eveline replied and turned back to the dishes.

"How did you know they were coming?" Marsh asked.

"They tried to convince me my children would do better boarding at their school," Fabrice told her. "The ones who came with the raiders, they came again last trading day, moving through the waystation and talking to folk about the children they'd seen with magical ability. 'Aptitude,' they called it. Said such children needed special guidance, and they were the best ones to provide it. Sent wrigglers down my spine."

She gave an exaggerated shiver.

"We were watching for them. Patrik saw them from the upstairs office, and he told me to take the children." She glanced at her daughter. "I couldn't find Eveline and didn't have time to look."

Marsh noticed the slight wave of color that rose up Eveline's neck but said nothing. It was something she'd look into later if she had time. Whatever the girl had been doing, it didn't matter in the light of what had happened after, and she doubted it would have made a difference to who the raiders took and who got left behind.

She reached across the table and touched Fabrice's hand.

"Is there no one you could stay with? Even if it's just until we get Patrik back?"

"You could come with us to the shadow mage monastery," Tamlin broke in. "They'd have room for the animals, and they could protect Ev and the little ones. Teach them how to use their magic."

Marchant caught the look on Fabrice's face and intervened.

"I'm not sure that's such a good idea, Tamlin. We don't know if those shadow mages are working with the ones who attacked with the raiders."

"Oh."

Tams wasn't slow to realize his mistake; Marsh would give him that.

"I'm sorry," he told Fabrice. "I didn't think. I mean, my parents wouldn't have been taking me somewhere that was bad, would they?"

Fabrice hurried to reassure him.

"I'm sure they knew what they were doing," she said and looked at Marchant. "Why don't we get Marsh to check them out? If they're not the same, we might come to join you."

She turned back to Marsh.

"In the meantime, I know some folk on the outskirts of Ruins. They've been after Patrik to mix our mouton bloodlines, so I'm certain I can strike a bargain in exchange for a place for my beasts and my family."

"So you're coming?" Marsh couldn't believe it had been that easy, but Fabrice nodded.

"We'll pack tonight and move the animals out in the morning. Hugo will keep them in line."

"If we take the mules from the waystation," Eveline said, "we'll move faster than if we just take the cart. We'll be able to take more with us, too."

She looked around the kitchen and back to the sink, and Marsh got the impression she wasn't looking forward to the trip. When she thought of moving through the caverns with the number of mouton she had seen in the barn, she wasn't looking forward to the trip either. It crossed her mind that Fabrice might be better off leaving the moutons behind and sending someone skilled to bring them back to the farms near Ruins Hall.

"How are we going to keep them all together?" she asked. "Don't they like to wander?"

"That depends on what the leaders are doing and how safe they feel," Fabrice told her. "If we take them away from their barn and out of their field, they'll stick pretty close to the rams and lead ewes."

"And the mules," Eveline added. "We bring those down

from the waystation and they'll walk with them, thinking the mules will keep them safe."

"And the dogs," Aisha added. "Moutons feel safe with dogs."

"I need to pay you for the food," Marsh said, getting out of her chair, "while I remember. And for the shelter…"

She stopped as Fabrice laid a hand on her arm.

"You take us to our friends' farm, and I'll consider us even. We wouldn't be able to make it without you, and I think you're right. We *do* have to worry about them coming back. I don't want to be here when they do. It would be foolish to keep the children out of their hands once, only to be caught by them later."

"Tell me more about them," Marsh said, and Fabrice shot a glance at the children before she began.

"The first time we saw them was two cycles ago. It was just the mages. We thought it was the folk from the Ruins Hall Monastery, but their robes were different, and they came from one of the tunnels leading to the mountains…or so folk say. I've never spoken to someone who set out on that journey and came back. Oh, and they were tall and big, too. I've never seen a man or woman built so big.

"Anyway, we listened at first, especially when they started talking about how much ability our children had." She blushed. "I mean, what parent doesn't like hearing that their little one is special or especially blessed?"

She paused, her eyes taking on a faraway look, and Marsh forced herself to sit still and wait. As much as she wanted to press the woman for details, she didn't want to shape her narrative. If she did, Fabrice might describe events the way Marsh might see them rather than the way she had seen them. Marsh didn't want that. She wanted to hear Fabrice's version. If she wanted more detail, she could always ask for it later.

"What really put me off was the insistence. We said no, that we needed the children's help on the farm, and they asked what gave us the right to deny our children the chance to develop their powers to their potential? I mean, Shadow's Teeth! How rude was that? As if we didn't care about our own children's welfare. Well, I wasn't going to be emotionally blackmailed. And Patrik? Well, he said that if they were so concerned about the children's welfare, they wouldn't mind staying in the cavern and setting up a school that everyone could attend, children and adults alike. But they wouldn't hear of it."

"Why not?" Tamlin asked, and Marsh shifted so she could see his face.

The boy seemed genuinely puzzled.

Fabrice shrugged.

"I don't know, but they took offense and left us to go see the next farm. Trouble was that Patrik and Alaine are good friends, and Alaine gave them the exact same answer. I think they visited every farm after that because everyone we spoke to at the markets said they'd come." Her voice dropped to almost a whisper. "Thing was, they even approached those whose kids had shown no magical ability at all. Claimed they could teach them new things that would make them better farmers with no magic!"

"Once we'd all gotten together and started comparing notes, it was pretty clear they were after our children, with little regard for what their abilities really were. When Patrik and Alaine went to their camp to ask them what they really wanted, they'd gone. Been gone at least a day, too. No goodbye. No final attempt to recruit anyone. Just gone."

"We should have been ready for the raiders. Should have known…" She let her words fade and sat staring past Marsh, looking at nothing as her eyes shimmered with unshed tears.

Marsh watched as the little boy wormed his way onto Fabrice's lap and wound his arms around her neck.

"No cwy, Mama. No cwy." Curt hugged her tightly, and a girl a little younger than Aisha ducked under Fabrice's arm and wrapped her arms around her mother's waist. That must be Tory

For a long moment, none of them moved, and then a strange barking cry echoed through the darkness outside. Hugo crossed to the door and growled, Scruffknuckle shadowing the big dog's every move. Everyone in the kitchen gasped and Fabrice stood, setting the little boy down on the bench.

"The moutons…" she began, and Marsh rose to reassure her.

"We put them in on the way down from the waystation. If you didn't let them out…"

Fabrice relaxed.

"Not today," she said. "We fed them, but the children didn't want to leave you, and I had business to attend to in the office."

She looked up.

"Ev, did you bar the doors?"

"*Oui*, Mama."

Fabrice relaxed, then blinked and focused on Marsh.

"We'll pack tonight. If we fetch the mules from the waystation early, we should be clear of the cavern before the joffra start to stir."

Marsh started to nod, then stopped, her head spinning. Fabrice gave her a shrewd look.

"You need to sleep. The children and I will take care of things here, but you need to rest."

Marsh wanted to ask her whose fault that was but resisted. The woman couldn't be blamed for her fear. Tomorrow they'd be on the road, and that much closer to reaching Ruins Hall and help. What worried her most was that Ruins Hall, like each of the Four Settlements, had just one appointed enforcer, and that wouldn't be enough to face down an organized force.

9

FLEEING THE FARM

Marchant felt much better the next morning. She rose with just the slightest hint of a headache and a dull throbbing to remind her of where the skillet had landed. She was in and out of the washroom before she realized anyone else had stirred. Fabrice was coming down the stairs as Marsh headed for the kitchen with her backpack in hand.

"If you get the mules, I'll have the children and moutons ready by the time you return."

Marsh nodded.

"Can you do it on your own?"

"Has Ev ever saddled a mule?" she asked, and Fabrice shook her head.

"No, but…"

"I have." Tamlin had arrived without either of them noticing, and he wasn't alone.

"Me, too," Aisha piped and caught Marchant's look of disbelief with raised eyebrows. "Can so."

Marsh looked from one to the other and saw only sincerity in their faces. She also noticed that Tamlin looked a little pale and that both children carried backpacks.

"We're ready," Tamlin told her. "I'll grab some shroom bread on the way through the kitchen, and we can eat while we walk." He looked at Fabrice. "If that's all right with you?"

"Yes. Take some cheese, too."

Marsh registered the faint tension thrumming through the air. Tamlin seemed most anxious, and Aisha was as taut as a bowstring.

"What's going on?" she asked, and Eveline answered.

"Tory had a dream. The mages will come back today. We need to hurry."

"Do you always…"

"Yes," Eveline said. "We'll talk about it later."

Her eyes held a pleading look Marsh could not ignore. She turned to Tamlin.

"*Bon*. When you're ready."

He didn't bother answering but turned and led the way through the kitchen, stopping in the pantry long enough to take the bread he found there.

"We need to hurry," he said. Marsh decided they could talk about why he was so sure on the way to the station.

As it turned out, Tamlin didn't give her the opportunity. As soon as they were free of the farmhouse, the boy broke into a jog, maintaining the pace past the barn as Aisha scrambled to catch up. To give her credit, the little girl didn't protest. Whatever was bothering her brother was bothering her too.

Marsh jogged with them, scanning the cavern around them. The last thing she wanted was for any of them to run right into a joffra ambush. She could only hope that Fabrice was right and the lizard-like monsters really did return to their lairs as the day cycle began. They were going to be in a lot of trouble if it wasn't true.

By the time they reached the waystation's gates, she was breathing hard. Tamlin had set a faster pace than she would have given him credit for. Together, they lifted the locking bar and opened the gates.

"Leave them open," the boy said when Marsh turned to pull the gates closed after them.

"Why?"

He blushed and looked uncomfortable.

"There's something in the shadows," he said. "We don't want to stay here any longer than we need to."

"How do you know?"

"You know how you ask the shadows if there are any towns nearby?"

"*Bien.*"

Tamlin led the way to the stables, talking as he went.

"Well, I asked them if Tory's dream was true and there really *were* mages coming." He frowned. "Thing is, when I asked the shadows down the tunnels we'd come by, they said there was no one there, so I had to ask the shadows in the cavern.

"When they said no one was here, I asked them where the people were, and they said they were coming."

Marsh gave him a skeptical look.

"Did they tell you *who* was coming?"

"No, just that there was someone." He led the way into the tack room, pausing to look at her as he reached the door. "They're coming, Marsh, and I don't want to be here when they arrive."

From the look on his face, he believed every word he was saying. Marsh decided she'd better pay attention. She picked up the first of the saddles and harnesses, noting that Tamlin and Aisha had a coordinated act going. He picked up a saddle and the little girl grabbed a bridle, and they headed to the stable.

Marsh stopped long enough to watch as Aisha cleared her throat to get the mule's attention, then stared intently at it until it dipped its head low enough for her to get the bit into its mouth and the bridle over its ears. Her eyes flared a brilliant green as she did so, and Marsh wondered just how long she'd been able to talk to mules.

Tams caught her look.

"Since she was four," he said. "Scared the Shades out of me the first time she walked up to a mule and gave it that look."

He cinched the saddle tight and gave her a meaningful stare.

"Scared our parents too, but they don't know of anywhere that can teach her more. It's not shadow magic." He frowned. "Are you going to put that saddle on a mule or just stand there hugging it all day?

Marsh decided he was the pushiest ten year old she had ever encountered, and that she didn't have either the time or reason to adjust his attitude. Without monitoring the pair any further, she began to saddle and lead out the mules as quickly as she could. When she returned to find all the stalls empty, she looked at Tamlin.

"Get them into line and I'll join you."

She didn't tell him why and he didn't bother asking, although he gave her a look full of apprehension. It didn't matter. Marsh had been stalked by a growing feeling of unease ever since they'd arrived, and it had grown strong enough to make her feel slightly nauseated. There was only one way she could think of to ease it.

As soon as she was clear of the mules, she took off at a sprint for the watchtower that stood on the farthest corner from the gate. Taking the stairs two at a time, she ran to the top and looked out over the caverns, adjusting her vision to take in as much as she could from the surrounding darkness. Any other time she would have paused long enough to admire the flaring luminescence that spread out over the cavern, but there was only one thing she was interested in now.

Steadying herself against the edge of the parapet, she took several deep breaths, closed her eyes, and then opened them, again, scanning the farthest reaches of the cavern. It really *was* almost as large as the cavern in which Ruins Hall had been built, and what made it more astounding was that it must have been empty and undiscovered when the waystation had been established.

It didn't take her long to find what she was both looking for and hoping not to find. In the distance, she saw a bright gleam of light. Sharp as a knife, it burned a hole in the dark and gave Marsh an idea of just how far away the force Fabrice's younger daughter had dreamed about was. On seeing it, she didn't stop to ask the shadows how many or who. She just turned and fled down the stairs, barely managing not to run to where Tamlin was leading the mules through the open gates.

"They're coming," she said, slowing her pace as she got closer. Tamlin didn't bother asking who either.

He just turned and scooped Aisha from the ground, settling her on the closest animal.

"This one's yours," he said, passing over another set of reins as soon as his sister was holding on.

Marsh took the reins from his hands and mounted. They booted their beasts into a trot that took them back to the farm at a faster pace than they could have managed on their own. Fabrice and her children were moving among a sea of woolly backs—or rather, Fabrice and Eveline were.

They had put Curt on the back of one of the biggest sheep, and the little girl Marsh remembered from the night before was holding its lead.

"Well, that's one way to keep them out of trouble," Marchant said, and Tamlin's eyes snapped open.

"We need to hurry," he said, his face paler than before, "but only after we get the moutons hooked on."

He slid from the back of his mule and rushed to lift Aisha to the ground.

"Stay there," he told Marsh. "Ask the shadows to keep watch for us."

Ask the shadows to keep watch? At first, Marsh had no idea what he was talking about, then she took a guess at what he meant. Gathering her reins, she rested her hands on the pommel and closed her eyes, trusting things would remain calm enough for her to concentrate on the shadows. The boy was right; they *did* need to know what was happening on the other side of the cavern.

"Show me the people coming through the dark," she said, reaching out and touching the shadow strands that coiled and gathered around her. "Show me how many and who."

She searched the strands, feeling for the ones that could tell her what she wanted to know and releasing those that could not. When she was sure she had found the right ones, Marchant focused on drawing the information through them. She wanted images. She wanted to hear the people talking. She wanted...

What was that? The voice sounded like it was right beside her, and Marsh's eyes snapped open. As soon as she did, the voice faded, to be replaced by the bleating of the moutons and the sound of their hooves as they moved over the road.

They were moving?

Marchant looked around and realized she'd spent more time in the shadow threads than she'd thought. While she'd been focused on searching for whoever was coming across the cavern after them, Tamlin and the others had finished organizing the moutons and clipped a lead rope to her mule's bridle.

"What did you find?" Tamlin asked.

"I heard voices, and it surprised me." She shook her head. "I lost the thread."

He scowled at her.

"We need to know how much time we have," he said, "and if you can hear them, we need to know what they're planning."

"Shouldn't I be keeping an eye on the trail?" she asked, and Tamlin gave her a look of scorn.

"I'm already doing that."

Marsh felt her face heat, more from outrage than embarrassment. The boy was all of ten—and the way he was going, he might not make eleven! What made him think he could read the trail? It was Fabrice who answered her question.

"He's following the trail glows," the woman told her, then added, "I'm sure he'll call you if we run into trouble."

Marsh was sure he'd call her too. What she wasn't sure about was if he'd call her in time. Fabrice had an answer for that too.

"There are five of us watching the trail, and the moutons have their own way of warning us when danger is near. Ruins Hall will need to hear about what happened after we left and what might be coming for them."

The woman had a point, not to mention a vested interest in knowing what might be headed toward the Hall. After all, she was going to be making her home in the cavern, and she wouldn't want to find herself homeless a second time. Marsh sighed.

"Okay. I will try."

If she was honest with herself, she wasn't sure she could find the threads again, even if what Fabrice said was true. However, they needed to know who was bringing the attacks and what they were planning next. Tightening her grip on the reins and the saddle, Marsh closed her eyes and sought the shadows around them. It didn't take her long to find the same threads again.

This time she followed them with more care. She

remembered the words she'd heard before and wondered if the raiders had somehow sensed her looking for them. Was there a way the shadows could hide her presence from those they touched?

Before she could pursue that thought, she felt the threads ripple, their answer an almost tangible wave. Marsh pushed the thought away and gave the shadows all her attention. Right now she needed to find out who was coming for them and what they planned. She needed to see them, by the Shades!

The thread leading to that detail steadied in her mind, and Marsh swept along it until she came to where a column of manlike shapes moved through a grove of tall calla shrooms. Their faces were lit by the faint fluorescence given off by the mushrooms' broad gills, and Marsh was surprised to find they looked nearly the same as she did. In fact, they looked like any of the folk in the four caverns, just a little taller and heavier, with less angular faces. Marchant frowned, studying them a little longer and noting how their clothes were different than what she was used to seeing.

Where her folk favored tunics over breeches, these men and women wore shirts with slightly baggy sleeves and trousers that hung loosely around their legs. It didn't make sense. How did they keep their clothing from snagging on things, and why did they need them to be so loose?

That didn't matter. Although they were dressed differently, they moved with the confidence of those who'd traveled through tunnels before. Even if they were used to the open skies of the surface world, the darkness did not bother them. They had no animals with them, but carried their supplies in heavy packs and bulging satchels slung about them.

And they were armed.

Marsh stared, plucking at the shadows until she found those most connected to their weapons.

"Show me," she demanded and studied the slightly curved blades, both long and short, that hung from their belts, and the spears they used as walking sticks or carried over their shoulders.

Some had small crossbows strapped to their packs, and quivers of bolts hanging from their belts on the opposite side from their swords.

I don't think they're here to parlay, she thought, noting the robed figures scattered throughout the line. These were armed with swords but carried neither crossbows nor spears. Each of them wore what looked like a broad collar from which draped a short length of cloth made of inter-linked chain. The odd-looking garment covered the top half of their chests and backs in a circular loop but looked like it would be useless in a fight.

"Shadow mages?" Marsh mused, noting how the chain links had been dulled as though their wearers had made sure they wouldn't reflect any light. She followed the thread down the line, counting a hundred men and women, a third of whom looked like they were mages. When she reached the end, she worked her way back along the thread and counted again just to be sure.

When she reached the head of the line, she saw the leaders' lips moving and wanted to know what they were saying. Surely the shadows could give her sound in the same way they could give her pictures? She couldn't have been imagining things before.

With the belief firmly held in her mind, Marchant searched amongst the threads. This time she did not open her eyes in shock when she heard words to go with the moving lips in the shadow threads' images.

"Not far, now. We'll have shelter by the first cycle of night," said the pale-faced man in the lead.

Despite the comfort he seemed to be trying to give, Marsh noticed a tightness in his expression, a wariness that said something preyed on his mind. His mouth was drawn and his eyes anxious.

The man beside him gave an amused snort.

"You're not afraid of the dark, are you, Berens? Not missing the sunlit world already?"

Berens scowled.

"Not missing it so much as wanting the feel of solid walls around me. You forget that joffra stalk this cavern, and they come out just as the night cycle starts."

His partner shrugged and gestured back to the line behind them.

"You think they'd attack a group this large and well-armed?"

"I know they would."

Marsh saw the look of disbelief that crossed the other man's face; saw him rally his thoughts to account for this new information.

"Then we will hunt them down as we prepare the cavern."

Prepare the cavern for what? Marsh wanted to know.

"It won't take them long to discover we are here," the

first man commented, but again the second man brushed his worries aside.

"It won't matter. The mages say they have nothing that can challenge a force this size, and we'll be here and gone in a few short months. We take out Ruins Hall, and there will be no reason for anyone at the Ledge to venture beneath the world."

At this, the first man turned on him.

"There are those at the Ledge who have family in Ruins Hall or in any number of holdings scattered in between. And here..."Marsh watched as he gestured to the cavern around him, which was mostly obscured by the tall calla and dangling rock formations. "You don't think someone's going to notice?"

His partner laid a heavy hand on his shoulder.

"By the time the first traders return, we will be settled. As you said, there is no force that can challenge us, and the master bids us establish an outpost here. These are not the only four townships in the region. Perhaps by the time we empty them, it will be enough."

Enough for what? Marsh wondered, but her attention was caught by the approach of one of the mages. And there were other towns beyond the Four? She didn't get far in her pondering before the man walking with Berens lifted his head.

"Someone watches," he said, and all who heard him looked hastily out at the surrounding shroom forest and cavern.

"No," the mage added with an emphatic gesture of his hand. "They watch through the shadows."

Marsh realized he might be talking about her.

The man standing next to the one called Berens lifted his head, his eyes growing dark as he reached out into the darkness around him. Marsh saw him raise his hand as though taking a handful of the surrounding shadow, and then she felt the strand she was using tighten.

"Shadow's Heart," she whispered as he twirled his little finger and she felt the shadow thread tangle around her.

She didn't stay to see what he would do next but let go of the thread, brushing it from her mind as she fled back through the intervening darkness to her place on the mule. Now was the best time to see if the shadows could be made to shelter them, if only she knew how.

She tried, but the darkness slid from her grasp, and a wave of dizziness overtook her. Startled by the feeling that she was about to fall, Marsh opened her eyes, grabbing for the pommel as she felt herself tilting sideways. Her scramble to retain her balance caught Tamlin's attention, and he turned in his saddle even as he tapped the sides of his mule to keep it moving forward.

"What did you do this time?" he demanded.

"They know someone was watching them," Marsh told him. "Not that it's any of your business."

Good one, she thought, *and you're supposed to be the grown-up.*

Tamlin didn't seem to notice.

"Do they know who?"

The boy had stopped his mule and let Marsh's mule come alongside.

"I don't think so."

"Then let's keep going." He handed her the shroom bread she hadn't taken that morning. "You need to eat."

Marchant might have argued with him, except she knew he was right. She *did* need to eat. Kneeing her mule forward, she raised the shroom loaf to her mouth and took a bite. Tamlin rode beside her and didn't say anything until she'd finished the small loaf.

"You think they can follow us?"

"They can try, but they're on foot, and they have to reach the waystation before the night cycle starts. The joffra won't be able to deal with them all but they'll try, and they'll take enough to feed the pack. We won't have to fret about them tonight."

"What about shadow monsters?"

Now that he'd started worrying, Tamlin looked like he was trying to find every problem he could think of and drag it out for consideration. At least this one was easy to answer. Marchant waved her hand at the glows lighting the trail toward Ruins Hall.

"Shadow monsters can't get past those. We'll be okay."

She glanced back at Fabrice, Eveline, Aisha, Tory, and Curt. Even though they seemed to be focused on the dark, she caught it when the older ones snuck glances in her direction.

"We will," she insisted. "We just have to keep going. We should reach Ruins Hall at around the same time as those people behind us get to the waystation."

Fabrice nodded and looked over her children and the herd of mouton.

"The traders say it's a day's journey to the Hall," she said, looking worried. "Will we make it?"

"We will push on until we do," Marsh told her. "As long as there are glows, we will be safe."

She didn't add that they would be safe from the shadow monsters, but from other forms of raiders? Not so much. It wasn't something Fabrice and her children needed to know. She spared a glance for Aisha, smiling when she saw the little girl had copied Curt and abandoned her mule to ride one of the mouton.

At least someone would have a fun journey.

10

REUNION AFTER RUINS HALL

Despite being sure they would make Ruins Hall late in the day, Marchant was pleased to see the soft phosphorescent glow coming from the township's roofs. With no sky to indicate the time of day and no sun to provide light, the town's founders had encouraged the growth of lichens over every wall and rooftop as well as planting luminescent fungi along the streets.

Tall calla shrooms spread their caps above street corners, and knee-high fuzzy antler fungi formed two-toned lines down the center of the main street. Guiding the tired mules and weary sheep down one side of the broad avenue, Marsh breathed a sigh of relief.

Not only was she safe, but she was close to being able to make good on the one delivery she *could* complete. The others were lost to the shadows of the road leading back to Kerrenin's Ledge. Guiding the mules through town, she looked over her shoulder at Fabrice.

"Which way to your friends' farm?"

The woman looked up as though Marchant's question

had startled her and Marsh waited. In the end, Fabrice pointed.

"We follow the road out of town and take the second turn-off. You'll see the marker. It has some kind of tower on it."

Marsh took her word for it. If they didn't see the marker, they would have to camp by the side of the road, which wasn't a good idea for Fabrice and the children. Their journey had shown that the family wasn't used to traveling. Marsh only hoped it wouldn't take too long for them to reach their friends' farm.

As they left the soft light of the town behind them, Marchant took comfort from the sight of the glows lining the road. At least this trail was still guarded. She only hoped it stayed that way.

After leaving Fabrice's cavern behind them, she had worried that the shadow mages might have some way of destroying the glows from a distance. It only made sense that if she could pull on the shadows to draw pictures and sounds from other parts of the cavern, they might be able to influence the shadows to affect the glows. She'd been very glad to discover she'd been wrong.

With that settled, she'd started worrying about the mages peering along threads of shadow to see who she was and where she'd gone. She hadn't been able to stop scanning the dark on both sides of the path, glad her eyes could pick up both light and heat and navigate the night of her world. It was hard to imagine being as blind in the caverns as someone with their eyes closed, yet she'd heard of children born that way.

Marsh shook that idea aside. It was ridiculous. Even if

she was one of the few who could adapt her eyes to the brightness of the outside world so that it did not hurt to wander beneath the surface world's sun, she found the idea of having to rely on bright light to see abhorrent. She was glad she had several different ways of looking at the world, and couldn't imagine what it would be like if she was limited to just one.

Her thoughts were interrupted by a sudden flare of light ahead, and she turned her head toward it.

"There!" Fabrice exclaimed, pointing excitedly in the same direction. "That's the sign. They do the best cheeses in the district!"

And so they might, but Marchant couldn't figure out why there would be a picture of a tower standing in the middle of a round of cheese.

The words Under-Paris Cheeses didn't make much sense either.

"Ooh, pretty!" Aisha said, clapping her hands together. "What dat?"

"It's the Eiffel Tower," Fabrice told her. "They say it used to stand in the middle of the city and that people came from all over the world to see it before things went bad."

Before things went bad—like that hadn't been a long time ago. Marchant took another look at the tower on the sign, wondering how any tower could have been built from latticework and yet have visitors come from all over the world to see it. Rather than say anything, she turned her mule onto the side road and shivered when she noticed the lack of glows lining the path.

How did they expect to stay safe from anything on a

path as dark as this one? Even knowing it was there, Marsh had trouble picking it out.

"Give it a minute." Fabrice's voice made Marsh pause. "The lights will come on soon."

What lights? Marsh wondered, staring hard at the shadowy edges of the path, but the road answered her question as patches of lichen slowly glowed to life.

"They react to the vibrations of the moutons and mules walking beside them."

Marsh stared.

Well! That was certainly new. She hadn't seen this kind of lichen before—and neither had her mule, she realized as the creature stopped short and snorted, its head lowered and ears pricked forward as it stared at the ground in mild alarm. Marsh reached out and stroked its neck.

"Easy there," she told it, nudging it forward with her heels. "Easy there. It's not going to eat you."

She hoped that last bit was true but figured the lichen would have been killed off long ago if it had a habit of eating anything that came along the path. The mule didn't know she had doubts. It just flicked its ears back and forth a couple of times and obeyed the tap of her heels.

Marsh was glad to see that the lichen seemed to be interconnected as more of the soft fuzzy growth lit the edges of the side road ahead of them. Glowing a soft blue, it marked the trail until they saw the outlines of the farmhouse proper. At first, Marsh was afraid that this farm had met the same fate as the farms in Fabrice's cavern. There was no light at all in the dwelling, not even the faint glow of a banked fire.

The windows remained dark until they had reached the

gates leading into the front yard. Marchant slipped from the saddle and led her mule over to them, glad when she caught sight of Tamlin doing the same thing. They stopped at the gate, trying to work out how to open it.

In the end, Marsh handed Tamlin her reins and lifted the metal loop holding the gate in place. He followed her through, the ram and ewes hooked to his saddle coming after. Marsh stood by the gate, watching as the moutons flooded into the field after them, well aware she could see very little of the cavern beyond the glowing lichen lighting the path. When the last moutons had passed through and Tamlin had led them a little farther into the field, she closed the gate behind them, making sure to secure it again.

"Fabrice?" she called. "It might be better if—"

Light blazed around them, scattering the moutons and startling the mules into bucking and braying with fright.

"Shadow's Heart!" Marchant snapped, shielding her eyes, which watered with pain.

She was glad she wasn't holding a mule when she heard Tamlin shout in alarm. She tried to brush away the tears obscuring her vision so she could see what was going on.

"Curt!" Fabrice shouted as the boy's shrill shriek split the dark. "Hang on tight, sweetie. I'm coming."

"Aisha!"

Marsh turned away from the light, blinking rapidly in an attempt to clear her vision. She was aware of movement on the stone veranda surrounding the house and could hear booted feet moving behind her. She placed her faith in Fabrice's claim that these were friends and focused her attention on finding where the mouton had carried Aisha.

Just as she started to make out shapes and color in the brightness, a whistle split the air. Short and sharp, it was followed by a series of shrill chirps that Hugo answered with a deep bark. Marsh heard the big dog run past her, followed by the eager patter of smaller paws, and knew Scruffknuckle was still shadowing the farm dog's every move.

She raised a hand to wipe her eyes and felt a large warm palm descend on her shoulder.

"Stay there. We'll see to the sheep."

"The children..." Marsh began, and the man chuckled.

"Them too. We'll bring them back. You just let your eyes adjust."

"Who are you?"

"Didn't Fabrice tell you?"

"She told me you were friends. I was helping her reach you. Why did you..." She stopped and gestured briefly at the well-lit home paddock before her.

"Hit you with bright glows?"

Marsh nodded, sniffing as her nose ran in sympathy with the watering of her eyes.

"We were making sure you weren't shadow mages."

Marsh snorted in disbelief and waved at the animals being brought back together by the dogs. Hugo wasn't working alone. He and Scruffknuckle had been joined by several other large dogs, and between them, they were making short work of bringing the scattered herd together.

"Didn't you see the moutons?"

"We wanted to be sure."

It was an answer that made Marsh wonder what had gone on in the caverns to make these men so cautious.

"I thought the local shadow mages were friendly."

The hand patted her on the shoulder, then moved to the center of her back and guided her toward the veranda steps.

"The *local* shadow mages are okay, and *they* take no for an answer. It's the new ones who have me worried."

Fabrice gasped when she heard him and Marsh turned her head to watch the woman approach, carrying a teary Curt in her arms. Behind her, Eveline carried Tory. Fabrice's dark hair was wild from the day's journey, her eyes ringed with shadow and her face pale.

"When did they come, Cleon?"

Having seen Marsh onto the veranda, the man's narrow face softened and he turned to offer Fabrice his hand.

"A week ago, maybe two. We told them no and they came again a few days later, suggesting we were neglectful. The third time, we hit them with the glows and set the dogs on them." He shrugged, a hard smile crossing his face but going no farther than his lips. "They haven't been back since."

He tucked Fabrice's hand through his arm, his face hawkish in profile as he turned away. His thick, dark hair did nothing to soften it.

"Come on in. You haven't told us what you're doing here." He glanced at the gathered moutons, his eyes taking on a worried look. "I don't see Patrik."

He shot another look at Marchant, who now had Tamlin and Aisha standing alongside her.

"Your friends can come too."

It hadn't crossed Marsh's mind that he might not welcome them with Fabrice, and the shock of it had her giving him a wide-eyed stare. He caught it but turned away, not offering her a clue how serious he might have been about leaving them outside. She followed before he could change his mind.

"We need to be gone in the morning," she said as another of those who'd come out to meet them followed them into the house and pulled the door closed behind them. It was a relief to find the inside of the house lit with gentler glows than the ones outside.

The sound of a locking bar falling into place made her jump, and Marsh turned with Tamlin to look behind them. The boy surprised Marsh by sliding a hand into hers. Him having a firm grip on Aisha was normal, and the fact she was shouting for her puppy, something Marsh should have expected.

"Scruffknuckle!" she cried, twisting in her brother's grip and reaching for the door. "Scruff!"

The rapid scrabble of paws against the front door answered her cry, and everyone shuffled to a stop.

"It's the pup," Marsh explained when Cleon turned toward her, eyebrows raised. "She needs him."

"We don't allow dogs in the house," Cleon retorted, but Fabrice slapped him on the shoulder, scolding him as she did.

"Since when, Cleon Sursees? Last time I visited, there were a full half-dozen under your kitchen table."

The man turned to meet Fabrice's eyes and sighed.

"Fine," he said and gestured toward the door. "Let them in."

The two men who'd come in after Marsh lifted the

locking bar, opening the door wide enough to let Scruff and Hugo through. Two more dogs followed.

"The others will be around back," Cleon explained. "These two have no manners."

From the way he said it, he didn't expect them to grow any either, and he didn't care. When they reached him, he ruffled each of their heads affectionately and pointed to a door at the end of the hall.

"Mats," he said, and the dogs went, leaving Scruffknuckle dancing around Aisha with puppy glee and Hugo sitting beside Fabrice, his dark-brown eyes switching between his mistress's face and the man standing beside her.

They followed him farther into the house, and soon after that Cleon's wife had the children fed and tucked into their beds. When she returned to the table, Fabrice told her what had happened in the cavern, and they turned to Marsh.

"How did *you* get to be there?"

It was a long time before Marchant was shown to a spare patch of floor beside the children's bunk. She woke the next morning to the bleating of the moutons and the sound of dogs at work and headed to the kitchen, leaving the children still sleeping. Tamlin would be mortified, but he needed the sleep, whether he'd admit it or not.

ARRIVAL AT RUINS HALL

Marchant bumped into Fabrice in the hallway, and the two of them walked in companionable silence to the kitchen. Cleon and his wife Marcelle were already there.

"Sleep well?"

"Yes, thank you."

"*Oui.*"

"What time you heading out?"

Way to make a girl feel welcome, Marchant thought, catching Cleon's eye. She gestured toward Fabrice.

"Had to see what Fabrice wanted to do with the mules," she said. "There'll be a reward from the traders for bringing them back. I'd like to see that she collects."

It was difficult to keep her eyes fixed on Cleon's face when she knew Fabrice was giving her a look of surprise. For a minute she thought Cleon wouldn't catch what she was doing, but then he spoke.

"We'll need to report what went on in Leon's Deep," he

said, "and to put in for a few more supplies. You could travel with us."

He said it casually, as if he was doing her a favor. Marchant knew it wasn't that, though. Going by the conversation they'd had last night, she got the impression he didn't show a lot of emotion, and that what Fabrice and Patrik had experienced was affecting him more than he cared to admit. Before she could garner more from his expression, Fabrice tugged on her sleeve.

"You can't do that," she said. "It was you and the children who found the mules and fed them."

"Eveline helped, *and* she traced their ownership so they could be returned. The reward is yours."

"But…"

Marchant held up her hand.

"You'll need it to get established here, and I have wages waiting."

It wasn't entirely true. Her wages depended on delivery, and the shadow monsters had put paid to that—not to mention that Kearick would want the cost of his mule repaid. Marsh frowned, trying to work out a way to reason with the man.

"Kaffee," Marcelle said, bumping a heavy clay mug against her hands. "You'll need to wake the children so they can eat before you leave."

From the look she shot her husband, this last was not negotiable, no matter what he thought.

Marsh shook away all thought of what Kearick was going to say or how much longer it was going to take before she'd made enough to pay him back so he would find her a mentor among the seekers. Remembering them reminded her of the tower on Cleon's sign, and she added the Eiffel Tower to the list of legends she wanted to look for—even if it meant she had to travel to the surface to find its remains.

She drank her kaffee, then went to fetch Tamlin and Aisha. To her surprise, Scruffknuckle growled when she shook Aisha gently awake.

"Put a sock in it, Scruff, or I'll turn you into a slipper."

"No!"

Well, that was one way to wake the child, Marsh thought.

"No turn Scruffy into slipper!"

"I didn't mean it…"

"No! Not funny!"

"But…"

The ruckus woke Tamlin, who slipped out of his bunk and hugged his sister until she quieted.

"You hungry?" he asked, and Aisha stopped fighting long enough to nod. "Good. Let's take Scruffknuckle to the kitchen. He'll be hungry too."

Aisha was out of bed in double-quick time, calling for the pup as she followed Tamlin out of the room. She shot Marsh a dark look as she went. Marsh held back the urge to tell them they were welcome and turned to make sure everything was packed instead. When she headed back to the kitchen, she had their gear in hand. She propped it by the kitchen door and joined the others at the table.

Breakfast was a simple affair of a puffy shroom pastry shaped into a crescent and another mug of milky kaffee.

"Boys will have the mules rounded up and saddled soon," Cleon told her. "We can leave when you're done."

As if she was holding everyone up... Marsh wanted to ask him what his problem was but decided she didn't want to know. It wasn't like he was going to be an issue for her much longer. Once they hit town and she'd made sure Fabrice was paid, they could go their separate ways. That should make the hawk-faced farmer happy.

"Have they restored the route to Kerrenin's Ledge?" she asked as they headed out to where the mules were tied.

Marsh noted that the sheep had been moved to a neighboring paddock and the mules had been groomed, their coats gleaming under the glows and their tails hanging smoothly. She headed over to the mule she'd ridden the day before, watching as Cleon moved to talk to the farmhands standing nearby. From the emphatic hand gestures in the direction of the moutons and the barn, she guessed he was giving them their work orders for the day. By the time he was done, she was mounted and waiting to leave, Tamlin and Aisha riding double on the next mule in the line.

"You ready?" Cleon asked Fabrice as he returned to them, and the woman nodded.

She blushed as she shot Marsh an apologetic look and turned her attention to where her children were standing with Marcelle on the farmhouse's veranda. For a moment her face clouded, then she gathered her reins and turned her mule in Cleon's wake. The look Marsh caught on her face when she thought she couldn't be seen from the veranda was heart-wrenching.

Something had to be done about the shadow mages. Something...

Tamlin's startled gasp pulled her from her thoughts and

she looked back to make sure he was all right. The look on his face was full of shock, but Marsh couldn't work out why because he was looking right at her. The look on Aisha's face mirrored her brother's, and Marsh shook her head clear of all thought of the shadow mages and the raiders.

"What?" she asked, and didn't like the disbelief that drove the shock from Tamlin's expression.

"You don't know?"

"Don't know what?"

"The shadows..." He frowned as though trying to find the words.

In the end, he shrugged and indicated the mules ahead of them.

"We need to keep up."

That much was true, and she didn't have time to stop and check the shadows herself right then. Cleon wasn't waiting, and Fabrice seemed too lost in thought to remember them. Marsh tapped her mule's sides and made sure to keep close to the end of the line. This time the gleaming lichens that came to life on either side of the trail did not come as a surprise. The journey along the main path back to Ruins Hall seemed nowhere near as long.

Scruffknuckle stayed close to the mule carrying Aisha, looking a bit lost without Hugo. The pup bounced excitedly around the little girl when Tamlin helped her to the ground. Watching them as she dismounted, Marchant caught herself thinking the pair had been traveling on their own for a long time—but she knew that wasn't true.

She wondered where their parents were and caught herself tweaking the shadow strands around her. It was no surprise when they came up empty. She did the same thing seeking Fabrice's husband, but none of them vibrated in answer. Curious, Marsh thought of the raiders' leaders, picturing them in her mind and trying to recall their voices.

Again nothing.

That was odd. Marsh knew the raiders' leaders were alive, and even knew vaguely where they could be found. Was there a limit to what the shadows could do? Just to be sure, Marchant turned her back on Fabrice and Cleon and asked the shadows to locate them. This time the vibrations rang loud and clear, snapping taut just before Cleon spoke from beside her.

"When you're done daydreaming, the traders' office is this way."

Marsh opened her eyes and found Cleon staring right into her face. She backed up a step, only to be stopped short by the mule standing behind her. The animal gave a protesting snort as she ran into its side.

"You a shadow mage, girl?"

Marsh pulled her face away from his and shook her head, watching his eyebrows rise in disbelief.

"Could have fooled me."

Marsh laid both hands on his chest and shoved him away.

"And you need to chew some ditch mint," she said, pushing past him to reach the traders' office door. "Hurry up, Tamlin, Aisha."

Ignoring their startled looks and the mild rebellion that flared across Aisha's face, Marsh stepped onto the stone footpath where Fabrice was waiting.

"I can't accept all of the reward," the woman told her, and Marchant smiled at her.

"Your children need it."

"And yours don't?"

Marsh looked at where Tamlin and Aisha were following her up the stairs.

"They're not my children, and they'll be fine."

"And what about you?"

"Our deal was bed and board for passage out of the cavern. We have both completed that part of the trade."

Before Fabrice could argue with her any further, Marsh pushed open the door and stepped into the traders' office. In the end, she didn't quite get everything her way.

"Because you were present at the feeding and retrieval," the clerk told her, "you are entitled to a portion of the reward."

"But..."

The clerk held up her hand, forestalling Marsh's protest as Fabrice covered her mouth with her hand.

"It is the law of the trade," the clerk explained and tapped another book bound in shroom leather, "and I have your details right here."

"Then I'd like to transfer my portion."

"No," Fabrice said too quickly for Marsh to silence her. "I won't accept it. Place it on her balance."

And that had been the end of that. The clerk had made the appropriate annotations and handed Fabrice a receipt. Marsh was glad to see that the woman had gotten the lion's share of the reward, but not so glad when the clerk continued.

"I will call a guild and town meeting," she said. "The

Ruins Hall leadership and the guards and merchants' guild need to hear about what happened in Leon's Deep and on the trail to Kerrenin's Ledge. We have sent runners to the monastery to fetch a mage to charge the glows, but they are not due to return until later today, and the visiting mage needs authorization to act since recharging the glows is outside his usual duties."

Marchant couldn't understand that. Didn't all shadow mages work the light as well? Wasn't that part of their philosophy? Balance?

"I will convene the meeting in two hours," the clerk informed them, unaware of Marsh's puzzlement. "The matter is of sufficient urgency."

She turned to Cleon.

"You are free to go about your tasks, but I respectfully ask that you be present. There is no time to call a full conclave of farmholds. You will be their spokesman until such time as a conclave occurs. I suggest it be within the week."

Judging by her tone of voice, it was not a suggestion so much as an order, and Cleon did not argue.

"Of course, Clerk."

He turned away, offering his arm to Fabrice.

"Since you will be helping Marcelle, I will be purchasing the supplies. If you could direct me about what we need?"

It was the politest Marchant had seen him, and she wondered what she'd done to deserve his ire. Again the clerk interrupted her thoughts.

"May I help you further?"

Marsh gestured toward where Tamlin and Aisha stood

quietly to one side of the office, Scruffknuckle sitting between them.

"The children..." she began, and the clerk frowned.

"What about them?"

"Well, they're not mine. I only rescued them during the shadow-monster attack."

"Then they stay with you. In lieu of relations or any other guardian adult, you shall continue in your care of them."

"But..." Marsh began, and Tamlin cleared his throat.

"You could always ask the shadow mages," he said, and Aisha wound her hand into his. "If you're too busy to take us on, that is."

Marsh wanted to argue that of course, she wasn't too busy, but she knew better. She would be traveling a lot, and the road wasn't any sort of place for children, especially if they weren't with their parents. On the other hand, she *was* the one who had snatched them away from the shadow monsters, her very actions promising that she'd take care of them, and it didn't seem fair to abandon them now.

She glanced at the clerk.

"Is there somewhere private we could go to discuss this?"

The clerk gave her a quick shrug and pushed back her seat.

"We have no conference rooms to spare," she said. "Maybe try the eatery."

She waved toward the door, indicating vaguely that they should turn left when they walked out and strongly that they should leave. Marsh was about to do so when one more idea struck.

"Have there been other incidents of settlements disappearing?"

"Recently."

From the way the clerk looked up at her and then back down at her books, the woman wasn't going to give her any more details. Marsh decided to push her a little.

"And were they visited by shadow mages beforehand?"

"Yes."

Marsh sighed.

"Local ones?"

The clerk shook her head.

"No." She looked up at Marsh with a heavy sigh. "Look, we'll be covering this in the meeting this afternoon. Do you mind?"

Did she mind what? Marsh wasn't sure what the woman was doing that was so urgent, but she knew the look on her face. If she pushed too much more, she was going to find it difficult when she came back looking for another package to deliver.

"Thank you," she said. "We'll see you at the meeting."

"Make sure you're there. We need your report of the Kerrenin's Ledge trail attack and what you found when you arrived at Leon's Deep."

The clerk didn't add that she would be very upset if Marchant didn't turn up. She didn't need to. The look on her face was eloquent enough. Tamlin, Aisha, and Scruffknuckle followed Marsh out of the office and into the glow-lit street beyond.

"Where to now, *Mum*?" Tamlin asked, and Marsh glared at him.

"Call me Marsh," she said. "Or 'Auntie,' or…whatever!"

"Sure thing, *Whatever.*"

"Scre…Go jump."

Tamlin snickered, but Aisha shifted her gaze between them, her expression showing she was horrified.

"Rude!" she said, and Scruff gave a muffled wuff at her side.

Great, Marsh thought. *Just what I need—commentary from the peanut gallery. Time to change the subject.*

"Where to?" she asked.

Aisha looked at her brother, and Tamlin frowned.

"Do you think the shadow mages knew Mum and Dad were coming?" he asked. "Maybe they were expecting me?"

From the way he said it, he didn't hold out much hope of it being true, but it was a good idea.

"Why don't we go check it out?" Marsh told him. "The clerk said there was a visiting mage. Maybe they have offices."

"Hungry," Aisha chimed in and patted the puppy sitting beside her. "Scruffy's hungry."

Oh, Scruffy is, is he? Marsh gave Aisha a disbelieving look and the little girl giggled. The sound brought a smile to Marsh's face, and she ruffled the child's hair.

"You sure you don't want anything too?" she asked, and Aisha gave her a coquettish look.

"Maybe…."

"Uh huh."

Marsh took a left turn and headed for the eatery, figuring it had to be the shop under the banner showing a kaffee cup and a crescent-shaped pastry.

12

RUINS HALL WELCOME

Despite the early hour, the eatery was busy. Unusually so, Marsh thought as she pushed through the doors. Tamlin and Aisha were two steps behind her. Men and women in traveling leathers gathered around the tables. They were dressed like every caravan guard she had ever seen, and every single one of them looked up when she came in. Marsh ignored them and headed for the counter.

After all, a mouton was free to look at a shadow mage.

She stopped halfway across the room when one of the caravan guards stepped into her path. The woman was a head taller than Marsh, and her platinum hair was tied back in a braid that would keep it out of her face in a fight.

"I know you."

Marsh took a step back, looking her up and down. Hard brown eyes stared back. There was nothing familiar in the guard's features.

"Pretty sure you don't."

The woman closed the space between them and laid a hand in the center of Marsh's chest.

"Yeah, I do. You were on the caravan scheduled to leave Kerrenin's Ledge after mine—and not happy with being put at the back."

Marsh shrugged, looked down at the hand and back into angry eyes, and she decided she wasn't backing up anymore. That wasn't how to win *this* game. She folded her arms across her chest and fixed the woman with a hard stare of her own.

"Name me a single traveler who is ever happy with being last in line."

She made a show of looking toward the counter.

"I need to eat."

"Not here, you don't."

To Marsh's surprise, several of those around her growled their agreement. Marsh held her ground.

"Only place that's open."

She resisted the urge to use the children as a bargaining chip and looked again at the woman's hand and back to her face.

"You need to clear a path."

"No, I need to toss your ass out of here."

"You can try." With that, Marsh twisted around the woman's hand, ducking under her reach to ram her shoulders into her waist and wrap an arm around her.

She'd been hoping to tip her over the leg she'd slipped past her ankles, but her opponent wasn't a stranger to a good fight.

Caravan guard, Marsh reminded herself as the woman got one hand on her shoulder. Idiot!

An elbow slammed into the center of her back and Marsh grinned as the woman yelped. The artifact was solid metal, and any good fighter should have known better than to strike someone's pack. Of course, if it was the only place she could hit, and the blow had been instinctive...

The heavy impact of a well-placed fist under the pack caught her in the side, and her opponent moved back, stepping over her foot.

"Nice try, short stuff."

The kick came faster than Marsh had expected, but she twisted enough that it only grazed her ribs. It was a pity she was too busy trying to avoid the foot to remember to grab it. She backed up, hoping for a bit of distance—and someone seized her from behind, pulling her arms back.

Well, fine! She hadn't grown up in a waystation to be bullied by every traveler's kid that came through. Marsh used the person at her back as a brace, lashing out with both feet as her first opponent closed and then trying to drop to her knees and pull the person behind her over her shoulders.

It didn't work. He was too big and had too good a hold, and her knees didn't hit the ground.

"Shadow's Heart," she muttered as the grip on her arms tightened and she was pulled hard up against an armored chest.

Why did caravan guards have to be so Shadows-cursed *big*?

And why did they always have to work together?

She tried for another kick as her platinum-haired opponent closed, but the woman knocked it aside. Well, this was going to be painful. Marsh tried again to twist out of the hands pinning her upper arms and then lashed back with one foot, trying to connect with a knee. She found a shin...covered by a hardened leather boot.

"*Putain!*"

The man holding her laughed, but Marsh didn't have time to reply before the woman drove a fist into her gut. Marsh tried to block with her forearms but didn't have enough range of motion to bring them down in time. She really hoped Tamlin could get Aisha out of the eatery before these guys beat her senseless. Actually, she really hoped he'd gotten his sister out of here before the fight had gotten this far. This wasn't the sort of thing kids should be seeing.

No such luck, as it turned out.

Marsh grunted as the second blow hit home. She wanted to double up but couldn't, and her mind drifted. She remembered wondering if the shadows could shield her from the shadow mages, and wished they would shield her now because she couldn't afford to be laid up for the weeks a serious beating would take to heal.

Trying to twist away from the next blow, she pulled her legs up in an attempt to protect herself. Somewhere outside the private world of hurt she was in, someone was shouting. Marsh wondered, if she pulled enough threads of shadow together, would they cushion the next blow? It was better than waiting for it to land.

What would a shadow shield look like?

The world slowed down as the fist crawled toward her, then darkness flickered before Marsh's eyes. Great, now she was going to black out. It would be interesting to see just how many additional bruises she would have when she woke up.

To her surprise, that wasn't what happened.

The blow never landed, and the shouting faded. The hands holding her arms loosened their grip and pushed her toward the female guard, who was now trying to pull her hand out of an oval disc of shadow.

Where had that come from?

Around her, the silence grew into a pervasive hush. Marsh let her feet carry her forward to where she could lean on a table. All she wanted to do was be violently and spectacularly sick, but she couldn't. That was a surefire way to get kicked out of the eatery, and she'd promised the children breakfast. Instead, she concentrated on getting her breath back and keeping the kaffee and pastry she'd eaten at the farm down.

She barely noticed when Aisha came to stand on one side of her, both small hands wrapped around one end of a rolling pin. Tamlin moved to her other side, also holding something between him and the guards around them. The small fierce growl coming from behind her legs was all too familiar, and it succeeded in pulling her out of her discomfort long enough to register that she was still standing in the middle of a crowd of caravan guards—and that they were all staring at her but not moving a single step nearer.

Marsh raised her head and realized there was something different about the way they were looking at her. Now there was fear mixed with their expressions of anger and dislike. She looked at the children standing on either side of her and noticed they were standing with their backs to her. Tamlin held a skillet in a two-handed grip, and

Aisha waved the rolling pin. Behind her, Scruffknuckle's growl was undiminished.

"What…" she began, making herself straighten and take a good look around the eatery.

The first thing she registered was that there was still shadow surrounding the female guard's hand, which, of course, was when the door to the eatery opened.

"You might want to dispel that."

Marsh turned toward the voice, wondering what new trouble she'd gotten herself into—and recoiled from the figure coming through the door, her hand going to the hilt of her sword. In a flash, the puppy and two children had interposed themselves between them. That was going to make things awkward.

"Tamlin, move!"

The boy shook his head, his attention not wavering from the shadow mage who'd just stepped into the eatery.

"Aisha!"

"Nuh-uh!"

Before she could say his name, the puppy growled, but whether it was because the shadow mage had taken another step toward them or in defiance, Marsh couldn't tell.

"You want to call your army off?"

Someone snickered.

"I promise I'm not going to hurt anyone. I just came for breakfast."

That struck a chord.

"Yeah, so did I," Marsh told him, letting go of her sword and reaching out to lay a hand on each of the children's shoulders. "Come on, guys. I don't think he's one of the *bad* shadow mages."

When neither of them moved, she tried again.

"He's probably one of the ones your parents wanted you to meet, Tams. Remember? We had to go find him after breakfast."

That got a reaction from both of them.

Aisha looked at her brother, and Tamlin lowered the frying pan. The shadow mage shifted his gaze from Marchant to the boy as though assessing him.

"Sorry," Tams said, but Marsh couldn't work out whether he was apologizing to her or the newly-arrived mage.

The boy looked up at her before pointing past her to where the female caravan guard was still trying to extract her fist.

"I'd leave her there if I were you," he said and walked past the woman to the couple standing behind the counter. His sister followed in his wake. "Thanks for the loan."

He held out the skillet, but they just stared at him. Finally, he sighed and put it on the counter.

"I borrowed it," he told them, "when you weren't looking."

"And I dis," Aisha said, waving the rolling pin.

She stood on her tip-toes, trying to push the rolling pin onto the counter. Tamlin took it from her, setting it carefully inside the pan. Marsh looked at the mage and held out her hand.

"Marchant," she said, and the mage smiled, accepting it.

He has a very cute smile, Marsh thought, and blushed. Fortunately, the mage didn't seem to notice it as he pulled her close and kissed her on both cheeks by way of greeting. Marsh froze.

"Roeglin." He paused, then said, "Over breakfast, you can tell me why your first option was a sword. For now, you really need to bust Lennie's hand out of there."

"Lennie?"

"Me." The guard sounded like she was choking down the urge to shout.

Marsh studied the way the shadow had bonded around the woman's fist.

"I don't know if I can."

The woman tried to jerk her hand free of the shadow ball.

"Don't...play...games. With. Me."

Marsh hoped her face showed the uncertainty she felt.

"No, I really don't."

"You just unthink it," the mage told her. "Unweave the threads. You wove the shield. You can unweave it."

"I can?"

Lennie wasn't impressed.

"You'd better."

Or she'd do what? Marchant wondered but didn't say it. For now, it was good enough that Lennie wasn't trying to beat the stuffing out of her, and she wanted to keep it that way, at least for a little while longer.

"What if I can't?"

Lennie made a sound that was a blend of frustration and outrage. She jerked her hand as hard as she could, trying to free it from the slowly turning ball of shadow.

"I'll help you."

Roeglin came and stood beside her and Lennie stilled,

glaring at the pair of them. The look on her face made Marsh wonder if she really wanted to cut the woman loose.

"Now, remember, all you have to do is feel the threads and ask them to let go."

He glanced at the caravan guards gathered around them.

"You just have to ask. The shadows will listen."

She just had to ask.

Like when she asked the threads to show her where the raiders were or to show her who was moving on the other side of the cavern? Just like that, only both those times she'd had her eyes closed and hadn't been focused on anything, let alone a single fist that was about to connect. When she'd wanted to shield herself from Lennie's next blow, she *had* focused.

Marsh took a deep breath and held it. Letting it out slowly, she concentrated on the cluster of shadow threads balled around Lennie's hand. They had woven themselves into something tangible; Marsh had never seen the like. She reached out to touch the ball and Lennie flinched.

Big brave fighter, my ass, Marsh thought.

"Screw you!"

Marsh realized she had spoken out loud.

"*Merde*. I'm sorry, I didn't mean..."

The woman's lips curved into a short, sharp smile that was gone seconds later.

"Sure you did. You just didn't mean to say it out loud. Now get on with it."

"Right."

Marsh bent to her task, focusing on the threads. At first,

she tried to gently tease them apart, but the threads wouldn't answer the fingers of her mind.

"Come on," she said, stroking her hands over the ball. "Thank you for protecting me, but please let her go. Please...."

As she said it, she thought about how Lennie's hand had looked without the ball of shadow around it. The image of the guard's fist coming toward her made her hesitate, but she reminded herself that the blow was no longer coming and she was no longer under threat.

"You have done what I asked, and done it well," she told the shadow, stroking her hand over it like it was a kitten or Scruffknuckle in a rare moment of stillness. "Thank you."

It happened between one stroke and the next. One minute the shadow threads curled under her fingers, arching into her touch, and the next they were gone, dissipating like mist in a sudden breeze. It left Marsh staring and Lennie looking at her, clearly contemplating whether to throw another punch. Roeglin preempted that by wrapping an arm around Marsh's shoulders.

"Come on," he said. "You owe me pancakes. The boy even gave them the right skillet."

As he ran his mouth, he pulled Marsh past Lennie, putting his body between them—which, in hindsight, was probably braver than he needed to be. Instead of stopping at a table, the mage waltzed past the counter to the serving door, and then he pushed right through it.

"We're eating in the kitchen today, Marc," he said, his tone not brooking any argument as he gave the dining room a meaningful glance. "Don't want to upset your usual customers. Come on, kids. Bring the pup."

That got a reaction from the woman behind the counter.

"No dogs in the kitchen."

Roeglin didn't pause.

"Not a dog," he retorted. "Krypthund. Whole different beastie."

Beastie? Like, seriously?

Apparently so.

"Come on, you two. Bring your beastie before the cook changes her mind."

The cook plucked the skillet from the countertop, hefting it as though she were contemplating using it on Roeglin's head as she followed him into the kitchen. Tamlin and Aisha followed cautiously behind, and Scruffknuckle bounced after them, yapping defiantly at the closest caravan guard.

Roeglin didn't stop moving until he'd guided Marsh to a table in a corner of the kitchen.

"C'mere, pup," he said, letting go of her and plonking himself down in a chair that put him between Marsh and the rest of the world. "Hurry up before she brains you with that skillet."

He snapped his fingers, and Scruffknuckle tilted his head toward him. Marsh's eyes widened as a piece of jerky appeared in his hand, and Scruffknuckle was lost. The pup bounced over to the mage and tried to snatch the treat from his fingers, but Roeglin tucked it out of bite range and fixed him with a stern glare, snaring Scruff's gaze as he did so.

For an instant, Roeglin's eyes flared green. Scruffknuckle sat, then stretched out beside Roeglin's chair.

"There's a good boy," Roeglin said, handing the pup the jerky. "Now, be a good pup and stay there. And you, young lady," he continued, addressing Aisha. "Come and sit down. You're safe now."

For a moment, Marchant thought Aisha was going to refuse. She watched as the girl stood her ground, resisting the draw of Tamlin's hand on her shoulder as she regarded the mage with serious eyes.

"Bad mens comed in de dark."

Roeglin didn't laugh. He returned the child's look and nodded.

"Are you going to help us stop them?"

Marsh opened her mouth to protest and caught Tamlin's hasty shake of the head, so she sat still and said nothing. Aisha continued studying Roeglin.

"I can talk with rocks."

"You can?" Roeglin sounded genuinely surprised. "And do they talk back?"

Aisha gave him a solid nod and took a tentative step forward. Roeglin patted the seat next to his.

"That might be a useful skill," he said. "You are not too little to sit at this table."

As if that was what she had been waiting to hear, Aisha walked quickly to the table. When she reached it, however, she didn't take the seat next to Roeglin. She sat on the floor next to the puppy, burying her hands in his fur as he rolled over to lean against her.

"I sit here," the little girl said, looking up at the mage. "You talk to Tams."

"Tams, hey?" Marsh knew Aisha had surprised the mage, again.

At the mention of his name, the boy crossed to the table and took the seat diagonally opposite the mage and Marsh.

"That's the most she's said ever," he told Roeglin, setting himself up so he could see the kitchen as well as the door leading into it. It made Marsh wonder if she'd misjudged his age, but Tams cast her a glance as though reading her mind.

"Someone has to keep watch."

"Just how old are you, anyway?" she asked.

"Nearly eleven." Tams paused. "Sort of."

"So ten and a half, then," Roeglin said with a hint of teasing in his voice, and Tams shrugged.

The mage pointed at Aisha.

"How old's she?"

"Fi...no, *seven*!" Aisha replied before her brother had a chance to answer, and she fixed him with a defiant look that dared him to say differently.

Tams rolled his eyes and Roeglin snickered.

"So it's kaffee all around then?" he asked, and Aisha frowned.

"Chocolate," she said, then opened her eyes really wide and looked up at him. "Please."

"And for me," Marsh added.

She'd always preferred chocolate to kaffee, but most adults never asked. They just assumed she liked the same brew as everyone else. Roeglin gave her a look that said he'd been about to make the same mistake and glanced at Tams.

"Kaffee's good," the boy said. Marsh wondered how old his parents would have wanted him to be before they let him touch the brew.

The way he avoided her eye said it was a good bit older than he was now. She caught Roeglin's brief look of question and shrugged. What the boy's parents might have ruled and what she was going to insist on were probably two different things, and given what he'd already been through...

"He's old enough," she said, and surprise and gratitude flickered across the boy's face.

While they'd been talking, the woman from the front counter had come through the back, frowning briefly at Roeglin and his small group as she headed for the stove. She'd worked while they discussed what they were going to drink, but she hadn't missed a thing. As soon as Marsh had given the okay, she'd set out five cups and began pouring from two large metal jugs that had been sitting at the back of the stove. Marsh watched her, wondering who the fifth cup was for.

The answer came when the woman brought Aisha her chocolate and set a cup of warm milk down in front of Scruffknuckle.

"Looks like he's in the same boat as these two," she offered as she straightened up. "They'll be fine together."

Marsh caught her unspoken question.

"I'm hoping to find someone to care for them until some relatives can be found. Do you know if anyone made it back from the last caravan to leave for Kerrenin's Ledge?"

The woman's lips tightened, and she looked down at the bowl she was using to mix the pancake batter. Marsh caught the brief shake of her head and felt her heart sink. Glancing down, she saw Aisha had frozen mid-sip of her chocolate. A look at where Tams had stopped, his cup halfway to his mouth, warned her that she might have made a mistake.

"I'm sorry," the woman murmured and carried the batter over to where the skillet was heating on the stovetop. Roeglin waved her apology away and turned toward the table, looking down at Aisha as he did so.

"Drink your chocolate," he said as though he was immune to the tears shimmering in her eyes.

"Drink," he repeated sternly when Aisha's bottom lip trembled, and he watched her as the child lifted the cup to her mouth.

Roeglin didn't give Marsh time to wonder why he was being so hard. He turned to Tamlin and got straight down to business.

"Your parents wanted you to meet me?"

Tamlin lifted his cup and took a large sip of the kaffee. Marsh caught the glint of tears in the boy's eyes and knew he was using the move as a delaying tactic to get his emotions under control. It was pretty effective. Roeglin eyed him while he waited, and after Tamlin had swallowed his mouthful, raised an eyebrow. The boy clutched the cup to his chest as though it would ward off what Roeglin's questions would bring.

"Well?" Again Roeglin's voice held a hard quality that demanded obedience—and an answer.

"Yessir."

"Why?"

"They said my magic... They said I would need guidance."

Roeglin made a show of looking the boy over.

"At ten?" he asked, and Tamlin lifted his chin in defiance.

"Ten and a half," he said, his voice firm and his eyes daring dispute.

Marsh was glad when Roeglin let it pass, but she almost choked on her chocolate when she heard Aisha's stubborn whisper drift up from near Roeglin's feet.

"Seven."

The mage sputtered and looked at Tamlin.

"Five," the boy mouthed, holding up a hand to show five digits and not making a sound.

He was very careful to keep his hand where Aisha couldn't see it. Marsh had no doubt that if the child caught sight of it, the resulting argument would carry out into the eatery proper. Aisha would have started a fight for sure if she'd worked out that her brother had given her secret away.

"Did your parents know your sister could talk to rocks?"

Tams shook his head, and Aisha confirmed it.

"Nope. It was a secret."

"A secret, huh?" Roeglin repeated, and Marsh looked around him in time to see Aisha's head nodding enthusiastically. It was a relief to see the small smile on her face too, even if there was no telling how long it would last.

"And you need help in harnessing your power," Roeglin added, turning to Marsh.

It was not a question.

She shrugged.

"If you say so."

She watched his eyebrows rise in surprise and cocked

one of her own. It might have been the after-effect of the attack on the caravan, the discovery that she had magic, or the unprovoked attack in the eatery, but she was in no mood to be pushed around, no matter how much she needed the person doing the pushing...or how cute he was.

Because he *was* cute, she decided, and blushed.

Before he could ask what she was thinking or try to convince her she needed training, Marsh lifted her cup and drank, closing her eyes to savor the chocolate and trying to ignore the growing stiffness in her middle and down her biceps. She was going to bruise like a wagonload of purple toads, not to mention feel like someone had slipped one in her supper.

She wondered if it would make the shadows go away.

13

ROEGLIN INTERVENES

The shadows drifted at the edge of Marsh's vision. They had grown slowly thicker in the corners of the kitchen and Marsh didn't know why.

"You sure you're okay?"

Roeglin's voice caught her attention.

"*Oui.* Why?"

He gestured toward the shadows.

"They seem to think you need company."

Did they?

Marsh forced herself to look at the shadows. They'd grown so dense that she could no longer see the wall. If that was her, she had no idea how she was doing it. She glanced toward the shadow mage.

"I'm doing that?"

Roeglin nodded, but before Marsh could ask him any more, the cook slammed a plate of pancakes down in the center of the table.

"I want that rubbish off my wall by the time you're done eating, or you'll be scrubbing pots until it's gone."

Marsh stared at her, startled by the crash of the plate but more so by the threat. She couldn't do that, could she? But the cook didn't answer. She just turned away and bustled back to the kitchen.

Roeglin laid a hand on her shoulder as though willing her not to speak. Marsh thought he might say something, but he didn't, not until the cook had come back and dumped a pile of plates and cutlery next to the pancakes and bustled out into the eatery.

"Yes, she can. The town's very firm about damage to personal property and the eatery is popular. She'd have a lot of help enforcing it."

Marsh caught the cut of his eyes toward the connecting door and remembered just how many caravan guards had been inside when she'd brought the kids in for breakfast. Roeglin wasn't finished.

"You need to let the shadows know you don't need their protection."

He leaned forward, hooked two pancakes off the top of the stack and onto a plate, and passed the plate to Tamlin. Aisha appeared on the seat beside him as if by magic, and Roeglin served her a pancake as well.

"Eat that, and I'll give you another," he told the little girl before she could complain, and Marsh stifled a smile at the glare he received in reply.

Where had *he* learned how to handle children?

"Lots of siblings," he replied.

Again, it was like he was reading her mind. He glanced at her, and she realized his eyes were an odd hazel color—almost green, not quite gold, mostly light brown. They were the most fascinating eyes she'd ever seen—and then they flashed white.

"You should see them in sunlight."

Marsh sat still. She was still staring, not certain she'd seen the white, when the cook bustled back into the kitchen. She glanced at their table.

"You need to eat those before they get cold."

She didn't stop, though; didn't come over to the table, just put a piece of parchment on the counter beside her and began gathering ingredients and pulling pans and utensils from the kitchen's cupboards and drawers. Roeglin didn't bother answering her. He handed Marsh a plate and a fork and gestured toward the pancakes. When she had served herself, he filled his own plate and then picked up the plate that was left.

"For the pup," the cook told him, and Roeglin shrugged and set a pancake down in front of Scruffknuckle.

Marsh watched as the woman worked. She'd only just caught the quick glance in their direction as Roeglin had served the pancakes and seen the slight smile as the mage gave the pup his breakfast. The woman was definitely the queen of her kitchen and a lot more alert than she appeared, even in the middle of preparing half a dozen different dishes.

Marsh started eating. They'd been brought butter and some honey, which had a soft smoky flavor suggesting it had come from the cave hives of Dimanche, although she couldn't be sure. She'd always thought of Dimanche as a center for gemstones and wool. Marsh shrugged the thought away, enjoying the taste of honey and butter on pancakes

Everyone focused on their food, the children hungrier than Marsh had realized. Their simple meal on the farm seemed too long ago. When Aisha cleared her plate and looked around for more, Roeglin was quick to give her another. Too much more of that, Marsh thought, and the little girl would look like a barrel.

Marsh let her mind drift as she ate, thinking over the last few days. So much had happened that she was having trouble coming to grips with it. The magic... Marsh wasn't comfortable that she could do the same kind of magic the shadow mages did. That wasn't her. She was no mage. She was just a seeker of ancient treasures, a finder, and a retriever of lost secrets.

Magic didn't come into it.

And yet, she *had* asked the shadows to show her where the raiders had gone, and they'd done so—and then she'd used them to fish for what or who might be coming across Leon's Deep toward the waystation. She'd encased Lennie's hand in a shield of shadow...or had that been a net?

Marsh lifted her eyes to the patch of shadows on the wall. It was still there, and slightly wider than before.

"Just tell them you're all right," Roeglin told her. "They'll return to their corners and wait until you need them again. Now that you have found them, they will always be there. Have no fear of that."

Have no fear? The man must be slightly out of his mind. She was no mage that the shadows should come at her beck and call!

"And yet they do." Roeglin's voice was calm. "And they always will."

Marsh speared another piece of pancake and concentrated on chewing it, focusing on the flavor and wishing Roeglin was right. If she told the shadows to stand down, *would* they really be there for her to summon again?

"Always," Roeglin whispered, and Marsh knew she would see white if she could see his eyes.

"But I'm not a mage."

"No?" For a moment Marsh thought he would argue with her, but Roeglin surprised her by continuing, "Then perhaps you are a shadow-caller or a speaker of shades. Come to think of it, though, you might be a wielder instead."

"A wielder?" Marsh swallowed a laugh and very nearly choked on her breakfast. "Like in the legends? Like that girl they talk about from the West, Rhona?"

"She was not the first."

"She's the one all the stories are about."

"Not all." Roeglin softened his denial with a slight smile. "Just most of the ones told by the wanderers."

"You've seen the wanderers?" Tamlin's voice was breathless as he interrupted.

"Once."

"It was a very long time ago, and more than enough trouble for a lifetime," the cook interrupted, setting another round of hot drinks in front of them and clearing their empty pancake plates away. She turned to Roeglin. "You're going to have to talk to them."

This last was accompanied by a slight jerk of the head toward the eatery proper, followed by a turn in Marsh's direction.

"They're saying she only survived because she was part of the attack."

"What?" Marsh pushed her chair back. "I'll go straighten them out."

Roeglin snapped out his hand and wrapped his fingers around her wrist.

"We'll both go," he told her, "but you need to let me lead, or they'll take you apart."

"Lennie?"

His expression turned grim.

"She lost her husband. Their child will grow up without a father."

Marsh felt her cheeks go cold as her face went pale. The caravan guard was pregnant?

"But I could have hurt her! She might have—"

The words jerked to a halt as Roeglin stood, pulling her toward him and laying his other hand over her mouth.

"You didn't, and the child will be fine, but she needs a place of refuge and calm, and I haven't yet convinced her to come to the monastery. With you, I might stand a chance." He paused, and his face turned pleading. "Will you follow my lead?"

Swallowing her instinctive retort that she could handle it, Marsh nodded, and Roeglin took his hand away from her mouth. He turned toward Tamlin, but the boy spoke before Roeglin could take more than a breath.

"We're coming too. We were part of the caravan, and we survived. It wasn't just Marsh."

"Marsh saved us," Aisha added, her little voice solemn as she slipped out of her chair. Her hand went to Scruffknuckle's head as the pup got to his feet.

Roeglin looked like he might argue, but Marsh shook her head.

"This time the kids have a point," she told him and began moving toward the door. "You coming or not?"

Just as she reached it, a man raised his voice.

"And I told you, you can't go back there."

"Step aside, Marc. It's not you we want to speak to."

Before Marc could answer, Marsh stepped out of the kitchen.

"No," she snapped. "You all want a piece of me."

"You—"

Marsh stopped Marc's protest with an upraised hand, but she didn't take her eyes off the crowd gathered in front of his counter. At sight of her, there was a moment's silence, then Lennie stepped forward, but Marsh didn't let her get a word out.

"You think I was part of the attack?" she challenged as Roeglin gently shouldered her aside.

"Well, do you?" he demanded, looking out at the gathering.

Lennie took another step, her movement mirrored by another guard. If Marsh hadn't known better, she would have said the big guy was trying to protect Lennie, and that he wasn't about to risk putting his arm around the female guard's shoulders. It was hard to imagine Lennie accepting any kind of comfort, but it wasn't something that made Marsh want to smile. She couldn't imagine loving someone enough to start a family with them and then losing them before their journey together had really begun. That was far from fair.

"You know we do," Lennie said. "No one else was found,

and here she waltzes through town with a line of mules that don't belong to her days later?"

Marsh drew breath to explain, but Roeglin laid a hand on her arm.

"And the children?"

It was clear from Lennie's face that the kids didn't fit with her theory of Marsh as a villain.

"They got lucky."

"Lucky?" Tamlin had made no promises about letting Roeglin lead the conversation, and the boy's tone trembled with grief and fury. He didn't give anyone time to reply either, sliding in front of Marsh and Roeglin and out from behind the counter before either of them could stop him. Aisha and Scruffknuckle ducked past them as they tried to catch her brother.

At first, Marsh thought the boy would back up against the partition to stop her and the shadow mage from following, but he didn't. He marched right up to Lennie and looked up into her face.

"My parents are gone!" he shouted. "My brothers are gone! My sisters..." His voice broke and he swallowed hard, his fists clenched at his side. "My whole family is gone, and she..." He pointed back at Marsh with one hand. "*She* is the *only* reason Aysh and I got out of there. She came back and grabbed us and dumped us on her mule, and then she ran for the glows..." a sob broke through the words, "and they went out and a shadow monster took the mule out from under us, but *she* didn't leave us. She grabbed us out from under its claws and got us out of there."

Marsh shook off Roeglin's hand and stepped out from

behind the counter. She laid her hands on Tamlin's shoulders and tried to move him behind her.

"It's okay, Tams. I've got this."

But Tamlin was having none of it. He shook himself free of her grip and glared up at Lennie.

"She's the only reason I have any family left."

Aisha came and stood alongside her brother, her little face matching his glare for glare, her eyes bluer than Marsh had ever seen them. Tamlin laid his arm across her shoulders as the little girl curled her hand in the ruff of fur at Scruffknuckle's neck. He gestured at Marsh.

"If she was part of the attack, we'd be gone too."

Lennie looked from the boy's angry face to Marsh.

"Did you?"

"Did I what?"

"Grab the kids when the monsters attacked?"

Marsh rolled her shoulders.

"What else was I supposed to do?"

"Why didn't you grab the rest?"

"I thought their parents had them, and I had no more space on the mule."

That much was true, but whether Lennie would buy it was another matter. Marsh watched as the warrior's face became thoughtful and waited until it cleared.

"Yeah. You *were* pretty heavily loaded." She still didn't look convinced, though, and turned to Roeglin. "What do you see, Roe? *Is* she telling the truth?"

"You want to see?"

Lennie nodded, her gesture echoed by several of the guards behind her, and Roeglin stepped up beside Marsh, his next question directed to the guards.

"Which one first?"

To Marsh's surprise, Lennie pointed at Aisha. The woman caught her look.

"Kids don't lie," she said and amended her meaning just as Marsh was thinking she was in for a surprise when her own came along. "They don't know how to hide things from Ro."

Ro, huh?

He cast her an anxious look and knelt beside Aisha.

"Aisha," he said, "if I look inside your head, can you remember what you saw when the shadow monsters attacked?"

Aisha frowned.

"Don't want to."

"If you don't, Lennie will hit Marsh again."

Aisha gasped. To give her credit, Lennie looked horrified at the thought, but Aisha wasn't daunted. She looked up at the guard.

"No hit."

Marsh saw when the guard decided to take the chance of finding out the truth and run with it. Lennie looked at Aisha with a face that said she meant every word.

"I will if you don't let Roeglin show me what happened."

Marsh watched Aisha think it over and saw when the little girl made her choice.

"I show."

She turned to Roeglin.

"How?"

"Just remember," he told her, and Aisha's eyes filled with tears. The shadow mage hurried to reassure her. "I will be here. I won't let *anything* hurt you."

"Promise?"

Roeglin dipped his chin.

"Promise. I don't want Tamlin cross with me."

His words brought a small smile to Aisha's lips.

"Okay."

14

THE FOUNDER OF RUINS HALL

As Marsh watched, Aisha sighed and closed her eyes. Beside her, Scruffknuckle gave an anxious whimper and leaned into her. Marsh saw the girl's hand tighten in the puppy's fur. She caught Tamlin's worried look and raised a finger to her lips, gesturing to where Roeglin had laid a hand against Aisha's face. With his other hand, he gestured in the direction of the gathered guards, and they all shuffled back to clear a space between them.

Roeglin looked at Aisha's face, his eyes burning silver even as white mist drifted from his open hand and shadows slid across the floor to mingle with it. After a couple of heartbeats, Aisha sat on the floor and Roeglin stood, both hands moving as the mist drifted into pictures and a miniature Aisha appeared. She had ducked down behind some rocks beside the path, and Marsh recalled being appalled that her parents would allow her to wander beyond the glows.

She had been relieved a few moments later when Tamlin had gone in search of her.

"Aisha!" he had said. "Come back! You're not supposed to—"

That had been as far as he'd gotten when the glows had gone out on the trail ahead. The sudden darkness had been accompanied by screams, and Aisha had looked out from behind her rock to see the shadows move and hear claws scrape on rock. With a shriek, she had run to her brother.

"Aysh!" he had called. "Aysh!"

Aisha had squealed again as the shadows roared, and she'd been snatched off the ground and tucked under a woman's arm. Now she was screaming because she'd been grabbed by a stranger, and her momma and poppa had told her *never* to talk to strangers.

"Hey! You let her go!"

Oh. Marsh remembered that. Aisha had seen it too because the rock Tamlin had thrown arced overhead as the stranger grabbed him by the arm.

"I'm trying to save you, stupid!" sounded strange coming from Roeglin's mouth when Marsh remembered saying it. "Now get on the bloody mule!"

Mist-Aisha ended up on the mule in front of a mist-formed Tamlin and Marchant could only stare as she saw herself grabbing the mule's reins and trying to tow it up the tunnel. She blushed as Roeglin reproduced her curses with more accuracy than she'd have given anyone credit for, and then the memory took on a faintly green glow as Aisha rested her hand on the mule's neck.

Oh. Well, that explained it. Horvin had been the most stubborn creature in all the tunnels and Marsh had never expected him to run so easily at her heels, as he had during the attack. She'd thought it had been because of the shadow monsters farther down the trail, but... Well, damn.

The sudden darkness and sweep of claws had the guards gasping even as mist-Aisha was pulled off the falling mule with her brother and carried into the darkness. The memory faded, and Marsh remembered that this was when the little girl had become dead weight in her arms.

The mist faded and Roeglin swayed.

Aisha opened her eyes and buried her face in Scruffknuckle's fur, the puppy licking her arm as if he could fix whatever had gone wrong. When Aisha kept crying, he whined and looked up at Tamlin. The boy was already responding. He knelt beside them, wrapping his arms around his sister and the pup and pulling them close.

"I'm here," he murmured. "I'm here. You're safe now. Safe."

He kept murmuring even when Lennie suddenly lunged forward to steady Roeglin before he could fall. Another of the guards grabbed a chair and brought it over as Marsh heard quick footsteps behind her. She stepped to one side, and the cook bustled past carrying a tray filled with cups. The strong, sweet scent of hot chocolate tugged at Marsh's nostrils, and she looked down at the children.

Aisha's sobs were growing softer, but Scruffknuckle caught sight of Marsh and wagged his tail at her, anxiety in every line. Tamlin followed the pup's gaze, and Marsh winced at the pain in the boy's face.

"Thank you," he said, and Marsh shrugged.

"Let me get you—"

"To the table," the cook snapped, cutting Marsh off.

"You all need a drink after a shock like that. You too, Lennie. Sit yourself down."

The caravan guard looked at the woman, and Marsh thought she was going to argue. So did the cook.

"Don't make me put your pregnant butt in the chair, girl. I know you're not made of porcelain."

Lennie sat, and Marsh did her best not to laugh at the look of consternation on the guard's face—a task that became easy when she realized she was going to have to sit at the same table. Tamlin tried to pull his sister to her feet, but Aisha was determined not to let go of the pup and refused to move an inch.

In the end, Marsh scooped both dog and child up and sat next to Roeglin, balancing the pair on her lap. Lennie gave her an apologetic grimace.

"You okay?"

Marsh figured that passed for an apology, and decided, given the circumstances, she'd accept it.

"Fine."

Lennie's lips tightened, but she didn't say anything more. Marsh didn't blame her. Beating the stuffing out of someone for something they didn't do rated pretty high on the stupid scale, and there wasn't really anything you could do to make it better except apologize and move on.

Speaking of moving on...

"I need an escort," she said, looking at Lennie. "You up for it?"

Lennie blushed and gestured toward the cook.

"You heard the chef. I'm pregnant. Might not be any good to you on the trail."

That drew a variety of snorts from the other guards in

the room, but Marsh couldn't pick out which had made them. The man that had come to support Lennie when she'd demanded Marsh be brought from the kitchen stepped forward.

"Don't you believe it. Unless you're chasing shadow monsters, Lennie's still one of the best for the trail."

That earned him a look of gratitude, then Lennie turned to Marsh.

"What did you have in mind?"

"Shadow mage monastery."

Fury crossed Lennie's features.

"Did he put you up to this?" she demanded, pushing back her chair. "Did he?"

Marsh shook her head.

"Nope." She indicated the two children. "Their parents wanted them taking lessons in magic and the monastery was the place. They had a farm near there."

"Treigon's old place?" Another of the guards stepped forward. "I know it."

"You for hire?"

The guard looked around at the others.

"Girl, we're *all* for hire. Ain't no caravans since the glows went down on the road to Kerrenin's Ledge. Hasn't been one from Dimanche for over a week, and no one's sure if there's one due from Ariella's. Can't remember when the last one came."

That couldn't be good.

Marsh watched the same thought cross the faces of those she could see and imagined it had occurred to everyone in the room. This wasn't the first time she had wished there was some kind of local law enforcement, but the guards here were the closest anyone came to that—them and the private security people who served the wealthy. There weren't too many of those, though, and Marsh couldn't think of any outfits that consisted of more than a half dozen men and women.

Nope. Not a one.

"We are so very screwed," she muttered, and Lennie gave her a sharp glance.

"What did you say?"

Marsh shrugged and tried to wave it away.

"It's no—" she started, but Lennie slammed a fist on the table.

"Like the Deeps it isn't!" she snapped. "Now, spill it. No more secrets."

Like there had been any secrets in the first place, what with Roeglin and his memory-thieving magic. Roeglin stirred weakly beside her.

"Hey!"

"If the boot fits," Marsh snapped. "Stay outta my head."

"And drink your chocolate," the cook added, returning with a large bowl of cookies. "Table first, and then everyone's welcome. Looks like we got things to discuss."

We? Marsh thought and wondered what she meant, which was when the crowd around them shifted and the heavy tramp of a dozen more boots announced the arrival of more folk from outside.

"Tell us what you saw, girl," the cook encouraged.

She glanced at Roeglin.

"We'll have to do without the shadow mage," the woman added, looking past Marsh to the newcomers. "He's all played out."

Roeglin didn't argue, but he reached over and snagged a handful of cookies, handing one to the pup and two more to each of the children before biting into his own. Nice to see a man who had his priorities straight, Marsh thought and was about to reach for one when the shadow mage snagged another two and tossed her one.

"Come on, girl. We're all waiting."

Lennie didn't even wait for Marsh to take the first bite. Judging from the murmurs of agreement from around the table, she wasn't alone. Marsh set her cookie down, took a sip of her chocolate, and told them what she'd found in the Leon's Deep cavern.

"Had a caravan due from there two days back," said the man who'd said all the guards were for hire. "Explains what happened to it. Wonder if…"

He was shushed by those around him, but Marsh guessed what he'd been pondering.

"The glows were still lit when I brought Fabrice and her three out of there."

"You were the ones who went through with the moutons last night?"

"Yeah. She's gone to stay with friends."

Before she could add more, a new voice broke in.

"So, girl, you for hire?"

"I beg your pardon?"

"Are you for hire?" The new voice sounded impatient.

Marsh looked toward it and pushed her seat back. The tall, narrowly-built man with his deep blue eyes and hawkish features was a well-known figure throughout the caverns, as the founder of any settlement and cavern community should be.

"Monsieur Gravine, I…"

"Sit down, girl. I mean after you have finished your duty to the children. Will you be for hire?"

Marsh sat. She doubted that her duty to the children would ever be finished, but was hoping they might find a secure home with the shadow mages until she could find their parents. With the road to Kerrenin's Ledge closed, she was going to need a new patron.

"I… Once those duties are done, I will be available," she answered.

"Good. May I?"

Not sure why he was asking her permission for anything, Marsh nodded, watching as he turned to the guards. Marsh realized he'd brought his own personal security force, a half-dozen hard-faced men and women.

"I hear you are between contracts," he began, addressing the gathered guards. "Is that true?"

There were murmurs of assent around the room. The founder turned his attention to Roeglin.

"And your people are not responsible for the glows going out?"

"No, monsieur."

"Tell me, are the shadow mages recruiting for the monastery?"

Roeglin frowned.

"No, monsieur. Not yet. There will be a recruiting drive later in the season, but not yet."

"Good. Keep it that way. I am hearing tales of shadow mages traveling to the farms and mines and trying to recruit apprentices. They do not like to be told no."

Roeglin looked confused and then upset.

"But we never force…"

Gravine raised his hand, and Roeglin faltered to silence.

"I know, but there have been incidents. Now that I know it was not your people, I can work toward repairing the damage that's been done to the monastery's reputation."

Marsh wanted to know why he would bother. What did it matter to him if the cavern folk were angry with the shadow mages? Her confusion must have shown on her face because the founder turned in her direction.

"I came to these caverns to build a new home for our people. I will not have some outside force destroy us as the ancients were destroyed." He looked the guards over, his gaze demanding and receiving their attention. "I need an army to meet the threat that is coming."

He cast another look at Marsh.

"If she had not escaped the ambush on the road to Kerrenin's Ledge and stumbled into Leon's Deep, we'd have had no warning. Now we do, and I need your help. The caverns need your help."

Again he looked at Marsh.

"This young lady needs…" He paused, and Marsh took the cue.

"I need four guards so that I can get the children to the monastery."

"And I need an emissary to the shadow mages," Gravine added, directing his next few words to Marsh. "This will fit with the duties you already hold. Will you and Roeglin be my representatives? I will need mages to assist in protecting the caverns and a way to ask the rock mages for their help."

Rock mages? It was the first Marsh had heard of *them*. Aisha squirmed in her lap, having heard the founder's words. Checking in with the rock mages might not be a bad idea for her, either. In the meantime, she hoped Aisha would keep quiet—but the founder wanted his answer, and he didn't like to be kept waiting.

"Well? Will you be my emissaries?"

"I'll go," Roeglin said, and Marsh nodded.

"Happy to," she said.

The founder dipped his chin in acknowledgment.

"Thank you," he said. "Your service is appreciated."

Marsh wanted to ask him what he was paying, but he had already moved on to the caravan guards.

"I am happy to pay for the hire of my emissaries' escort team, and I'd like to start signing on any of you interested in helping me found the Ruins Hall Protectors."

He gestured in the direction of the door, where one of the tables had been pulled up parallel to one side. Behind it sat a woman with a quill and a heavy ledger. Just behind her at a second table stood two men with a heavy chest and a box of small leather pouches between them.

"My clerk is waiting, and I have the tailor reserved for uniforms."

Marsh raised her eyebrows. That sort of organization spoke of more time for preparation than her arrival in town the evening before afforded. She stared at the founder. For a moment his eyes rested on her face and his expression stilled, then he let his attention rove over the guards again.

"Anyone interested?"

"What are your terms?" Lennie asked, and the guards

stopped moving, their expressions attentive as they waited for his reply.

The man named a price for a year's service that most guards wouldn't see for ten trips, and Marsh held her jaw closed as he added that it was for the lowest rank, with increments for specializations and increases in rank and responsibility.

"You're already trained in fighting and guarding," he said, "but I will need you trained to fight in formations and coherent groups."

He indicated his men.

"My men can teach you that if you're not afraid to learn it."

This brought a growl of protest from the room, and Marsh caught the satisfied twitch of the man's lips. It made her wonder where Gravine had come from. She searched her memory but didn't recall anything that said he'd been born locally, which only meant he had come from somewhere else. Come to think of it, she hadn't heard where he'd recruited his men, either.

As far as she knew he'd always had them, and he'd arrived shortly after Kerrenin's Ledge was established. That made him very old, a lot older than he looked. She frowned and didn't realize she'd been staring until Gravine spoke.

"Something displeases you, Seeker?"

Seek... How had he known that?

Marsh shook her head, shaking the question to one side.

"No, Monsieur. I was just wondering how you were going to select those who would accompany me."

He gave her an easy smile that said he didn't believe a word of it but was willing to let it slide. He gestured to one of the men at his side.

"Gustav will be the first—"

"And I will be the second," Lennie cut in before he could say any more.

Instead of protesting, Gravine dipped his head.

"Then I shall place you and Gustav in charge of who accompanies you." He paused, then continued. "You are pregnant, are you not?"

"That will not prevent me from carrying out my duties."

"No. I did not think it would, but I would like you and Gustav to ask the shadow mages if they could recommend a safe place for the children and families of my soldiers. I believe their holding is the only real fortress in the area."

Roeglin frowned, and Marsh wondered what he thought of Gravine's unspoken expectation that the monastery would provide refuge for his force's loved ones. Whatever it was, he didn't voice it, and Lennie didn't protest that the task wasn't what she'd signed up for. From the expression on the woman's face, she was turning over the idea.

Marsh had to admit that it *did* have possibilities.

15

ALTERNATIVES

As Marsh contemplated the idea that Monsieur Gravine would provide protection for the Ruins Hall cavern complex and that the shadow mages might be convinced to work with him, the caravan guards filed over to the table where the founder's clerk sat, each signing their name and accepting the equivalent of a week's wages as a retainer.

"From now on," Monsieur Gravine said, "I will be protecting the roads into and out of Ruins Hall. We will need masons and engineers to secure all routes into and out of our lands. Your main task will be to protect them, but first we have a meeting to attend."

He turned to Marchant.

"The Merchants' Guild is about to become very unhappy with me. I will need your assistance."

Just like that, he switched his attention to Roeglin.

"Are you strong enough to draw the memory of what she saw both in the tunnels prior to arriving at Leon's Deep and what she caught on the shadow threads?"

Roeglin drained his cup and grabbed a handful of cookies, which he stuffed into one of his trouser pockets. Marsh watched him and wondered just how deep the pocket was. He caught her glance and waggled his fingers at her from halfway down his thigh. She rolled her eyes, but he was already giving Monsieur Gravine his answer.

"I will do my best. Which is more important?"

"I need both if you can do it." Gravine directed the next question to Marsh. "Can you recall these things?"

Marsh nodded.

"I can remember both, and I do not mind the mage drawing them out if it stops what happened to Leon's Deep."

Gravine's face was solemn as he replied.

"That is what it is designed to do. What the result will be when so much greed is riding on the answer is not guaranteed."

Lennie stepped forward with a grim smile on her face.

"They will comply if the caravan guards refuse to walk the dark for them." Her smile faded, and her eyes grew hard with determination as she gestured to the men and woman at her back. "We can make that happen, especially if the guards know there is another employer for them to go to."

Gravine shook his head.

"We cannot guarantee their safety beyond the bounds of Ruins Hall," he said, and Lennie cocked her head.

"Monsieur, correct me if I am wrong, but our security depends as much on being linked to the other three settlements as it does on having a force stationed here, does it not?"

She watched as he considered that and then ceded the point.

"Yes."

"So we have to secure our borders, and then reopen the trade routes and secure them."

"*Oui*, but—"

"If you speak to the other founders and explain to them that you can only man checkpoints and provide guards to the halfway point, and should they employ the guards stranded in their own settlements, they should be able to do the same."

"Or you could form a separate entity tasked with guarding the routes and cavern complexes of the Four Settlements..." Marsh suggested, then raised her hands as though in surrender. "I didn't mean to interrupt."

"You did," Gravine argued, "and the idea has merit. Once this threat is defeated, we will come to it again. For now, I will take the steps I deem necessary to secure the Ruins Hall complex. I cannot protect the others, but I can do this much. When we are secure, we will assist the others —starting with Ariella's Grotto."

He caught her look and sighed.

"As I said, the idea has merit, but we don't have the time to implement it. At the end of this crisis, we will. An independent body funded by allies would be preferable to four private armies."

That made sense.

Marsh looked around for Aisha, then took her hand and set the little girl on her feet.

"Hold onto Scruffy," she said as she passed the child

another cookie and pretended she didn't see Roeglin sneak one to the pup.

Contented crunching followed, and only when it was done did Roeglin get to his feet. He still looked pale and Marchant shifted to his side, tucking her arm through his so he could lean on her without drawing too much attention. As soon as the children had fallen in alongside them, Monsieur Gravine pivoted on his heel and marched toward the door, five of his six guards falling in behind him.

The sixth, Gustav, walked just ahead of Marsh, and Lennie dropped in behind them.

And so it begins, Marsh thought. *Even if I'm not exactly sure what "it" might be.*

She kept a firm hold of Aisha's hand as they left the eatery and followed Gravine down the street to a large gray-stone building on the left. Marsh remembered passing it the night before, and how imposing it had looked in comparison to the rest. Then she remembered just wishing they could reach the farm and have the journey over and done.

Well, so much for that, she thought, realizing she'd just promised to head out onto the road as soon as Gravine and his meeting were done.

Except it wasn't Gravine's meeting. Fabrice was standing on the footpath outside the hall, Cleon on one side and the clerk from the merchants' office on the other. Fabrice's face lit up when she saw Marsh, although her brow creased with puzzlement when she saw who, or rather, *what*, Marsh was walking with.

"Didn't take *you* long," Cleon muttered, and Fabrice looked at him askance.

"It's not what you think," Roeglin told the farmer as they followed Monsieur Gravine and his escort into the hall proper.

Fabrice and Cleon hurried after them, confused when they registered that Marsh and Roeglin were part of the founder's entourage. Marsh followed the founder and his guards to the front of the hall and sat to one side at the front as directed, Fabrice and Cleon sitting in the row behind them.

It didn't take long for the hall to fill, and Marsh snuck a few quick looks to see who else might have come to the meeting. She was looking for one face in particular, but she didn't see her—Madame Monetti. Marsh made a note that she would have to look the woman up after she had returned from the monastery.

She sighed. It would have been so much better if she could have delivered the package straight into the woman's hands. Stifling a second sigh, she forced herself to pay attention to the proceedings. Monsieur Gravine's clerk was speaking.

"As many of you know, the road to Kerrenin's Ledge is now closed. All that was left of the last caravan were the bodies of its mules. No goods, and not a sign of any of those traveling with it or guarding it. Today we have both good news and bad."

As openings went, Marsh had to admit that was a good one, guaranteed to get attention.

The clerk gestured for Marsh and the children to stand up and come to the front of the hall. Giving Tamlin and

Aisha a quick glance, Marsh stood and stretched her hands toward them. She was relieved when both stood with her and took hold. Together, they went over to the clerk and waited in front of the gathered towns- and farm-folk.

"There were survivors."

Small sounds of relief and happiness erupted around the hall, but the clerk ignored them and continued, indicating Marsh, the two children, and the dog.

"Marchant Leclerc, and Tamlin and Aisha Danet." Her hand fluttered over the dog. "The pup they found along the way."

Whispers of "Krypthund" filled the hall. When Scruffknuckle twisted under Aisha's hand to face the crowd, keeping his body pressed against her leg, those whispers were joined by others: "bonded," "loyal," "druid," "fey child," and "rock mage." Aisha's grip tightened on hers, and Marsh looked down.

The child's face was troubled as she returned Marsh's gaze.

Hang on, kid, Marsh thought. *I won't let them hurt you. You are mine.*

In the front row, Roeglin's eyes flashed white and he stood, moving swiftly in front of the clerk and maneuvering so that he and Aisha and March were side-on to the crowd. The clerk hesitated and then continued with her spiel.

"The bad news is that Leon's Deep has been cleared of all its residents." She paused as gasps of shock followed her announcement. When the sounds had died away, she continued. "With the exception of Fabrice Jeter and her children Eveline, Tory, and Curt, who escaped the raid and were escorted to safety by Leclerc."

A patter of applause rippled through the hall but stopped the instant the clerk raised her hand.

"The danger is not over," she added, and silence fell over them. The clerk pretended not to notice and continued. "We have asked shadow mage and mindwalker Roeglin Leger to show you two of Leclerc's memories to give us a clear idea of the dangers the caverns face. After that, the Ruins Hall founder, Monsieur Gravine, will outline his plans to keep our homes safe."

She gestured for Roeglin to continue.

"May I?" Roeglin asked, and Marsh nodded.

"Be my guest," she told him. "I have nothing to hide."

It must have been the right answer because his lips twitched and he stretched out his hand and set it in the middle of her forehead.

"Show me the first time you heard the raiders," he said, and Marsh closed her eyes.

A heartbeat later, she felt Roeglin lift his hand away but ignored that in favor of remembering the events of their last night of sleeping rough. It all started with Scruffknuckle's growl, followed by the raider's voice.

"I tell you, it sounded like children laughing."

Marsh held the memory as clearly as she could, not trying to hide anything from her audience, just trying to remember what she'd heard and seen. To her surprise, Roeglin pulled the scene of her searching the shadow threads, making sure to highlight the impression of many people moving away from them.

"She abandoned them!" came Cleon's indignant exclamation, and Marsh lost the memory.

She pulled the children behind her and placed herself between them and the people gathered in the hall. To her surprise, no one else seemed angry. Well, no one except Fabrice.

"Cleon Jarvay Sursees!" Fabrice snapped, and the big farmer turned to her like he'd been slapped. "You take that back!"

"But…"

"She did *not* abandon them! If she had gone after them, she would have lost the children, and I would have still been trying to keep Patrik's legacy when the second force arrived."

Her words sent a shockwave through the hall, but she ignored it.

"If she had gone chasing after them, I would not be here now—and my Patrik's sacrifice would have been for nothing. And all my…my children would have been taken. The moutons would have died in their barn, and you would not be getting the warning you need to be ready for what is coming."

Roeglin, Marsh, and the children were all staring at her when she turned to them.

"Show them, mindwalker. Show them what Marsh has seen is coming for us. Repeat their words for all to hear."

She lifted her hand and clipped Cleon under the ear with an open-handed slap.

"And I will seek another place to keep my moutons since this one is so set against the girl who is trying to save us."

Cleon colored a brilliant red and opened his mouth to protest, but Fabrice merely glared at him and pointed to the seat.

"Close your foolish mouth and *sit!*" she snapped, then turned to Roeglin and waved for him to continue. "Show them, shadow mage."

Again Roeglin turned to Marsh.

"May I?" he asked, tentatively raising his hand again.

Marsh shot Cleon another wary glance and then nodded.

"Please do."

This time she kept her eyes open as Roeglin placed his fingertips on her forehead.

"The memory, please."

It took Marsh a moment, but she found it. She took it from the feeling of unease she'd had at the waystation stables. Roeglin's eyes burned white, the mingling of shadow and mind magic reflected in their color as they suddenly flared to silver when mist and shadow combined.

When Marsh had gotten a firmer grip on the memory, he lifted his fingers away and Marsh closed her eyes, letting the hall drift away as she remembered running up the stairs to the towers while the children prepared the mules.

It didn't take her long to find the force moving through the grove of calla shrooms and highlight the differences in their build and clothing as they moved beneath the faint fluorescence of the calla—and then she worked out how to get the shadow threads to deliver sound. Some snickered when they heard the leader speak his first real lines.

"You're not afraid of the dark, are you, Berens?"

Their mirth rapidly faded to anger as they heard the raiders plan to "take out Ruins Hall" and how they intended to drain the Four Settlements of all their inhabitants. She opened her eyes as Roeglin ended the connection between them, her words to Tamlin falling oddly from his mouth.

"They know someone was watching them. Not that it's any of your business."

In front of her, Roeglin was pale as a ghost, his face glistening with sweat. Silence cloaked the hall, and tension filled the air as if lightning were about to strike. Marsh started when heavy footsteps jerked her attention to where Cleon was crossing the floor toward her.

"Forgive me," he said. "I thought you…might be responsible."

Marsh shook her head.

"Help the founder protect the caverns and you will be forgiven," she told him, lunging forward in barely enough time to catch Roeglin as he collapsed.

Aisha gave a shriek of fright and Tamlin wrapped his arms around his sister.

"He's okay, Aysh. Just a little tired. He only needs to sleep. It's okay."

Scruffknuckle wuffed and licked the little girl's hand, butting against it until she scratched his head. The people in the hall stared. Marsh wanted to shout at them that the show was over, but she couldn't. She was too busy pulling Roeglin's arm over her shoulder with the aim of carrying him back to his seat. Cleon surprised her by coming around the mage's other side and lifting him from the floor.

"Where do you want him?"

"Just where we were sitting," she managed, and Cleon took him to where she wanted, leaving her to collect the children and lead them back to their seats.

She was grateful when Monsieur Gravine stood and drew the attention from them.

"People of Ruins Hall," he said. "We need to be ready to defend our caverns."

His announcement was met with an outcry of disbelief.

"But we're not warriors!"

"We have no weapons."

"I have no idea how to wield a blade."

"How do we stop a force that size? By asking them nicely to leave?"

Getting Cleon to settle Roeglin against her shoulder, Marsh watched as the town's founder let the protests ride over him, waiting for the noise to start subsiding before raising his hand for quiet.

"We *do* have an army," he announced, his voice quiet, calm, and sure.

He gestured to the caravan guards who had filed in and now stood around the edges of the halls.

"They are trained warriors, many of whom have seen bloodshed—and they have no work while the roads are closed."

The looks of outrage on the faces of the merchants who were sitting to one side of the dais beside him had Marsh choking down the urge to laugh. They hadn't seen *this* coming. Some raised their hands and others tried to voice a protest, but Monsieur Gravine pretended not to notice.

"They have said they are willing to protect the caverns

like they protected the caravans I'd like to hire them, to do just that."

Murmurs of approval rippled through the townsfolk, and many of the farmers turned to each other, seeking the opinions of their fellows. Within seconds, it was clear how the town- and farm-folk would vote. The merchants were outraged.

"But we need the guards!" one finally managed to protest and was nearly shouted out of his seat.

Another tried to reason with the people gathered before them.

"Who will guard the caravans and take your goods to market?"

Well, there was only one reply to that, and their protests were met with scorn.

"What caravans?"

"Which market?"

"There *is* no trade while the roads are closed."

Marsh listened as the questions rapidly degenerated into mockery and shouted insults, and Gravine chose that moment to step in. Raising his hands, he patted the air in placation. Slowly the uproar died down, and when all was relatively still, the founder spoke again. Turning first to the merchants, he began.

"I think you will agree that trade is the lifeblood of the Four Settlements."

Several of them nodded emphatically, and Gravine continued.

"You also have to agree that the caravans from Dimanche and Ariella's Grotto are overdue." He held up a hand as one started to protest. "I know the Grotto's shipments are unpredictable, but tell me when you last saw an interval between them as long as this?"

Several of them opened their mouths and closed them again. It was like watching fish trying to breathe on dry land. If it hadn't been for Roeglin's weight resting against her shoulder and the smaller burden of Aisha and Scruffknuckle leaning on her legs, Marsh might have laughed. When it became clear that the merchants had no answer for him, the founder went on.

"As long as there are no caravans, these folk..." His gesture took in the gathered guards. "These folk don't have any way of earning a living. They cannot feed their families, and they cannot take on other employ because *you* demand they hold themselves in readiness. Well, I want them to be ready too. I want them fighting at my back when the raiders reach this cavern. I want them guarding my town, my friends, my family, and my home—and I am willing to pay them to do so."

He paused, letting his gaze sweep over the assembled cavern dwellers; letting them think about that before finishing his speech.

"Are you?"

For a moment Marsh was sure she could have heard a pin drop, then the hall erupted into agreement. One of the merchants rolled his eyes and slumped into his chair. Another threw up his hands in disgust. But there were others who were nodding, and one who began to softly applaud. Soon everyone in the hall had joined him.

Marsh saw some of the tension leave the founder's frame. He let the gathering applaud a little longer before calming them with a gentle motion of his hands.

"I am sending an envoy to the shadow mage monastery," he announced, and there were several indrawn breaths. He acknowledged these with a frown and a nod. "I know some of you have been approached by a group of mages who were very persistent in trying to recruit your children. Those mages are not *our* mages. *Those* mages belong to the raiders. I want you to continue to tell them no, and I want you to report them immediately. I will send a contingent of the Ruins Hall Protectors out to capture them. We cannot have them roaming our caverns. We *will not* have them roaming our caverns."

His words were met with cheers, and again he had to wait for the noise to die down.

"I will be meeting with the leaders of each of the groups in the cavern. Look for my emissary in the next couple of days. In the meantime, I also need any volunteers with a knowledge of engineering and masonry. Their expertise will be required in planning our defenses. And I need to speak to anyone who knows of tunnels leading into our lands. We need to secure them, so we know who enters and how many—and so the raiders cannot get through unseen. Are there any questions?"

Marsh let the tide of noise wash over and around her, not really tracking who was asking what or what was being said. She already knew the next part she would play. What she had to decide was what she was going to do next.

16

HUNTER IN THE DARK

Marchant was still trying to work out what she was going to do about her magic when she got to the monastery. She knew what she was doing for Monsieur Gravine and she knew what she was doing for the children, but she didn't know what she was doing for herself. Her world had changed, and she had to change with it. What she still couldn't figure out was the part she wanted to play in it. She couldn't even work out if there was a part she *could* play.

She only had the skills of a seeker trying for an apprenticeship—a seeker wannabe. What good was that to anyone? The same went for her skills as a courier. Anyone could play that part, and she wanted more. How much more, she didn't know, but she did know she couldn't walk away.

She hadn't been able to walk away from the children or from Fabrice, and she hadn't known she'd been walking away from a whole cavern's worth of captives. If she had, she'd never have made it to Leon's Deep, and Ruins Hall might very well have fallen. Marsh shook her head. Even though everyone else thought it better that she hadn't intervened—and that included Fabrice—she had trouble accepting it.

Marsh felt like she'd failed; like she'd just abandoned all those people to whatever fate the raiders had planned. What had they meant when they'd said "perhaps that will be enough?" What did their master want with all these people? Why would it take four settlements or more before their master was satisfied?

"Enough for what?" she muttered. "Enough. For. *What*?"

She was back on a mule again and leading another borrowed mule, Fabrice's herd bleating in her ears. The woman hadn't been making idle threats when she'd told Cleon she was moving her household and her herd. Granted, Marsh hadn't expected Tamlin to step forward and offer Fabrice his family's farm. The boy had told Marsh the night before and sworn her to secrecy.

She'd been sitting in a corner of the eatery the next morning when Fabrice and the children had come in. Catching Marsh's eye, Tamlin had slipped from his seat and intercepted the family as they'd walked toward the counter. Aisha had followed him, Scruffknuckle at her heels, and nodded solemnly when he'd made his offer.

"I can't take that!" Fabrice had been shocked.

"Borrow it, then," Tamlin said. "Consider it a kind of trade. You look after the place, and we lend you the pasture in return."

"But where would the children and I stay?"

Tamlin had smiled and played his final card.

"You look after Aisha and Scruff an' me and the house

as trade for staying there until Marsh rescues Patrik and we get your old farm back." He'd stopped and given her a pleading look. "Please? Marsh is going to be busy. We'll need a grownup around."

Marsh had caught that in time to look up and catch Fabrice's questioning stare. She'd nodded and kept the rest of Tamlin's plans a secret. What the boy hadn't told Fabrice was that he expected that he and Aisha would be staying up in the monastery. He'd whispered it to Marsh when he'd asked for her support in his plan.

"She needs somewhere to go," he'd said. "She can't stay with Cleon; they'll only end up fighting. And Aysh and me won't need the place unless you get our family back. You can do that if we've got another adult to look after us, right?"

Marsh had felt a lump forming in her throat and bowed her head so he wouldn't see the tears in her eyes. When she'd raised her head again, the tears were gone, and she'd been able to stop them from showing in her voice.

"Right."

"So you'll let me do this, then?"

"I will."

Those two words had been the hardest she'd had to say in a while, but they'd been necessary. Tamlin needed her to try to find his parents, and Fabrice needed somewhere safe for herself and the children. Whatever came of this could be dealt with when it arose.

"Are you okay, Marsh?"

Marsh remembered nodding and forcing herself to smile.

"I'll be fine, Tams. Get some sleep. We've got a busy day tomorrow."

She hadn't been joking, either. Once Tams had gotten Fabrice's agreement, Marsh had needed to convince Gustav to stop at Under-Paris Cheeses so that they could collect the sheep on the way to the shadow mages' cavern —and they hadn't arrived a moment too soon. Cleon's farmhands were already moving the herd toward the paddocks containing the farm's existing stock.

"Stop!" Fabrice commanded, and it might have gone very differently if Gustav hadn't added four more men to the guards to cover the extra duties required for looking after three more people and a herd of moutons on the trail.

When the guards had stepped between the herd and the gate, Cleon's hands had understood the situation very well. Marsh and Lennie had escorted Fabrice and the children inside to collect their belongings. At first, Marcelle had protested about the cost of lodging the herd and the family for the night they'd already stayed, but Fabrice was more than prepared.

She slapped a quarter of the reward for returning the mules on the table and counted out the cost of Cleon's resupply on top of it.

"We square?" she asked, and Marsh hadn't missed Lennie's hand drifting to the hilt of her sword.

Marcelle hadn't missed it either.

"Square!" she declared, and Marsh and Lennie were quick to close the deal.

"Witnessed," they stated, and Marcelle stared at them in shock.

She obviously hadn't expected the hired help to know the tradition.

Well, too bad for her, Marsh thought. She'd agreed, and it was witnessed. They'd left her counting the payment at the kitchen table, escorting Fabrice and the children out to the caravan and helping them load their gear onto the mules.

"You're well out of there," Lennie had said, and Fabrice had sniffed.

"Thank you," she'd said, not quite stifling a hiccup that nearly made it to a sob. She'd leaned over to Tams and patted his cheek. "And thank you too, boy. I'm grateful for what you've done."

He'd blushed bright red and tried to scowl.

"Well... Well, can you cook pancakes tomorrow?" he'd asked, and Fabrice had laughed.

"I will make you croissants if you like."

The boy's face had brightened.

"Really?"

"Yes," she'd said, and Gustav had sidled over to her mule.

"Is that offer open to all of us?" he'd whispered loud enough for them all to hear, and Fabrice had laughed again.

"Of course it is, you dear man."

"Dear man" was clearly something Gustav wasn't called often because several of his fellow guards had coughing fits and Lennie gave a most unladylike snort.

"Come on, *dear man*," she'd snarked. "You're on point with Marsh."

Her declaration had caught Marsh by surprise. "I'm on point?"

Lennie had given her a toothy smile.

"You are now, sweetie."

Honestly, Marsh had liked it better when Lennie was hitting her. She'd pulled a face and gone out front with Gustav. They'd counted the number of times the sand ran through the hourglass and stopped the caravan on the fourth turn.

"We eating while we ride or stopping?" Gustav had asked, looking at Roeglin.

"It's another half-day to the monastery," the mage had replied. "Choice is yours."

"The moutons are happy to keep going," Fabrice had said, "and the children and I only need a short break."

By which she'd meant only one thing, and everyone needed to do that after a half-day in the saddle. Gustav had insisted on digging a quick latrine beyond the line of glows, and he and the guards had taken turns guarding the pit until everyone had finished. Fabrice, Roeglin, and Marsh had filled it in.

"You made sure we didn't get caught with our pants down," Marsh explained. "Least we can do is save you some digging."

That had pretty much ended the discussion and now they were back on the road, eating meat-and-mushroom-filled pasties as they sat their mules. This time it was Lennie and her supporter taking the lead. His name was Henri, and he reminded Marsh more of the raiders in build than any of the folk of the Four Settlements. She wanted to ask him where he'd come from but didn't quite know how to go about it.

In the end, she'd been content to let herself drift,

keeping a half-eye on Tamlin, who shared his mule with Aisha. The little girl seemed lost without her puppy, but Scruffknuckle had rekindled his acquaintance with Hugo and the pair was running with the moutons, nipping at their heels if they slowed too much.

The steady pace of the mules and the slow and constant bleat of moutons had lulled Marsh into a state of half-sleep. She'd only just thought she'd figured out what she was going to do next when her mind started to drift. She'd also figured out what she needed to do for Monsieur Gravine. All she had to do was talk it over with Gustav.

She also wanted to discuss shadow mage recruitment with him, because if the farm folk had been spooked by the false shadow mages, it would be a bad idea to send the monastery mages out to do the same thing. Someone was liable to get killed. It would be better to have the Protectors scout for hidden talent. Perhaps even train mages of their own, splitting the responsibility.

It was worth a thought.

"Mind if I cut in?" Roeglin's voice interrupted her and Marsh sighed.

"I can see what you're thinking," he added, and Marsh knew he meant that literally, not figuratively.

That should have been a lot more disturbing that it was. "Yeah, and?"

"Pitch it as a split between adult and child recruits to start with, then ask the mages for a liaison to do the training. A fighting force with immediate practical application might be the best place for adult learners anyway, especially since they have less time to acquire the skills. The monastery needs to diversify as well. Not all of our mages have the same gifts."

It gave her some idea of how he'd ended up in the town, something he confirmed when he nudged her.

"They wanted me to hone the skills the wandering mages had brought and thought a town would be a better place, given the number of minds that were available." He grimaced. "You have no idea of the minds I've touched."

From the look on his face, there were minds he didn't want to touch again and wished he hadn't gone near in the first place. Marsh didn't pry. It wasn't like she'd asked anything out loud. If the man chose to dip into her head, what he found there was his problem.

"Nothing wrong with your head," he muttered. "I *like* dipping into *your* head. It's a nice space."

"You keep your grotty little mindwalker paws out of my head, or I'll make you very sorry you visited."

"Oookay, then." Roeglin didn't seem too afraid.

Marsh scowled but didn't pursue it. If he kept it up, she figured she could always knock him out to get some peace and quiet.

"Hey!"

Marsh ignored him. She was tired and in the company of strangers, and she had two tired kids to protect, and then there was the way she could tweak the shadows and look into a hoshkat's eyes and convince her to go away. She really had to decide what to do about that.

To her surprise, Roeglin had nothing to say about it, which was funny, really; she would have thought he'd have had some opinion. When he remained silent, Marsh slid him a sideways look and saw he'd wrapped his hands around the pommel of his saddle and closed his eyes.

Each to their own, she supposed, and let herself drift, just as she'd seen the guards do. As she'd taught herself to do on the numerous errands Kearick had sent her on without a guard. It let her keep a vague awareness of her surroundings as she descended into a state of near-sleep. She knew when the mouton bunched closer to the center of the path and when the guards straightened in their saddles, knew when they saw nothing but did not relax.

She also knew when Lennie turned the hourglass at the second hour and the third and noticed when the mouton grew quieter, their bleating dying to almost nothing. Without saying a word, she straightened in her saddle and searched the groves of fungi and clusters of rock beyond the glows, but she saw nothing. That didn't mean nothing was there.

Instead of relying on her eyes, she followed Roeglin's example and gripped the pommel of her saddle, keeping her reins taut but not tight enough to make the mule stop. Slowly she reached out to the shadows, asking them what lay concealed beyond the path. At first, they showed her nothing but the rocks and fungi.

"I'm looking for something else," Marsh whispered, startled to hear the words hit the open air. "Something that scares the moutons but remains hidden from the guards."

The pace of the caravan slowed, and a mule came alongside hers.

"I've got your reins."

Marsh registered Tamlin's voice and relaxed a little bit.

"And I'll watch the children," Roeglin and Fabrice said in chorus.

Marsh let herself descend farther into the dark, tweaking each thread and seeking what living things lay along its length. Whatever stalked the edges of the trail eluded her. Many times, the threads would tighten, but when Marsh drew the information to herself, all she found was a brief warmth, as though something large had passed and left only its presence behind.

"Nothing," she said when she opened her eyes and saw Gustav riding to her left, splitting his attention between her face and the terrain around them.

"Nothing?"

"Nothing I could catch," Marsh amended. "There's something there, something big, but it's moving too fast for the shadows to register what it is."

"Then how do you know it's so big?"

"I can feel its warmth like a hollow in the dark."

"How big?"

Marsh thought about it.

"Bigger than a mouton but not as big as a mule."

"We need to speed up," Gustav snapped, looking at Lennie and Henri. "I can think of only one thing that size that can move as silent as the shadows and leave close to no trace."

Now that she thought about it, so could Marsh. As if to confirm what they were all thinking, a series of grunting coughs echoed through the dark, and Marsh caught a glimpse of mottled fur. One of the guards raised a crossbow, but Tamlin was quick to stretch out a foot and nudge the man's mule so it sidled underneath him.

The movement drew Gustav's attention.

"Don't shoot!" he snapped. "No one shoot. We've got nothing that will do more than make it angry, and a pissed-off hoshkat will have us down before we can bleed."

The guard froze, lowering his weapon as he steadied the mule.

"What do you want us to do?"

"Keep riding," Gustav told him. "It hasn't attacked yet. If it wanted a mouton, it would have grabbed one by now, and there'd have been sweet nothing we could do about it. Same if it wanted a mule or any of us. If we're lucky, we're just sharing the path."

Sharing the path. Marsh liked the idea of that. She tugged on the reins until Tamlin handed them back and then she nudged her mule forward. But why would a hoshkat be anywhere near the path in the first place?

She nudged her mule again as Gustav and the guard with the crossbow dropped back to the rear of the herd. She let herself fall back to what she guessed was about halfway along the column, leaving Tamlin and Aisha to ride in front of her while Fabrice paralleled her on the other side of the herd. If the kat wanted a mouton, it could still have taken one, but it hadn't.

Marsh knew it was still out there. She could sense it keeping pace with the caravan, but she could also sense that it intended no harm. It was keeping them company...

In the shadows.

In the cavern dark.

Because that wasn't as scary as the very Deeps.

17

SHADOW MAGE MONASTERY

They arrived late in the cycle of hours, Lennie having turned the hourglass twice more since Marsh had first sensed the kat traveling with them through the dark. Gustav signaled for her and Fabrice to bring their mules up beside him as he rode up and knocked on the gates.

"It's late. The gates are closed for the night."

The rough reply did not deter Gustav.

"We seek refuge."

"The gates will open in the morning."

"We bring news of invaders."

Silence, followed by the sound of footsteps retreating deeper into the fortress.

"At least let us wait in the barbican!"

Subdued voices conferred beyond the gate, but Marsh breathed a sigh of relief when the reply came.

"Only the barbican."

Well, where else were they going to go? Marsh rolled her eyes, confident the expression would not be seen from within the fortress. When the gate finally opened, she directed her mule slightly to one side, gesturing for Tamlin and Aisha to bring the mouton through before her. When the mouton milled and turned before the opening, Aisha slid off her mule and stepped up to the first of the rams, catching his gaze.

"Come," the little girl said, her eyes blazing emerald as she scratched him under his chin.

He hesitated, but then followed her in. The lead ewe was nowhere near as cooperative. She bleated anxiously, turning her head to look from the ram and the open gate to the cavern around her. Marsh could guess what she was thinking: the journey had been a long one, and they'd barely stopped to graze—and then the hoshkat had come along, so no one had *wanted* to stop. But now that they had...

The mouton started to turn, and Marsh saw what they were about to do. Before they could take more than one step in the direction of the open cavern, she gave a short, sharp whistle and the animals turned their gaze toward her. She tried to do with them what she had done to the kat.

"Please come inside," she murmured, imagining piles of fodder and buckets of cool, clean water. "Come where you will all be safe." Here she thought of the hoshkat lurking in the dark, waiting. "Come where it may not follow. Please come."

She moved her eyes from one woolly face to the next, picturing safety and food in the dark hollow between the walls and beyond the gates.

"Please..."

The moutons stilled, then turned as one and trotted

into the space between the walls. No sooner had they done that than heavy fatigue dropped onto Marsh and she almost fell from the saddle. If it hadn't been for Roeglin reaching out to catch her, she'd have landed heavily on the cavern's floor. As it was, only Gustav's quick lunge to capture Roeglin by the belt stopped the mage from tumbling to the floor with her.

"Now what?"

The mercenary sounded more angry than worried, and he slid from his mount to push Marsh firmly into Roeglin's arms.

"Don't drop her until we're all through safely. After that…"

"I won't drop her," Roeglin assured him, and Marsh felt slightly comforted because it sounded more like the mage was making her a promise than Gustav.

Which was a good thing, because Gustav was still annoyed.

"I was going to say you could drop her all you liked."

Roeglin gave a snort of amusement, but Marsh didn't have the energy to do a thing. She wouldn't be able to do anything if Roeglin *did* drop her. She couldn't even find the strength to grab the saddle or his arm, or…anything. Whatever the mouton had done to her, it was pretty thorough.

Not the mouton, Roeglin said, his voice sounding in her mind and not her ears. *You talking to the mouton. Tell me you haven't done that before?*

Well, duh! Marsh thought before letting sleep take her. *If I'd done that before, I'd have had a better grip on the saddle…*

When she woke, she was inside the monastery in a bed of her own, still dressed in her traveling clothes but without her boots. She sat up, and looked around the room, feeling like she'd been run over by a million moutons. Seeing her missing footwear by the side of the bed was little comfort.

Suppressing a groan, Marchant swung her feet out of bed and reached down to pull her boots back on. She needed to find out what had happened to Tamlin and Aisha —and Fabrice. She needed to know if Gustav had spoken to the shadow mages yet, or if she needed to prepare for a meeting. She needed—

"You need to rest, Marchant."

The voice was unfamiliar. Female, but with a ring of authority that Marsh decided she should pay attention to. Looking toward it, Marsh saw it belonged to a slender woman with a strong-featured face and dark brown eyes. She continued speaking before Marsh could think of anything to say.

"That was quite a display you put on."

She had?

"To move the moutons into the castle. We wondered how you would manage it, because our fields are very enticing. Thank you for keeping them out of the crops."

She really had?

Some of her puzzlement must have shown because the woman smiled.

"So, Roeglin is correct? You don't know what you have done?"

Marsh shook her head, and her world spun. When it

steadied, the woman was crouched before her, one hand on her shoulder.

"You have stretched a muscle you didn't know you had, and now your body and mind need to rest."

As she spoke, she took the boots from Marsh's hands and tucked them back under the bed. Her nose wrinkled as she leaned close to Marsh.

"I'd tell you to take a bath, but I don't think you could stay awake, and I'd hate for you to drown. Sleep now. There will be food waiting when you wake again."

Marsh wanted to do as she was bid, but she had duties. Responsibilities. No matter how tired she was, she had to make sure the children were all right.

"Tamlin and Aisha..." she began, fatigue slurring her words.

The woman nodded.

"They are safe, and a fine pair of rascals, too. We are keeping them busy while you rest. Tomorrow we will send a team to accompany Fabrice and her family out to Tamlin's farm. They will need help setting it up. *Now* will you sleep?"

The children were fine? Even as she thought it would be good to see some proof of the mage's words, Marsh caught movement just behind the woman's shoulder. Lifting her head, she saw Tamlin peering around the door, Roeglin's head and shoulders above him. Aisha had no such sense of subtlety.

She slid past her brother and their keeper, circling around the female mage to clamber up onto the bed beside Marsh.

"You *bon*?" she asked.

Marsh started to nod but was pushed back when Scruffknuckle forced his way between her and the mage, leapt onto the bed, and put his paws on her shoulders.

"Scruff, no!" The command was lost in laughter when the persistent beast started licking her face, worming his way onto her lap even as the mage tried to scowl.

In the end, the woman gave up and stood, setting her hands on her hips.

"*Now* will you get some sleep?"

Marsh shot Aisha a swift glance and focused on pushing Scruff out of her lap and back onto the floor.

"*Oui*," she said and tucked her feet up off the floor. Aisha got off the bed and returned to where her brother and Roeglin were waiting. Marsh curled back under the covers as the mage headed for the door. She was asleep before the woman reached it.

There was food when she woke, some kind of sweet pastry and a cup of thick chocolate. Someone had guessed her preference...or not, as it turned out.

"You need the sweets," the mage said. "I'm Lucille, an instructor here. Roeglin tells me you have only just discovered your powers."

Marsh frowned, glad to be too busy eating to be able to reply. Roeglin needed to keep his tongue still.

"He only has your best interests at heart."

He had a heart? Marsh kept that thought to herself, even as her heart leapt at the idea.

The mage mistress continued, completely oblivious to what was running through Marsh's head.

"You stink, by the way. When you've washed and

changed, come to the offices. The Shadow Master wishes to meet you." She turned for the door. "Do not be long."

She wrinkled her nose again.

"But *do* be thorough."

Marsh felt color flood her cheeks and wanted to argue that it wasn't her fault she stank so much. It had not been her idea to sleep after the day on the road. She'd wanted a good wash and a meal. Her stomach rumbled as she thought about it, and Marsh hoped the meeting with this Shadow Master person involved more food.

It didn't.

"I understand you come to us with several intents," he began once she was seated in his office, and Marsh's heart sank.

It looked like this was going to be a long meeting.

"Tell me of them."

At first, Marsh struggled to remember each one, so she started with the most important.

"I rescued the boy and his sister. Their parents were bringing them to this cavern so that they could grow up near you, and Tamlin could learn to harness his gifts."

"The girl too, no doubt."

"I don't think they were aware of her abilities."

"And you were hoping to dump them into our care?"

Marsh felt her skin warm and looked down at her hands.

"At first, but now I am hoping you will allow them to learn what they need. Tamlin has engaged Fabrice to care for them."

This brought the slightest quirk to the Shadow Master's lips.

"Yes, the boy has explained his arrangement, and the woman agrees. We are satisfied the children's needs are covered…"

Marsh heard the "but" before he spoke it.

"But we must be satisfied that they have no relatives waiting to claim them before we can make their situation among us permanent. You will do that for us."

It was an order, not a request. Marsh opened her mouth to protest, but the Shadow Master held up a hand, commanding silence, and she subsided. When he spoke, it was to demand another answer.

"Your second purpose?"

"To learn more about my own powers."

"Hmmm."

His lips compressed into a thin line but he said nothing more on the subject.

"And the third?"

Again Marsh felt her face coloring even though she had done nothing wrong and had nothing to be sorry for, neither of which explained how she could feel so guilty and uncertain.

"I bring a message from Monsieur Gravine of the Ruins Hall cavern complex."

"Go on."

"I was to deliver it with Gustav."

"He has already delivered his version of the message. I wish to hear it from you."

So it was like that, was it? Marsh took a deep breath and tried to remember the words exactly as the founder had said them. In the end, she settled for paraphrasing,

"He wishes the shadow mages' monastery to be a refuge

and home for the families of his soldiers, and for the wounded and sick. He wants his men to know that their loved ones are cared for and safe as they go about protecting the caverns, and you have the only fortress capable of that."

She paused, catching the Shadow Master's upraised eyebrows before continuing.

"He also wishes for you to continue recruiting and training shadow mages, although I believe he thinks it would be better if you went in the company of his men so that the people of the caverns know that you are to be trusted."

"And?" the Shadow Master pressed when she hesitated.

"And he would like for you to train his men in the art of shadow magic—the ones who have the gift. I believe his idea is for adults to be trained as part of his Protectors while the youngsters come here for a proper apprenticeship."

"Are you sure that was *his* idea?" the Shadow Master pressed, and Marsh's face became even redder than before.

"I may have suggested the separation," she admitted. "Roeglin agreed it might work better if the adults had something more concrete to practice their skills on."

The Shadow Master nodded.

"I agree."

"It's..." Marsh stopped, registering what he'd said. "You do?"

This time his mouth curved into a small, firm smile.

"Yes, Marchant Marie Leclerc, I agree to this order of shadow mages assisting Monsieur Gravine, Founder of the Ruins Hall cavern community, in protecting the Four

Settlements, starting with this one." He raised his head, clearly speaking to someone waiting just beyond the door. "Send in Gustav Moldrane. We will finalize a proposal for the founder."

He turned to Marchant.

"I believe you have done your part and are overdue a meal, as well as an interview with the Training Mistress Varangarde. You are dismissed."

Marsh stared at him for a moment and realized he meant it—and was acting as though she were already a trainee in his order. For a moment she thought of protesting, but then she thought it would be better if she discussed it with the training mistress. Catching the look on his face, Marsh decided talking to the training mistress would definitely be a much better option.

Something troubled the Shadow Master, but she doubted he was the sharing kind. She discovered she'd made a mistake as she reached the door.

"You forgot to ask me to help you contact the rock mages. The girl, Aisha, will need them, and so, I think, will you." He paused, catching the look of puzzlement on Marsh's face. "What is it?"

"Rock mages," she said. "I know Aisha speaks to rocks, but I…"

"Ah." His face softened with understanding. "Rock mages deal with more than rocks. They are in touch with the natural elements of the caverns: the rock, the fungi and plants, and the creatures. In other parts of the world, they would be referred to as 'druids.'"

He paused, watching Marsh's face as she absorbed the information before he continued.

"Please ask the mistress to send a request to their Master of Stone—and have her inform the Master that we need to speak in the name of the Guardians."

"Yes…yes, Shadow Master."

He did not reply, but the doors opened before she could reach them and Gustav strode through. His eyes rested on her for a moment, and he paused.

"You told him what the founder asked?" Marsh realized the Shadow Master had not been as honest with her as she thought.

What a surprise!

She didn't stop to challenge him, though. He had, after all, agreed to what the founder wanted, and even agreed to contact the rock mages on their behalf. If he hadn't wanted to see the caverns safe, he'd have sent her away without adding that in…or agreeing to anything at all.

She caught the Shadow Master's eye. "I told him what I remembered of the founder's request. You should go over it with him to make sure I didn't forget anything."

18

SHADOW MAGIC AND COOKIES

There were two shadow mages waiting in the hall when Marchant left the Shadow Master's office. One brushed by her, going into the office as she stepped into the hall and pulling the door closed behind him. Marsh looked at the other and he pointed down the corridor.

If ever an order could be conveyed by a gesture, this was it.

"Follow the dark flame," he said, and a tongue of dark blue and purple fire sprang from his fingers, folding in on itself and then unfolding into a dark-winged moth.

"Go," he added, gesturing again when Marsh hesitated.

Marsh followed the flicker of his fingers and saw the moth fluttering away from her.

"You'll get lost if you don't."

Marsh resisted the urge to stamp her foot and insist he tell her the way; it would have been rude. Besides, there was something appealing about chasing the flutter-winged creature through unfamiliar corridors. She pivoted after it, not looking back—and not letting her smile escape until the mage was well behind her.

The moth fluttered on, and Marsh concentrated on following it. The happy curl on her lips faded as she found the task more difficult the farther she got. After the third turn, she caught herself reaching into the shadows to find the threads connecting her to the moth. They twitched unevenly under her hands, but she found that by concentrating on them and asking them to show her the moth, she could make the elusive creature glow.

An intense halo of purple and blue surrounded its form and Marsh trotted after it, trying to stay aware of her surroundings as she kept the moth surrounded by light. It got easier the farther she went—and she was glad because the little creature sped up until Marsh pushed her trot into a jog and chased it into a stairwell.

Halfway down the steps, the damn thing vanished.

"Well, *merde!*"

Marsh let her feet carry her to the next level and then she made herself stop.

This wasn't funny! The Shadow Master had ordered her to see the instructor. The instructor would be waiting. Why in all the Deeps would the mage have played such a mean trick? When she saw him again…

Marsh took a deep breath and forced herself to calm down. She had to see the training mistress, and she wasn't going to let a mean-spirited prank stop her. After she'd seen the mistress, she was going to find a way to deter the man from ever playing such a trick again. The idea of having him carried out the nearest window by a cloud of fluttering shadow-moths crossed her mind, and Marsh smiled.

Later... Later she was going to find a way to make that happen. Now, though...

She took a second breath and let it out slowly, looking around the stairwell. If she was Roeglin, she'd probably just try to contact the woman with her mind, but she wasn't—and as far as she knew, she didn't have the magic of the mind. The thought snagged, and Marsh gave a snort of derision.

Then again, she hadn't had the gift of being able to speak to the shadows either until a couple of days ago. For all she knew, she *could* talk to someone mind to mind.

"That is a trick for another day," she told herself, pushing the idea away. "Right now, what would I do if I needed to find..."

She sighed. The answer was obvious when she thought about it.

"Well, of course I would, wouldn't I?"

This time the shadows gave her no answers—or rather, they gave her too many. Just how many 'training mistresses' were there, anyway? Oh...

"Training Mistress *Varangarde*."

This time when the shadows answered, there was only a narrow band of threads for her to follow. She took a firm hold and let them guide her back up three flights of stairs and along the narrow corridor to a door set into the outer corner of the next turn. Resisting the urge to push the door open, Marsh raised her hand to knock instead.

"*Entré*." The command came before her knuckles touched the wood.

Marsh turned the handle and pushed the door open. She opened her mouth to explain why she had come, but the training mistress didn't give her a chance.

"Come and sit," she commanded. "You are late."

Again Marsh opened her mouth to explain, and again she was cut off.

"I do not need an explanation. It is I who will do the explaining."

Marsh closed her mouth and sat, her mind a momentary blank. This was not at all how she'd imagined it would be. The mistress waited until she was settled and then raised her hand, moving it in a circular motion. A heartbeat later, Marsh felt a swish of air and then the office door slammed, almost startling her out of her chair.

"Tell me how you got here."

"The guard outside the Shadow Master's office summoned a moth..." Marsh paused as the training mistress's face twisted. "Did I do something wrong?"

The mistress shook her head.

"No, but it is an old trick—and one often played on new students. Tell me, where did the moth disappear?"

"In the stairwell at the other end of the corridor."

Now Marsh felt stupid. She should have asked the Shadow Master for directions, should... The training mistress interrupted her thoughts.

"Mmhmm—and how many floors down?"

At least the mistress wasn't making fun of her.

Marsh remembered her hurried run up the stairs.

"Three, I think."

"And how did you solve the problem?"

Marsh studied the woman in front of her and saw she

was asking the question in all seriousness, curiosity rather than mockery coloring her tones.

"I asked the shadows," she said, trying to sound confident. She was pleased when her voice came out firm and clear rather than quivering and small.

There was no need to be afraid; she had done nothing wrong.

If they chose to reject her now, it wouldn't matter. She'd already started to figure out how her magic worked, and she could continue to do that even if they sent her away.

"How?"

"I asked, then listened to the threads that knew the answer."

The training mistress looked surprised but quickly smoothed the expression from her face. Finally, she leaned forward, put her elbows on her desk, and rested her chin on her interlinked fingers.

"Tell me, what else can you do?"

Like a dog doing tricks. Marsh scowled, but the mistress's gaze didn't waver, so she obeyed.

"I can see what lies in another part of a cavern."

The mistress raised her eyebrows as Marsh continued.

"And hear conversations too, if I ask nicely enough."

The mistress folded her hands together, still resting her chin on them.

"Go on."

Marsh thought about it. She'd already shown she could find things by asking the shadows; get them to reveal distant visions and sound. What else could she do?

"And I once trapped someone's fist in a ball of shadow."

"Is that everything?"

Marsh thought about it.

"I think so."

"What about the things you've done that *don't* involve shadow?"

It wasn't a question she'd expected, so Marsh took a moment to gather her thoughts.

"Like talking to the moutons?"

"Yes. Have you done anything like that before?"

Marsh instantly remembered talking to the hoshkat and her mouth went dry. She swallowed and licked her lips.

"I talked to a hoshkat once."

"Tell me about it."

So Marsh did, describing the way she had fallen into the hoshkat's eyes and spoken to her, and then telling how she had left and not come back.

"But there was a kat on the trail yesterday, was there not?"

"*Oui*, but..." Marsh caught a breath. "D'you think it was the same one?"

"It is the first kat we've had along that trail, so it is a possibility."

"But why would she have followed me? *How* would she have followed me?"

The training mistress shrugged.

"That will be something for the rock mages to explain," she said. "They're the ones who deal with animals and plants. I take it the Shadow Master sent instructions for me to contact them?"

"Oh, yes. He said Aisha would need instruction from

them...and maybe me, too."

"Definitely you," the female mage told her, "and you will need instruction from that scamp Roeglin as well."

"But I don't have mind magic!" Marsh protested.

"What you do when you seek the words or the presence of people in the shadows is not purely of shadow, and not purely of mind. Of all of our people, he is the most versed in that kind of working."

Marsh remembered Roeglin taking the memories from Aisha and her. She recalled him giving them life using a blend of shadow and mist and heard his voice speaking her words, Aisha's words.

"If you say so."

The mistress' eyes snapped with suppressed anger and fire, and Marsh found herself momentarily trapped in her obsidian gaze.

"I do, young lady, and you'll find that what I say is generally correct."

The training mistress blinked, and Marsh felt like she'd tumbled out of a cage. She gripped the edge of the tabletop to steady herself, then remembered the argument she wanted to make.

"What makes you think I want to become one of your trainees?"

The mistress stared at her with wide eyes.

"You *did* come here for help in learning the extent of your abilities, did you not?"

Marsh nodded.

"And you *did* want to learn what else you could do, did you not?"

"*Oui.*"

"And you really want to learn to control what you can do, don't you?"

Control? She hadn't thought of that. What if she trapped more than someone's fist in a ball of shadow? What if it had been a head? Could the guard have breathed through that? The training mistress was watching her face closely and saw when Marsh caught the implications.

Marsh swallowed.

"*Oui.*"

There was no doubt in her mind that she wanted control. Too much could go wrong. Too…

Wait. If she could control the shadows, did that mean she could control the monsters? She was about to pursue that thought when the training mistress spoke.

"So you're happy, then?"

That pulled Marsh from her thoughts.

"Happy with what?"

"Happy to become a trainee here."

"Trainee?"

"Rather than an apprentice." The mistress looked her up and down. "No offense, but you're a little old for that, and already showing skills beyond the apprenticeship stage despite what you lack. With some effort, you could develop the discipline to be a journeyman in a couple of months."

"A couple of months?" Marsh was horrified. "But I can't! I…*we* don't know how long we have before the raiders attack. I have to be ready. I—"

The mistress cut her protests off with a lift of her hand.

"Then you'd best work hard, or we won't be able to send you out where you will be able to do the most good when they come."

"What else?" Marsh wanted to know. "I mean, I have the children to care for, and…"

Again the mistress held up her hand, stopping her in her tracks.

"You and the children have already solved that problem. Tamlin hired Fabrice, and Fabrice will care for them when they are at the farm, while we will care for them here. We have made arrangements with the farmer's wife in this domain."

"And the Shadow Master's instructions that I should find out if there are any living relatives?"

"He will not want you out there until you have gained sufficient control of your abilities, and neither will the Master of Stone." She paused, watching Marsh's face as she worked through what she'd said. "I don't think the cavern founder will want you left untrained. You're no use to him if you can't be relied on to call the skills his people need at the moment they need them."

As if he was her employer now. Marsh hesitated, then said nothing. Before yesterday, she hadn't thought of who she'd work for now that the road to Kerrenin's Ledge was closed—or who would pay her wages even if she *did* deliver the artifact. The commission was with Kearick, after all, and Marsh would have to return to him with the payment if she was to receive her fee—and that was only if Kearick didn't decide to fine her for the loss of the rest of her shipment. He wouldn't care whose fault it was.

Besides, now that she was able to wield shadow magic and talk to animals, maybe she could find artifacts for herself, no apprenticeship needed—and no Kearick. She could trade direct. The training mistress cleared her throat, bringing Marsh back to the present.

"Well?" she asked and rolled her eyes at Marsh's blank look. "Are you willing to sign on as a trainee here at the monastery?"

"And I could go where I was needed?" Marsh asked. "You wouldn't keep me from the fight?"

Because there was a fight coming; she was sure of that.

The mistress regarded her intently.

"We wouldn't do that," she assured Marsh. "These are our caverns too, and we will do all we can to protect them. We will expect your help in that as well."

Marsh felt a piece of tension unknot inside her and let out a slow breath.

"Then yes, I would like to be a trainee here."

The mistress pushed a piece of paper across the desk.

"Sign this, then," she said. "It will make our agreement official, and give you some protection from being pulled this way and that by others who might think they can order you where they will."

Marsh took the piece of paper and looked at it, turning it around so she could read it. She was relieved when the training mistress did not rush her but let her take her time to go over the script. She was also relieved to find that it bound her only for the length of her training, and asked only that she provide assistance in emergencies thereafter unless she accepted the position of journeyman. She wondered how likely it was that they'd offer her a permanent place among them—and then wondered if she'd take it.

In the end, she decided that was a question to be

answered later. Once she was sure she'd read it correctly and missed nothing in the fine print, Marsh signed the sheet and returned it.

The mistress signed it and rose from behind her desk.

"If you'll follow me," she instructed, moving to the door and pulling it open, "I'll show you where your quarters are. I take it you only have what is in your pack?"

"The rest was lost in the ambush."

"We'll provide you with the tunic and trous of a trainee, and ceremonial robes, should you need them. You are being paid. If you require more, you may speak to the tailors."

There were tailors?

Marsh followed as the training mistress stepped into the corridor and led the way, descending three flights before stopping on the landing and opening a door.

"You will be across the hall from Tamlin and next door to Aisha. Apprentice Journeyman Petitfeu will be your main supervisor until we've worked out what instruction each of you requires. It will be a busy few days of assessment, then we'll place you with an instructor and your sleeping quarters will change."

"Thank you," Marsh managed, although she wasn't sure if it was the right thing to say.

The training mistress accepted it and continued hurrying ahead of her. They traveled the full length of the corridor before turning to the right. Halfway along, the mistress stopped and knocked on one of the doors set in the wall. Marsh heard the scrape of a chair followed by soft footsteps, and then the door opened.

"Yes? Oh, Mistress Varangarde, I didn't know it was

you. The children are…" She let her words fade and raised her head when she caught sight of Marsh behind the trainer.

Marsh saw her in the dim light of the glows set in the walls and gasped. She had laid a hand on the training mistress's shoulder and was pulling her back and behind her even as she started to pull her sword from its sheath. To her surprise, the mistress resisted her grasp, shrugging herself free of Marsh's grip and turning to push Marsh's sword back into its scabbard.

"I'm sorry," she murmured, but she wasn't speaking to Marsh; her apology was addressed to the apprentice journeyman.

For her part, the girl was watching Marsh without a hint of surprise on her ebony face.

"I am only colored like them," the young woman said and stepped a little to the side so Marsh could view her fully. "See?"

She brushed aside the hair that partially obscured her eyes.

To Marsh's surprise, those eyes were a stunning blue, not the craze-filled red of the shadow monsters that had attacked the caravan. She lifted her hand from her sword hilt.

"I… I'm sorry," she stammered, her face coloring with embarrassment for what felt like the millionth time that day. "I… It's just…"

She sighed.

"I'm really sorry, okay?"

To her surprise, the girl gave her a reassuring smile. It was a fleeting thing, soon replaced by sadness.

"Who did you lose?" she asked. "And how long ago?"

The look made Marsh pause, and she realized that hers wasn't the first hostile reaction the girl had faced. It made her ashamed.

"I was part of a caravan that was attacked a few days ago." She thought about that. "Almost a week, now."

The attack was beginning to feel like it had happened to someone else a whole other world ago.

The girl's eyes widened.

"You're the one who rescued Tams and Aisha?"

Marsh nodded and then wondered how the children had reacted, but the apprentice journeyman hurried on, not giving her time to ask.

"I'm so glad you've arrived. We can't convince her to open the door."

We? Marsh looked around but didn't see anybody.

"Her brother is trapped in the room with her."

Trapped? *Tamlin* was trapped?

"But how?"

The apprentice journeyman shrugged.

"I don't know. The little one took one look at me and bolted into the nearest room. He ran after her, and the door slammed shut." She turned to the training mistress, distraught. "No one warned them."

Mistress Varangarde laid a hand on the girl's shoulder.

"Don't fret. We'll sort it out." She hesitated. "I'm sorry. I will speak to the others."

The mistress turned to Marsh.

"See what you can do to fetch her out."

Marsh looked at the journeyman apprentice.

"Which door is it?"

"That one."

Marsh turned abruptly on one heel and strode to the door, pulling her sword from her scabbard as she did so. Turning it in her hand, she rapped on the door's hard surface with the pommel.

"Aysh!" she shouted. "Aysh! You get your tiny tail out here right now. You owe the journeyman an apology!"

For a long moment, there was silence, so Marsh banged her sword hilt on the door once more.

"Aysh! Do not make me come in there!"

That got a response from Tamlin as well as his sister.

"Like you could!"

"No come in!"

"Just open the door!"

"No! Monsters!"

"No monsters out here except me."

"Are not!"

"Am too!"

"Not!"

"Too!"

"Kick your tail!"

"Can't get me."

"Open the door!"

"No!"

"Fine!" Marsh turned her back to the door and leaned on it. "No cookies for you!"

Seconds later, she gave a startled shout as the door opened and she fell into the room. No sooner had her butt hit the floor than a blur of paws and fur bounced onto her chest and began licking her face.

"Oh! Hey! Get off!" Marsh sputtered, dropping her

sword as she tried to defend herself from the pup. "Hey! No cookies for you either!"

"Scruff!" Aisha's reprimand got the pup's attention straight away, and he bounded over to sit before her.

Marsh pushed herself up onto her elbows and sat across the doorway, pulling her sword to her side.

"You know that's not a shadow monster, right?" Marsh asked, and flinched as Aisha made a gesture and the door moved toward her.

She closed her eyes and braced, but the expected blow never came. When she peered cautiously at her surroundings once more, she saw that the door had stopped and Aisha had come close enough to stare down at her.

"Monster," she said with all the conviction a child could muster. "Bad, bad monster."

Marsh did not let that conviction daunt her.

"Nope, and you owe the apprentice journeyman an apology. She cannot help it that the monsters look like her."

Tamlin snorted, and Marsh noticed that the boy had moved out of the room and into the corridor opposite his sister's door. She didn't bother trying to work out if he was mocking her or laughing at the way she made it sound like the monsters were the ones with the unfortunate similarity. Either way, she had Aisha leaning through the door to peer carefully out.

At first, the only other person in the corridor other than her brother was the Training Mistress. The little girl eyed the woman carefully, then scrambled over Marsh and ran to her brother. Tamlin crouched beside her.

"You know how to tell she's not a monster?"

Aisha shook her head.

"Check her eyes," Tamlin whispered, his voice carrying along the corridor. "Monsters have red eyes."

Aisha glanced up at his face, her expression full of suspicion and distrust. Marsh saw the training mistress make a gesture toward Petitfeu's door. Tamlin saw it too.

"And monsters don't do what they're told," he added, this whisper carrying just as far as the last.

Petitfeu appeared in the doorway and lifted her face so that Aisha could get a really good look at her eyes. They blazed as blue as before, and Marsh wondered if the woman was working an enchantment to brighten them. Aisha gave a little gasp, backing up a step to shelter under Tamlin's arm—and Marsh held her breath.

The little girl stared at the apprentice journeyman, her own blue eyes wide—and Petitfeu stared back. Neither of them moved for a long moment, then Aisha took a cautious step forward. Marsh held her breath and Aisha took another step, her small face determined and her fingers curled through the fur at Scruffknuckle's neck.

Petitfeu did not move. She waited as the little girl came forward one small step at a time. When Aisha reached out to touch her skin, the apprentice journeyman flinched but did nothing more. Aisha froze, then ran her fingers lightly over the woman's hands, hesitating when she reached her fingernails.

"Pretty!" the child exclaimed, and Marsh wondered if an apprentice was allowed to paint their nails.

That did not matter to Aisha or to Petitfeu as she knelt beside the little girl and let her examine her fingers. When she was finally done, Aisha looked into the apprentice journeyman's face and patted her cheek.

"Not monster," she said as Petitfeu pushed back to her feet, and Tamlin groaned.

"Aysh! That's rude."

His words made the child pause. She turned and looked up at Petitfeu.

"I sorry."

To Marsh's surprise, Aisha waited, looking up at the apprentice. For a long moment, Petitfeu looked back, then she sighed.

"It's okay. Grownups have run away too." She glanced at Marsh.

Aisha followed the glance, her small face lighting up with curiosity when she saw Marsh.

"What you do?"

"I didn't run away!"

The child regarded her carefully, then her eyes fell on Marsh's sword and her mouth fell open.

"Dat's *rude!*"

Marsh scowled at the kid.

"You locked yourself in a room," she snapped, grabbing her sword and getting to her feet.

Aisha had closed her mouth and was now glaring.

"And I already apologized."

For a moment, she thought Aisha was going to argue. Instead, the child pouted.

"Where's my cookie!"

19

SECRETS AND A NEW START

In the end, Apprentice Journeyman Petitfeu had to give up another of her secrets and reveal her stash of cookies, given that it was clear Aisha was going to throw the mother of all fits if Marchant didn't deliver on her promise.

"You owe me!" she muttered when Aisha took the first cookie and handed it to Scruff before holding out her other hand for a second.

"Bad Marsh," she said, and Petitfeu laughed, handing her another.

"You make sure she behaves," the apprentice said, casting a teasing look at Marsh. "She looks like trouble to me."

Aisha nodded solemnly but didn't say a word.

Not that she could have, Marsh thought, given the amount of cookie that had gone into her mouth.

Having seen the newcomers settled, Training Mistress Varangarde turned to go.

"See they make it to the dining hall for breakfast on

time, Petitfeu," she said, and the apprentice journeyman stiffened.

"Yes, mistress."

She watched the training mistress walk away and let out a soft sigh of relief, tensing up as the woman spoke again.

"And make sure those cookies are put away by inspection. You know the rules about food in your quarters."

"Yes, mistress."

Petitfeu sighed, and Aisha sidled over to her. The little girl said nothing, merely watching as the training mistress disappeared down the corridor and around the bend. Even after she'd disappeared, they waited, their heads turned to observe the direction she'd gone. Several breaths passed, and the mistress didn't reappear. Aisha reached up and tugged on Petitfeu's sleeve.

"I hide cookies," she offered, her voice firm. "I very good at hiding."

Petitfeu looked down at her.

"You are?"

Aisha vigorously nodded and Petitfeu put one hand on her hip, cocking her head as she returned the child's gaze.

"You know *I'm* supposed to be looking after *you*, right?"

The child nodded again, a little uncertainly.

"So you know I'm supposed to make sure there are no cookies to find, don't you?"

Aisha looked confused and then disappointed, and Petitfeu laughed.

"You can help me with that, okay?"

Aisha's face brightened, but the apprentice put a finger against her lips.

"It will be our secret."

Aisha clapped both hands over her mouth and nodded again.

"Right, now, your room is over here. I'll clean up the mess in the other one. What did you do?"

"I talked to the rocks."

"Oh, you did, did you?"

Petitfeu went over to the room that Aisha had hidden in. She looked in, sighed, and looked back.

"Will you ask the rocks if they'll go back into the wall?"

"'Kay."

Aisha went to stand beside the journeyman and looked into the room. For a moment her eyes went from blue to black, and Petitfeu stuffed her knuckles into her mouth. After a few more moments, she patted Aisha on the shoulder.

"Very good," she said as she knelt beside the child. "Do you want to meet someone else who can talk to rocks?"

Aisha clapped her hand and bounced on the spot.

"*Oui, oui, oui-oui-oui.*"

"I'll talk to Mistress Varangarde and ask her to help, okay?"

"'Kay!"

"But you have to sleep *all* night. I will wake you in the morning."

At the mention of sleeping all night, Aisha shot her brother an uncertain look. Tamlin hastened to reassure her.

He tapped on a door a little farther up the hall.

"I'll be in here."

"No close door."

It looked like Tamlin was going to argue, and he even shot Marsh a pleading look as though asking her to intervene, but she shook her head. Tamlin frowned and then sighed.

"*Fine.* I won't close the door, but you'll owe me a cookie."

Aisha hesitated, and Petitfeu took that moment to open the door opposite Tamlin's room.

"This is your room."

"*One* cookie," Aisha told him.

"Two," Tamlin argued, and Aisha folded her arms.

"One or I scream."

"You scream and I'll—"

"You'll both be in trouble for fighting," Petitfeu interrupted, "and you both have to keep your doors open."

"Cookie," Aisha muttered rebelliously.

"No cookie," Petitfeu said firmly, "or I'll tell the mistress."

Aisha thought about that, then turned on her heel and marched into her room.

"Fine. Story."

Tamlin groaned as he followed her into her room.

"Not you!"

Tamlin stopped, a surprised look on his face. Aisha stuck her head back around the doorframe and looked at Petitfeu.

"You!"

"Me?"

"You."

"But what story am I going to tell you?"

"Shadow's Heart."

Marsh's eyes widened in surprise and she looked at Tamlin. The boy shrugged.

"It's her favorite." He glanced at Petitfeu. "You know it?"

What he was really asking was if she minded telling it, but the woman smiled.

"It's one of my favorites too."

Aisha reached out and took the apprentice journeyman's hand, leading her into the room.

"Tuck me in," she demanded.

Marsh stared at the doorway, stunned by how quickly Aisha had formed the attachment.

"It used to worry Mum and Dad too," Tamlin told her. "It was my job to make sure she didn't get too friendly with strangers."

He rolled his eyes.

"It was a job and a half!"

As Petitfeu's voice took on the lilt and timbre of story-telling, Marsh believed him. She and Tamlin stood in the corridor a bit longer, and Marsh tilted her head.

"You going to bed, or do you need a bedtime story, too?"

Tamlin glared at her and pushed off the wall he'd been leaning on.

"Puhlease," he said, stepping into his room. "It's not like *I'm* five!"

Marsh waited for the inevitable protest from his sister, but she was silent. All she could hear was Petitfeu's rhythmic voice. She thought about going to her own room, then realized she didn't know where it was, aside from being beside Aisha's. With a sinking heart, she glanced around and realized it could be the room Aisha had "rearranged" in her attempt to escape the "monster."

With a sigh, Marsh leaned against the wall and waited for the apprentice journeyman to finish her story.

This didn't take as long as she'd dreaded; Petitfeu appeared shortly afterward.

"Well, she *looked* asleep," the woman offered. "Sorry I took so long. Let me show you where you're sleeping."

To Marsh's surprise, the room was beside Aisha's and farther from Petitfeu's, not nearer, leaving the damaged room for someone else. Petitfeu caught Marsh's curious glance.

"That one's already taken, and it's a good thing the owner's away, or Aysh would have had a bigger fright than when she saw me. Gina's not fond of children." She pushed open the door for Marsh and stood back. "The name's Brigitte, by the way."

"Brigitte?"

"Brigitte Petitfeu."

Marsh felt stupid.

"Sorry." She held out her hand. "It's Marsh, short for Marchant, but Marsh is fine."

Brigitte took her hand.

"Nice to meet you, Marsh. Get some sleep; it'll be an early start in the morning."

In the morning? Marsh stared at her. Just how long had she been asleep? Surely the day hadn't been so short? Her stomach rumbled, and Brigitte paused.

"When did you last eat?"

"When I woke up? Honestly, I don't know what time it was. They gave me a cup of chocolate and a couple of pastries and sent me off to talk to the Shadow Master, then the Training Mistress…"

"…and then here," Brigitte finished for her. "I get it. The kitchens are closed, but I can offer you a cookie."

They ended up eating most of Brigitte's secret cookie supply while they talked about what the monastery was like.

"They say you've got a few skills already," the apprentice said. She sounded almost envious.

Marsh hurried to put her at her ease.

"Yeah, but there's a lot I don't know. I only worked out how to talk to the shadows because the kids needed me to. Tamlin said anybody could do it if they just believed, and I really needed to find a way to get them to Ruins Hall. I thought there might be someone waiting."

Marsh let her voice fade, and Brigitte picked up on what she hadn't said.

"But there wasn't, and now you don't even know if they have anyone they could go to—or if they'd want to if there was."

"Something like that." Marsh yawned and stood up. "Thanks for the cookies. I'll have to figure out a way to pay you back."

"Just keep talking to me like I'm a normal human being," Brigitte said, then ducked her head. "That would do for a start."

Marsh heard the loneliness behind those words and figured it couldn't be easy to look so much like the shadow monsters but not be one of them. Most people wouldn't even register the girl's eyes. She wanted to ask Brigitte how she'd ended up at the monastery, but couldn't quite find the courage. She was only just getting to know the woman, and she didn't want to offend her.

She knew what it was like to be different, but being an orphan was one thing. Looking like the demons of the deep would be a whole other degree of misery.

I'll give it time, she thought. *Maybe when we get to know each other better...*

"I can do that," Marsh said and looked for something to add.

When she couldn't find anything, she stood and moved toward the door.

"Hate to eat and run, but someone said I had an early start in the morning, and I get the feeling it's quite late."

Brigitte stuck out her tongue.

"Get going, trainee. I expect you to be dressed and ready when I arrive."

Marsh resisted pulling a face in return and smiled instead.

"Thanks for the talk," she said, and added almost as an afterthought, "and the cookies."

Brigitte rolled her eyes.

"Of course, the cookies," she answered with a sigh. Marsh was relieved to see she was smiling.

Maybe things would be all right after all.

20

BREAKFAST BEGINNINGS

Marchant was up and dressed just before Brigitte made it to her room. She had strapped on her sword and was turning back her bedding when the apprentice journeyman knocked on the door.

"Ready."

Marsh smoothed the sheets and then hurried to open the door. Brigitte gave the room a cursory glance and nodded.

"Nicely done," she said. "Let's get the kids and head to breakfast. You must be pretty hungry."

Marchant was, but she didn't want to admit it.

"Getting there," she said. "How about you?"

"I should be stuffed from all those cookies," Brigitte said, "but I'm not. Too much excitement, I guess."

"I'll get Aisha if you like," Marsh said, not knowing how well the little girl would wake up...or how well Scruffknuckle would take to a stranger coming into the room. Brigitte shook her head.

"I'll be fine," she said. "You go and see if Tamlin is up. I'll get Aysh."

Marsh gave an internal shrug. She guessed this was one way to find out just how Aisha woke up, and how well Scruff dealt with strangers. She hurried to Tamlin's room and knocked on the open door.

"Time to get ready for breakfast," she said when she saw the boy was still asleep.

"Hey!" she called when he didn't move, and he stirred.

"What?"

"Breakfast. Unless you want to starve."

Just as she'd hoped, that got him moving, and she turned back to see how Brigitte was faring with Aisha. To her surprise, the blue-eyed apprentice emerged with Aisha and Scruff in tow as Tamlin appeared in his doorway. If the boy was as surprised as she was, he didn't show it.

"Did someone say something about breakfast?" he asked and Aisha bounced up and down, clapping her hands.

"Cookies!"

"Not cookies!" Marsh told her sternly as Tamlin and Brigitte said the same thing just as sternly.

Aisha's lower lip quivered.

"No cookies?" she asked, looking for all the Deeps like she was going to burst into tears.

"No cookies," they all replied, and Scruff gave an anxious whine.

"But there will be hot chocolate," Brigitte told her, "and pastries."

Aisha looked happier and Scruff's ears pricked up.

Aisha slipped a hand into Brigitte's and coiled her fingers through Scruff's fur, and the apprentice journeyman led them down to breakfast. Marsh found herself falling into step beside Tamlin as they went.

"So," she said, "the Shadow Master approves of your arrangement with Fabrice."

Tamlin looked relieved.

"He does?"

"Yup. He said I still have to look for any relatives and make sure they're okay with the way things are set up here, but that if they had no objections, you could stay."

"Phew."

His shoulders sagged with relief.

"I was worried he wouldn't let us stay." He glanced around as though the walls had ears. "We've got nowhere else to go. Dad said something about a brother in Dimanche, but he lived across the caverns from us and we never saw them. To be honest, I don't think they got on all that well. Maybe I wasn't the only reason we left."

He stopped, realizing he'd said more to Marsh than ever before. She watched as he closed his mouth, pressing his lips together tightly. Marsh tried to ignore the way he squeezed his eyes shut and she took a deep breath.

"I'll do my best to keep you here," she said. "Even if I find them, I'll try to make sure that what your parents wanted still happens. Okay? I'll do everything I can to make it happen."

After a few more steps in pained silence, Tamlin nodded. It took a few steps more before he tossed her a quick glance and nodded again.

"You need to find my parents too," he said. "If there's any chance they…" he glanced at Aisha and continued, "*escaped*, you need to find them."

Marsh gave him a quick nod. It was yet another reason she had to master her powers. If she was to be of any use in the battles to come or in finding out if the children's family had survived, she had to have a better idea of what she was doing. It was just that she didn't know how much time she had to do the search or what would happen if she delayed, which meant it was lucky the roads out of the cavern were closed or she'd have to leave so she could pick up the trail.

"I'll do my best."

"Thanks."

He didn't look at her, but looked for all the world like he was observing his surroundings. Marsh knew better. The boy wasn't with them at all; not in his mind, at least. He was worrying himself sick about his family and his future and the raiders. He was probably worried about Fabrice too, even though he'd done the best he could to see her right.

"Don't thank me yet," she said. "It's going to be a while before they let me leave to go looking. I need to learn some control before they let me loose on the caverns, and then I'm going to have to help get the trade routes up and running so I can even think about getting to Dimanche—and who knows how long *that's* going to take."

She gave him a sideways look.

"I mean, it could take years, and then we're going to have to reach an agreement. I don't know how old you'll be by then. You see what I'm trying to say?"

He held her gaze for another four steps, then nodded, his shoulders relaxing as he took a breath and let it slowly out. Marsh watched as he connected the dots. If it took long enough, he wasn't going to need his relatives, and then he was going to have to have to decide what he was going to do about the farm and about his sister's care, and he and Marsh were going to have to agree on what was the best path for all of them to take.

"Yeah. I hear you."

They'd followed Brigitte into a stairwell and descended another two flights before he spoke again.

"Thanks, Marsh."

She resisted the urge to ruffle his hair.

"No problem, kid."

He scowled.

"I'm not a kid. I... I'm nearly eleven."

"Are not," Aisha snapped. "Are *so* not!"

Before an argument could break out, they reached the dining hall and forgot their quarrel, focusing instead on the food at the other end.

Breakfast was simply a matter of choosing what they wanted and taking it back to their table. The dining hall was on the ground floor of the fortress, with arched and buttressed walls that were reassuringly solid on one side and stood open between a series of pillars on the other. Through the arches, Marsh saw a stone patio leading out into a garden lit by glows bright enough to allow plants from the surface to grow and thrive. Brigitte chose a seat near one of the arches.

"We'll sit here once we've got our food," she said, indicating the garden. "The former Master of Stone helped us build this. He and a stranger from the northeast, a wanderer. They said it was important for those of us below to know there were people on the surface who would be there if we needed them. We had only to call."

She sighed and stared at the flourishing plants.

"This was supposed to give us hope and encourage us to seek them out," she continued. "But all it does is remind us of what was lost when the surface world went mad and our founders fled to the safety of the dark."

Her words carried sadness and maybe a touch of longing, and they were silent as they gazed across the portico to the garden's brightness. It was a relief when Roeglin joined them.

"Why so sad?" he asked when he saw their faces. "And why are you just standing there? Breakfast is waiting, and we have a long way to go today. Brigitte, why don't you get the children started?"

Marsh saw Tamlin take a breath to protest about being called a child—and noted when he caught Roeglin's gaze and let the breath out without saying a word. The boy held out his hand to Aisha.

"Fine. Come on, Aysh—and don't let Scruff get loose this time."

This time? Marsh tried to remember when the pup had gotten loose before.

Brigitte turned with them, and the three of them headed for the food. Roeglin waited until there were several tables between them before he leaned toward Marsh and began to speak.

"Today we're going to take a trip across the cavern to

ask if the Master of Stone will assist in your and Aisha's training. We'll be away from the fortress for the night."

Marsh nodded, wondering why he couldn't have told her that while the others were still there. Roeglin's next words explained it.

"There's a good chance the rock mages will want to keep the girl with them, while most of Tamlin's training will be conducted here. I need your help to convince the children it's okay." He glanced over to where Aisha was slipping a meat pastry to Scruffknuckle's waiting mouth while Tamlin distracted the server. "Something tells me it's not going to be easy."

"We'll play it by ear," Marsh told him, then lifted her chin toward Brigitte. "Does she know?"

"She received her instructions last night while you were sleeping. I'm surprised you slept through it."

To be honest, so was Marsh.

"I guess I was more tired than I thought." She stared at where Brigitte was helping Tamlin juggle his breakfast and two cups of chocolate. "She's an apprentice journeyman, right?"

"Yeah."

"So, who is she apprenticed to? I haven't seen her master or mistress."

Roeglin frowned.

"They're out on the road, which is where she should be, too, but with all the shadow attacks, lately…" He shrugged. "It's not safe for her to leave the fortress."

"And yet she's going with us?"

"On this journey, she'll be fine. The rock mages know her well."

"But isn't journeying the only way she'll complete her apprenticeship?"

"It is." Brigitte sounded a little annoyed, which was understandable given that they'd been talking about her behind her back. "But being dead makes that hard as well."

She banged her plate down on the table.

"What I need is someone willing to take the risk with me, and that's not something my current journeyman is ever going to do. If either of you can come up with a solution to that one, let me know."

She sounded angry and sad, and Marsh couldn't blame her. If her own reaction was anything to go by, the girl faced open hostility every day because of her coloring. When she added that to not being able to complete her apprenticeship, Marsh thought Brigitte had every reason to be angry...and sad. It was the kind of thing that would upset Marsh too.

Before she could find anything to say to that, Brigitte sat and waved her and Roeglin toward the food.

"Better go and get some food," she told them and looked at Marsh. "I gather he's told you what we're doing today?"

Marsh nodded and managed to force a smile.

"Yes, and thank you. I'm sure Aisha will be excited to see other folks who can talk to rocks."

"Really?" Aisha squealed, looking at Brigitte. "More like me?"

"More like you. They can help you."

"Help me talk to rocks?"

"And more."

"Are they nice?"

Marsh and Roeglin stood and headed over to select

their breakfasts. Behind them, they could hear Tamlin joining in the conversation, working to reassure his sister that rock mages were very nice, but she'd better behave or they'd shut her in a cave forever. By the time Brigitte managed to calm Aisha down, Marsh and Roeglin had collected their food and returned.

"You really have to stop teasing your sister," Marsh told Tamlin. "Now eat your breakfasts before we decide to leave you both behind."

"But…" Aisha started, and Roeglin raised his hand and pointed to her half-full plate.

"Eat," he said, making it sound like she had no option.

Tamlin didn't wait to be told but focused on clearing his plate, glowering at the shadow mage as he did so.

"You have to teach me how you do that," Brigitte said, and Roeglin smiled.

"Just watch," he said. "You'll get the hang of it."

Brigitte glared at him, but she lifted her cup of kaffee and didn't say anything. They all hurried through breakfast, clearing their plates before leaving the hall. As she ate, Marsh found herself staring at the garden from the surface world, the gift of a stranger she'd never heard of or seen, and she wondered if she'd ever have the chance to see any of those plants beneath an open sky.

The thought made her shiver until her mind adjusted to the idea of not having stone above her head, and then she wondered what it would be like—and just how many artifacts had survived the more volatile weather above ground. It was something she might look into once the threat to the caverns was over. Following Roeglin, Brigitte, and the children from the hall, she wondered if any of them would want to come with her, then she shook the thought away.

First, she had to help remove the threat to the Four Settlements. After all, what use was exploring the surface world if she had no home to return to? She stowed the thought for another time and hurried down the corridor behind the rest.

21

THE HOSHKAT RETURNS

Roeglin surprised them by stopping at the fortress's storehouse.

"I've brought them," he called to the woman behind the counter, and Marsh found herself being assessed by a shrewd pair of steel-gray eyes that traveled from the top of her head down to her toes.

The woman turned the same gaze onto Aisha and Tamlin and turned to Brigitte.

"Do you know what disciplines they'll be?" she asked, and the apprentice journeyman shook her head.

The woman raised her eyebrows and turned to Roeglin.

"I thought you said she was ready?"

Roeglin shook his head.

"No, I said she'd be ready once this journey was done and that you'd need to prepare."

"Excuse me?" Marsh exclaimed.

Both Roeglin and the quartermaster ignored her. The woman made a soft harrumphing sound.

"Well, at least you were right about the rest of it."

Her eyes returned to Marchant.

"Except maybe that one. She's a little taller than you guessed."

Marsh stared at them.

She was? And he had? But before she could say anything, the quartermaster put her fingers to her lips and let loose with a shrill whistle. Running footsteps answered the summons, and three straw-haired youngsters appeared.

"Ma'am?"

Instead of answering, the woman handed them each a strip of paper. As soon as they'd received it, each one thanked her and disappeared at a run. The quartermaster flipped over a small sand-glass as they departed. Marsh was curious as to what she was doing, but the woman didn't seem to be the kind who appreciated questions, so she stayed silent.

If she had to guess, the youngsters were learning the business of stores, and the quartermaster was timing just how fast they could fill each order.

Very fast, as it turned out—and Marsh's guess on timing proved correct. When any of her assistants returned carrying a bulging pack, the quartermaster turned that apprentice's hourglass onto its side, stopping the flow of sand. She tipped each of their packs out onto the bench before her and checked off the pile of items against her list. Only once did she send one of her assistants back, and she tipped the hourglass up so the sand started flowing again as he bolted from the room.

When he returned with the required item in hand, she stopped the glass once more and returned to checking off the list. By that time both of his compatriots had returned, something he noted with a dejected sigh.

"Very good," the quartermaster said, stowing the items back in their respective packs and handing the gear to Roeglin.

As she did, Marsh's pack caught her eye.

"Pass that over," she ordered, and Marsh shot a glance at Brigitte.

"She'll store it while you're away," the apprentice journeyman assured her. "You'll be able to collect it when you get back."

Well, that made sense. Marsh handed over the pack, feeling a twinge of unease as she did so. If the quartermaster felt the extra weight she didn't show it, just upended the pack onto the bench and made a note of the contents. Marsh breathed a sigh of relief when the woman didn't open the carefully wrapped package containing the artifact.

"Delivery?" she said, raising an eyebrow.

"It's nothing urgent," Marsh told her. And it wasn't, since the road was closed. "I'll hang onto it until I can deliver it and then return the payment to my... To Kearick."

She had been about to call Kearick her master, but that would have been wrong. He wasn't her master any longer —and might never be her master again if she didn't get the roads open. Not only that, she was pretty sure she was going to have more important things to do than play delivery girl in the hopes of him organizing a seeker's apprenticeship that probably wasn't going to materialize.

After all, Kearick had been promising to speak to a seeker for more than a year.

If she was honest with herself, her ex-boss probably had no intention of ever doing so. Marchant was too useful as a courier and cheap, too, given he was taking her "training" out of her wages. She watched as the quartermaster carefully stowed her delivery back into the pack, surprised when the woman asked another question.

"May I ask who it's for?" she asked. "You know, in case you don't return?"

Well, that was grim.

Marsh shook her head.

"If I don't return, there won't be any point in making the delivery. Just send word to Kearick in Kerrenin's Ledge that it's here and waiting for pick-up. He'll send someone he trusts."

"You work for Kearick?"

From the look on the woman's face that wasn't a good career option, but Marsh didn't let it bother her. Beggars couldn't be choosers, after all. She shrugged.

"I *used* to work for Kearick. With the roads down, I'll be looking for another employer once my traineeship here is done."

The suspicion didn't go away.

"And when the roads are back up?"

"I'll make the delivery, return the payment, and hope I have another employer to return to by then."

At her reply, the woman relaxed, and the suspicion that had crept into her expression eased. She glanced at Roeglin.

"You might help her with that," she said, and Marsh got the impression it was more an order than a suggestion.

Roeglin's reply was equally solemn, a promise just as much to Marsh as it was to the quartermaster.

"I will."

Marsh shook away the feeling that those words held another significance, shouldering her pack and adjusting the straps before moving to help Tamlin with his. The boy had already seen to his sister.

As they finished speaking, two of her assistants disappeared through a door in the back, returning with packs for Roeglin and Brigitte. The quartermaster glanced at Scruffknuckle and then at Roeglin.

"The stablemaster's been working on a harness for the hund. He'll be carrying his own food."

Marsh wondered if that was such a good idea, but kept her mouth shut. She didn't think the woman had a sense of humor, even less when the joke questioned her competence. Still, she wasn't so sure it *was* a good idea for the pup to be carrying his own supplies. Keeping the thought off her face was easy, especially when the quartermaster's gray gaze swung toward her.

It rested on her for a short moment, and Marsh realized the woman was checking her straps. When she said nothing, Marsh breathed a sigh of relief.

"Thank you, Quartermaster," Roeglin said, and moved toward the door.

Brigitte took Aisha's hand, Tamlin fell in beside his sister, and Marsh followed them. The quartermaster's voice stopped her as she reached the exit.

"Trainee Leclerc," she said, "the monastery has its own seekers if that is where your path takes you."

Marsh froze, shooting a stunned look at the woman's face and receiving a secretive smile in return. She didn't elaborate though, shooing Marsh out with a gesture.

"Don't fall behind," she advised. "Roeglin is a hard taskmaster."

He was? Marsh jerked her head around to see where Roeglin had gone and realized her companions hadn't waited. Not sparing another glance for the woman behind the stores counter, she rushed out the door, hurrying in the direction she'd seen her friends take. It wasn't long before she caught up with them, and she was very careful not to let them out of her sight again.

It was quick work to fit Scruffknuckle's harness, especially after Aisha had caught the pup's gaze, her eyes flaring green as she talked him into standing still.

"That's a neat trick," the stablemaster told her. "If you ever want to come help me with the mules…"

Marsh watched Aisha's face light up as the little girl turned to her brother.

"I can help!"

"Not right now, you can't. You have rock mages to meet."

"Oh." Aisha's face fell, and the stablemaster sighed.

"Some other time, then," he suggested, and the little girl's expression brightened.

"Okay!"

As they headed toward the gates, Marsh glanced back. The stablemaster was still smiling as he turned toward his office. It made her smile, too. Aisha's happiness was infectious, much as her sadness would be if anything harmed her brother or the pup. Marsh swore not to let that happen. To *never* let that happen, and to bring the girl's parents and other siblings back.

Sometimes the happiness of a child is even more important than delivering a package, especially when it gave those around her a reason to make the world a better place. Marsh took that thought and held it close. She was going to make a difference—not just to Aisha, but to the caverns. The raiders and their shadow monsters had to be stopped, no matter what it took.

When they arrived at the gate, Henri, Lennie, Gustav, and Jakob were waiting. Their armor had been patched or replaced, and their weapons and harnesses gleamed with care.

"Shadow Master says we're to go with you," Gustav told Roeglin, and Marsh stared.

What about his duty to the cavern founder? It was a question that went unanswered as the shadow mage on the gate nodded his confirmation and Gustav and his guards formed up around them.

"We're to keep you safe on your journey to see the Stone Master, and we're to bring you safely back. Shadow Master says the cavern might not be safe to travel with both raiders and a hoshkat on the loose."

Well, she couldn't argue with him there, even if he *had* missed another danger. Raiders, hoshkats, and shadow monsters were *all* on the loose, and Marsh was glad they had more weapons protecting them than just her blade. It made stepping into the dark space between the gates much easier.

"Is it much of a walk?" she asked, and Roeglin laughed.

"Should take us most of a day," he answered. Marsh heard Tamlin groan, but the shadow mage had no sympathy. "Strong young man like you shouldn't have *any* trouble. Let's get moving."

They set out as soon as the last gate opened, stepping into the caverns' perpetual dark. Marsh found comfort in the soft luminescence of different fungi, shrooms, and mosses. She noted patches of glow worms on a distant wall and knew there was water nearby. She wondered how Fabrice and her children were settling in.

She strode along, taking one step after another and wishing the quartermaster hadn't been quite so generous with her stores. The weight soon became part of her, though. She followed the pace Roeglin set as he turned off the road leading to the fortress and took a smaller, less well-defined trail around the monastery's side. As she walked, she let her eyes adjust to the cavern's darkness, seeing the ripple and shimmer of heat around the fungal growth.

She'd lost track of the time they'd traveled before Roeglin called a halt. He instructed them to eat and drink and to relieve themselves in the sturdy stone structure set beside the trail for exactly that purpose.

"We're halfway," he told them, and the children groaned.

Marsh didn't blame them. She felt like groaning too, but someone had to be the adult. Still, she couldn't suppress a sigh when the shadow mage got to his feet, lifted his pack, and headed back out onto the trail. The journey continued, the children keeping pace, Aisha stubbornly refusing to go slower than her brother. Tamlin, for his part, was also being stubborn and pushing to keep the pace Roeglin set. Between the two of them, they were keeping up, and the group was making swifter progress than Marsh had thought it would.

By the time they stopped for a mid-afternoon snack at yet another of the solid stone facilities, Marsh had noticed that the fungi and other plant life were growing thicker, their colors more vibrant than before. She had also started noticing more animal and insect life around them, as well as a flash of heat from something larger.

She tried not to think about that larger thing. Tried really hard not to imagine what a hoshkat would be doing stalking in perfect silence beside the trail or why it would be accompanied by two smaller flashes of heat that were never very far from its side. She tried equally hard not to wonder why Scruffknuckle was pressing closer and closer to Aisha's side, looking very much like he was torn between trying to protect the little girl or asking her to protect him.

Marsh scanned the fungi and the quiet shadows between stalactites, stalagmites, and boulders. She studied each shadow before the children drew alongside it, her hand creeping to the hilt of her sword. Around her, the guards seemed to grow more wary, their heads in constant motion as they surveyed the surrounding cavern.

Roeglin led the way, seemingly oblivious to the tension flowing through the group, but Brigitte kept a tight hold on Aisha's hand, and the little girl's other hand never left the ruff of fur at Scruffknuckle's neck. They traveled that way for what seemed like hours until shouts and the clash of stone on metal caught their ears.

Now more than tension crackled through the air. Marsh felt power tugging at the shadow strands around her, reminding her that she wasn't limited only to her eyes. She walked swiftly to where Roeglin stood, his hand upraised to command them to halt. Gustav joined them.

"Let me look along the shadows," Marsh said as a man screamed.

"Will it take long?" Gustav demanded.

"Coupla breaths," she told him, hoping it was true; also hoping that he wouldn't want to go charging in blind.

She was true to her word, relieved to be able to find the relevant strands of shadow quickly and easily. It didn't take her long to draw the images back, although it surprised her when Roeglin plucked them directly from her mind and shared the situation with Brigitte, Gustav, and the rest of the guards.

"You know what to do," he said, and Gustav led the guards forward, sharing his plan of attack for Roeglin to relay.

Marsh went with them, glad that Gustav didn't care what Roeglin thought of him using her as another sword. The shadow mage made no argument but stayed back with the children and Brigitte—or he would have, except that Brigitte put Aisha's hand into his palm and ran after Marsh and the rest.

"You keep forgetting what I can do," the apprentice journeyman snarled as she raced forward, pulling swords from the air around her as she ran.

Roeglin sent them a mental warning, so none of the

fighters turned to confront the woman as she joined them. Instead, they took in the scene before them, noting that the raiders had fallen on a small group of men and women in brown robes. The group had clearly stopped to eat when they'd been attacked.

Food lay scattered around their feet, and one man was fighting by swinging his water canteen in one hand as he tried to edge toward a long staff propped against the trunk of a calla shroom. When his opponent's blade smashed against the canteen with a crack, Marsh realized that the canteen wasn't made of wood, leather, or steel, but some kind of stone.

It met the blade, causing it to ring, and then the man moved his wrist and the canteen deflected the blow, forcing the raider to swing again. All around them, the fighting was similarly mismatched. There seemed to be one raider for each robed man and woman, and then there were the mages. Three in all, they were starting to call the shadows to entangle the group.

"You should have agreed to join us peacefully," a shadow mage called. "Things would have been a lot easier."

"For you, maybe," replied the man with the canteen, "but not for us."

He ducked under another sword swipe and drove his fist into the raider's gut, only to gasp as his hand hit metal. Marsh winced. That *had* to hurt. At least he was in grabbing range of the stick...until another raider snatched the staff away and threw it into the surrounding fungal forest. The man backed up, trying to keep out of reach of both his opponents—which was when Marsh decided to even things up.

She charged, her shout drawing the attention of the raider who'd tossed the staff. Beside her, she could hear Brigitte laughing, and she caught a glimpse of twin blades gleaming ebon in the cavern's darkness as the journeyman leapt forward. They both struck at the same time, Marsh trying to take the head off the raider who'd thrown the staff and Brigitte driving one shadowy blade through the other raider's gut even as she parried his sword with the other.

After that, Marsh didn't have time for watching. She usually fought with a leather buckler strapped to her left forearm, but she'd left it on the fallen mule when she'd grabbed the children. It was just something else she wasn't going to get back. She missed the shield, barely remembering she needed to parry with the blade and not block with the non-existent buckler. It would have been nice to be able to conjure one the same way Brigitte had conjured her matching blades.

She marked it down as something to try to learn and changed her fighting style to suit the single weapon she had. A block, a feint, a parry, and a swift thrust, and the raider was backing off, his sword wavering in front of him in useless defense as Gustav sliced through his back from behind.

"Not bad work, girl," the soldier said. "You're out of practice and need some time in the yards, but you'll do."

Well, that was nice of him to say. Marsh turned, looking for another raider to fight. What she saw instead was a shadow mage making the final sweeping gesture that tore a rent in the fabric of shadow clustered between a calla shroom and a stalagmite. Screams rang from within, and

Marsh almost froze. Only Gustav's panicked shout broke through the horror conjured by the sound.

"Don't let them through!"

Hearing his voice, Marsh leapt forward to meet the first shadow to emerge.

Get the mage, echoed in her mind as Gustav repeated Roeglin's order, but Marsh held her ground. She didn't know how many shadow monsters were behind the rift, but she couldn't break away from it without risking that one of them getting through—and if one got through, then more might follow, and there weren't enough of them to handle that kind of flood.

Behind her she sensed movement, but she couldn't shift her focus. She had to rely on the others to have her back. And speaking of back, Marsh took a step away from the rift, trying to avoid the clawed arm that slashed out at her. The arm was impossibly long, and the claws tore through her tunic like butter. Heat scored lines across her chest and stomach, but Marsh didn't stop to check the damage.

She spun her blade, parrying another attack, and then reversed the strike, taking off the arm. The shadow beast howled beyond the portal and began to push through. As it did so, it shoved the beast facing off against Gustav, which lost its balance, momentarily dropping its guard. It was all the invitation the guard needed.

He swept his blade in a clean arc, taking the monster's head from its shoulders as its mouth stretched impossibly wide in another scream. There was no time to celebrate, however. More monsters appeared, three forcing their way through while Gustav was off balance, three pushing them back so another two could begin clawing their way through behind them.

Marsh kept fighting; losing ground, but opening up enough space beside her for Lennie to fill.

"You mages have all the fun!" The blonde guard laughed, carving through one monster's chest and wrenching her blade free. "How about you leave some for me?"

Another claw got through Marsh's defenses, scoring a series of lines down her ribs as she kicked the monster back. A hand grabbed her by the shoulder and yanked her out of the melee, spinning her out of the way so its owner could take her place. As she turned, trying to regain her balance, Marsh caught sight of the shadow mages who had led the attack sliding in behind the monsters.

"Stop them!" she cried, but it was too late.

The shadow mages slipped behind the first row of shadow monsters and slithered, wraithlike, between them. To Marsh's surprise, the creatures' attacks went through them as if they were smoke, their bodies parting around claws, and coming together on the other side as though the attack had never happened.

Marsh stared, slowly relaxing as Lennie dispatched the monster before her, stepping smoothly into the attack of the creature behind it. She watched as another monster came out of the rift, then another, then saw the rift snap shut behind them.

As it closed, the shadow monsters roared, their attacks becoming more frenzied and vicious, but the guards held them back and defeated them. Marsh stood behind them, ready to step in and protect anyone overcome by the attacks. As the last monster fell, she swayed, lowering her sword and dropping to her knees.

"I'm okay," she said, waving off the first guard who came to help.

She had just registered the blood seeping through the rent in her armor when the hoshkat leapt from the nearest clump of calla shroom to land right in front of her.

Great, she thought. Now she's gonna eat me.

THE HOSHKAT'S REQUEST

To Marchant's surprise, the hoshkat didn't eat her. It snapped its head right, then left, hissing fiercely at the guards as it stepped over and lowered its head so it could look into Marsh's eyes. She managed to hold up a hand to stop Gustav's rush toward her before she tripped on the edge of the hoshkat's gaze and fell.

This time she landed in the midst of sorrow, outrage, and need, and she rested her forehead against the kat's and brought the palm of her upraised hand to its cheek.

"Tell me," she said as a small part of her stared in shock at what she was doing.

She should have been afraid. She should have been asking the kat not to eat her; should have been feeling the tear of her claws and teeth as she took her apart. Instead, she was asking her to tell her what was wrong, tears running down her face as the mother kat's grief washed over her, her fury rising to meet and mingle with her outrage.

"Tell me," she repeated, and the answer came in a flurry of images.

The kat had been hunting and returned to find the raiders at her lair. Her kits were fighting, but it was doing them no good. Two had already been trapped by balls of shadow, held tight inside the darkness, unable to escape. They'd been carried through a portal as she'd arrived and were beyond her reach before she'd discovered they were in danger.

The other two she had been swift to rescue, leaping into the fray before the raiders had known she'd returned and crushing the skull of the mage who'd wielded shadow before he could encapsulate another. One kit had leapt to her back and she'd seized the other in her teeth, lifting it out of harm's way and vanishing into the cavern dark before the other raiders had been able to bring their crossbows to bear.

She'd known of only one human she had any chance of asking for help. Need rushed over Marsh.

Could she help? *Would* she help? The kits were young and vulnerable. They needed to be rescued!

"Yes," Marsh said, "but..."

The kat understood; first Marsh had to heal.

She did?

Marsh slipped out of her mind and looked down. She'd pressed her free hand over the gash in her tunic while she'd been speaking to the kat, and blood now trickled over her fingers.

Oh. She looked over at the humans standing a wary distance from the feline, their eyes full of concern. Marsh figured that if she didn't do something soon, someone was going to try something stupid. She glanced at the kat once more.

"Don't hurt them," she said. "They will help us."

The big beast turned her head and moved forward, sliding around Marsh so she didn't fall. When the kat had settled, she raised her head and gave a curious whistling mew. Marsh registered surprise and shock on the face of one of the mages they'd rescued and made a note to talk to him later since he clearly knew more about kats than she did.

He stared, rapt, as the two half-grown kits leapt out of the middle of a clump of brown noses and blue buttons, bounding swiftly to their mother to settle between her forepaws. Marsh had time to register a furious bark and groaned as Scruffknuckle forced his way between the humans' legs and raced over to confront the big kat, a furious Aisha in his wake.

"Scruff! You get back here!"

The little brat ducked past Gustav's startled grab and sidestepped Lennie's lunge before coming to a stop face to face with the seated kat. Marsh twisted just enough to watch as the child put her hands on her hips and looked the kat in the eye.

"You are a bad, bad kitty!" Aisha scolded, and the kat yawned, showing dagger-length fangs and a purple-pink tongue as long as her arm.

Marsh would have laughed if she hadn't been hurting so badly. The look on the child's face said that Aisha might for the first time be having second thoughts about the creature she was confronting. The kat caught the little girl's eyes and they stared at each other.

To Marsh it was obvious they were talking, but the watching adults didn't know that. Marsh was grateful when the mage who'd recognized the kat's call to her kittens put his hand on Roeglin and Gustav's arms to stop them from rushing forward.

A short moment later, Aisha nodded.

"'Kay," she said, then, "Promise?"

The kat gave a rumbling growl and curled her paw around her kits, resting her chin on the nearest one's head.

"'Kay," Aisha said and looked at the gathered adults. "Dis is Mordanlenoowar. Mordan. She is a friend and needs our help. She says help Marsh. She won't hurt us."

When no one moved, Aisha stamped her foot.

"Help! Marsh!" she shrieked, her voice bouncing off the cavern ceiling, then she hurried around to Marsh, grabbing her hand and pulling it off her side.

When she had a firm hold of it, she lifted it so they could see the blood covering Marsh's fingers and palm.

"Help!"

She dropped Marsh's hand and turned to wrap her arms around the kat's neck. The stunned adults gaped as the child buried her face in the big kat's fur, and one of the kits edged close enough to lean on her. Scruff bounced closer, his barking becoming uncertain as he gazed at the kat. Finally, he sat just out of paw's reach and whined.

Aisha looked at him and patted her leg.

"Come, Scruffy. Come." The puppy trotted cautiously forward so she could tangle her hand in his fur.

As he did so, Roeglin hurried over to Marsh, kneeling in front of her. She hissed in pain as he brushed aside her tunic so he could see the wound better.

"*A la putain!*"

"You say the sweetest things," Marsh joked, but her voice was ragged and she felt like being sick. "You mind if I lie down for a bit?"

Gustav and Brigitte crossed to them, and one of the mages followed them. When the kat didn't move, they walked with more confidence, their attention shifting from the beast to Marsh.

"*Merde*," Brigitte exclaimed. "Of all the stupid, bull-headed, idiotic things to do, you go and get yourself shadow-clawed."

"Is that bad?"

The rock mage settled beside her.

"It could be," he said, pulling a knife from his belt and reaching for her tunic. "Let me see that."

Roeglin had lashed out as soon as he'd seen the knife. Now he let go of the mage's hand.

"I'm sorry."

"I'm not offended," the mage told him, "but if you could fetch me some lava-weed, golden gleams, and yellow glow-moss, I'd be grateful."

"We'll help," said one of the mages, and they split up to look for the plants and fungi he'd named.

Lennie sighed.

"I'll get a fire going, shall I?"

"If you would."

The mage seemed to completely miss the sarcasm in the guard's voice.

Gustav spread a blanket on the ground, and they lifted Marsh onto it. The mage peeled her tunic back and whistled.

"What?" Marsh asked, her voice creaky with pain.

"You're lucky you were wearing armor."

"Did I break it?"

"It did its job."

"Quartermaster is going to kill me."

"You make sure to thank her when you see her next. She gave you good gear."

"Damn."

He was examining the gashes as he talked and glanced up as Roeglin returned with an armful of moss and small golden mushrooms.

"Two things," he said, and indicated Marsh. "She needs to be asleep, and I need you to fetch the Herb Master. You know the way?"

Roeglin nodded, setting the shrooms and moss down beside him.

"Hurry. I'll need his advice before I'm done."

Roeglin was about to rush away when the mage grabbed his leg.

"Put her out first."

Put her out? Marsh wondered. Exactly how was he going to do that?

The answer came as Roeglin settled himself beside her and looked into her eyes.

"Hey," he said, managing to send her a smile.

"Hey," she replied as he leaned forward, catching her eyes.

"You need to sleep," he told her.

For a moment Marsh thought about arguing, then his eyes flashed white.

"Sleep," he repeated. "I'll tell you when to wake."

He'd better, Marsh thought. She didn't want to be trapped in some kind of magical sleep forever. If he got himself killed while he was on whatever errand... The need to sleep vanished in a wave of anxiety for Roeglin's safety, and he rolled his eyes.

"I'll take Gustav and Lennie," he said, speaking quickly, and his eyes flared white again. "*Now* will you sleep?"

She seemed to remember someone else asking her that not too long ago. What was it with people thinking she needed to rest? Marsh shrugged.

"Sure," she said.

She'd been going to add that he'd better come back when she fell into a sleep so deep that she did not dream. When she woke again, she was stretched out beneath two blankets between two roaring fires. Roeglin knelt beside her.

"*There* you are!" He looked relieved. "I thought you were ignoring me."

"Wouldn't dare."

Marsh heard the gravel in her voice and tried to clear her throat. She pushed slowly onto her elbow and wished she hadn't moved. Pain lanced across her stomach and side. Roeglin didn't try to stop her, but slipped his arm around her shoulders and lifted a canteen to her mouth.

The liquid inside was slightly warm against her lips, and she took a cautious sip. It was sweet and bitter at the same time, and Marsh twisted her mouth away from it.

"What in Shadow's Deep *is* that?"

"Something to help you heal."

She didn't know that voice. Marsh turned her head as the mage who'd come to her aid crouched in front of her.

"You should have let the fighters do their job."

"I was closer."

"You're an idiot."

Marsh recognized the voice and tilted her head to look up at Lennie, remembering how the woman had pulled her away from her shadowy opponent before she took another hit.

"Thanks, Lennie." Whether she was being grateful for being pulled clear or sassing the platinum-haired fighter for her comment wasn't clear.

"Don't thank me yet," Lennie said, regarding her with worried eyes. "I might have been too slow."

Aisha gave a squeak of dismay at this, and Marsh heard Roeglin murmur assurances to the little girl. The hoshkat growled. Lennie rolled her eyes.

"I'm only telling you how it is." She nodded toward the flask. "I'd drink all of that if I were you, and then I'd go back to sleep. You've got a rough ride ahead."

"Anyone ever tell you that you suck at patient care?" Marsh quipped, trying for light-hearted but sounding slightly angry instead.

"Most of my patients prefer not to be fed shit about their chances," Lennie snapped and turned away.

Marsh didn't have anything to say at that. She watched the warrior until she moved out of sight, not resisting when Roeglin lifted the flask to her lips once more. This time she drank it all and then turned her gaze to the rock mage.

"You a healer too?"

He shook his head.

"Not the kind that heals by magic anyway," he told her.

"I just use the medicine we find in the world around us. You are fortunate we cultivate as much of it as we can inside our cavern's borders."

Caverns had borders?

Fatigue made Marsh's head spin, and she looked at Roeglin.

"I'd better lie down again," she said, and he helped her lower herself back to the ground.

"Magic can heal?"

To Marsh's surprise, the question came in Lennie's voice, but she was asleep before she heard the reply.

Of course, magic can heal, she thought. It was just a pity none of them knew how to ask it. When she woke again, it was to the sound of a lively argument being carried out not two feet from her head.

"Let me try it on myself first."

Now, why didn't it surprise her that Lennie was in the middle of a verbal spat?

"We can't afford for you to lose the use of a hand."

"And I'm not letting anyone else risk themselves if I can't pull it off. It's my idea, and my risk to take."

"Look, Lennie—"

Whatever else Gustav might have been going to say was lost to an agonized yelp.

"What in all the Deep!"

Lennie was clearly not impressed.

"Now neither of you need to do it." Roeglin sounded like he was in a lot of pain. "And I don't need my hand to be useful."

Lennie let loose with a description of his heritage that involved a lot of fornication and a physically impossible mismatch. It made Roeglin laugh. The sound was followed by the sound of him hitting the floor, and Marsh struggled to open her eyes. She was in time to watch Lennie drop to her knees beside the mage, uttering another heartfelt expletive as she did so.

"Give me your hand."

Turning her head allowed Marsh to watch as Lennie took Roeglin's hand and carefully unfolded the fingers. Blood flowed over his palm, and Marsh wanted to protest as both Tamlin and Aisha crowded closer. One of the rock mage's knelt beside them, his face creased with concern. Try as she might, Marsh didn't recognize him.

She saw Lennie lift her face to Tamlin.

"You say we all have magic, right?"

The boy nodded, his face pale beneath its crown of dark hair. Lennie pressed her lips together and turned back to Roeglin's hand.

"Helluva way to find out if I can actually do anything with it."

"You have to want to," the boy told her and Aisha nodded vigorously beside him, her blue eyes never leaving the gash in Roeglin's hand.

By the Deep! What had the man done to himself? Sliced his palm open so Lennie could prove a point? Marsh stared.

"You have to *want* it," Tamlin repeated, and Lennie cast him a determined look.

"Oh, I want it, boy. I've had too many good people die on me and not been able to do a damn thing about it. I just don't know how to start."

"Think of what my hand should look like," Roeglin

suggested, his voice harsh with pain. "It's how I call the shadow."

"Me too," Brigitte chimed in. "I need blades, I call blades. I want a spear, I think of a spear and just how much I need it."

Lennie looked from one to the other of them.

"And neither of you ever wondered how to fix what you were busy breaking?"

"It never occurred to us that we could," Brigitte admitted.

"I wish one of you would fix this," Roeglin said. "I can't focus enough to even begin."

That got Lennie's attention. She took a deep breath and spread his hand wide.

"These should be attached," she murmured, using her other hand to touch the wound.

Roeglin whimpered and then went limp.

"That should make it easier," the closest rock mage muttered, and Lennie glared at him.

"I'll try that again."

As she moved her finger, Aisha crept closer. The child was chewing on her lower lip and watching Lennie's every move. From where she was lying, Marsh watched too. At first, nothing happened and Lennie gave a moan of frustration, but instead of giving up or turning on Tamlin, she kept her eyes on Roeglin's hand.

"No one's going to get hurt on my behalf," she muttered. "No one. The tendons should be whole. Please, Mother of the Dark, have mercy."

Light gathered around Lennie's fingertips and the

guard's eyes widened, flaring briefly green. Aisha bounced on her toes.

"Again!" the little girl cried.

"Again?" Lennie's voice had a slightly faded quality.

"Again," Aisha repeated, firmly.

Lennie sighed.

"I don't know if I can."

"You have to want to," Tamlin said, and the rock mage added, "Unless you want to give up now and leave the man a cripple."

"No!"

Lennie traced her fingers over Roeglin's palm.

"Mother of the Dark, Shadow's Heart and Shadow's Deep, let me do this. No one else has to die beside me. No one."

This time the green light was much brighter, leaping from her fingers to flow over Roeglin's palm and making her eyes burn with emerald fire.

"I *can* do this," she murmured, her voice fierce with determination. "Shadow Mother! The world cannot *all* be a shroud."

She succeeded if Aisha's excited jiggle was anything to go by, and the rock mage breathed a sigh of relief before he looked at Tamlin.

"You know, boy, not everyone can call the magic within…"

Lennie stared at him in horror.

"Well, it's a Shadow's-cursed good thing that no one told me *that* when I was busy believing I could."

Tamlin frowned, giving the mage a troubled look.

"But the magic is inside everyone," he insisted. "I *know* it is."

Roeglin came to with a gasp before the mage could say anything else. He raised his hand in front of his face and studied it carefully.

"Oh, thank the shadows that's over," he said and got unsteadily to his feet. "Remind me *never* to try that again."

He spun on the spot, staring at his palm.

"Never," he repeated and came to a stop when he saw Marsh's eyes were open. "Hey, look who's awake?"

Marsh managed a trembly smile, but it faded quickly when she tried to move. She'd been so busy watching the drama play out between Lennie and Roeglin that she hadn't registered the fire burning over the skin around her wound.

Roeglin came over to crouch beside her.

"How are you doing?"

"*You* tell *me*, because I don't feel so good."

"Lennie." Roeglin looked over his shoulder, but Marsh could already see that the warrior wasn't going to be any good.

Lennie looked drained, her face pale and the heat signature from her skin noticeably cooler. Marsh shook her head.

"She needs to rest." She turned to the children for support. "Isn't that right, kids?"

"Marsh!" Aisha was clearly glad to see her awake.

Tamlin cast a glance at Lennie.

"Yeah." He seemed strangely despondent, even though he'd been the one to encourage the woman to try. "She really does."

"I'll be fine," Lennie protested and tried to get to her feet.

The rock mage was close enough to catch her when she collapsed. Lennie looked grieved.

"What in the Deep is wrong with me?" she asked, then looked at Marsh. "I can do it. I have to…"

The mage laid a hand on her shoulder.

"You have to rest," he said, "or you won't be able to do anything."

"Think of your child," Gustav urged when Lennie tried to get up. "Jorj does not want either of you to join him so soon."

That stopped her, and Marsh guessed that Jorj was the husband Lennie had lost in the caravan from which Marsh had escaped.

"But…" Lennie began. Her eyes darted to Marsh, and then back to Gustav and the rock mage.

The latter laid a hand on her shoulder.

"There will be a later," he said, and Lennie seemed about to protest that until he added, "I will see to it."

Again Lennie slid Marsh a worried look, but this time she nodded and let Gustav help her to her feet. Tamlin watched the guard settle the woman by the fire, then came and sat beside Marsh. It was the most subdued she had ever seen him.

"What's up?" Marsh asked him, because clearly, something was. Tamlin just shook his head and cast Roeglin a miserable look.

Marsh shivered, feeling cold despite the warmth coming off her skin. It didn't take her long to figure out what was wrong.

"So," she asked, "how bad am I?"

Roeglin gave her a careful look.

"You're going downhill."

"Nice... How long?"

"Since this morning."

Marsh shook her head.

"How long have we got to change it?"

His face closed over as if a shutter had been pulled.

"Uh huh. And Lennie's only just learned she might make a difference, and now she's learned she can't."

Roeglin broke eye contact and looked out into the cavern, his throat working as if he were trying to swallow something...or maybe not give in to the urge to cry. She slowly reached out from under the blanket, her arm as heavy as lead, and laid her hand on his knee.

"Not your fault."

Movement caught her eye—Aisha coming over to stand beside Roeglin, her small face pinched with worry. Before she could say anything, the rock mage arrived with another flask.

"I need to change the dressings," he said, his face a professional mask although his eyes were sad.

"Tamlin says we all have the magic," Marsh told him, and his expression froze. "You could try."

The man's face softened into regret, and he shook his head.

"I...can't," he said, and from the look on his face, there was nothing she could say to convince him otherwise.

He tried to explain why.

"It's not my gift. No man can call every magical effect to

hand." He glanced at Lennie. "No matter how badly they want it. The herbs are my limit. I *am* sorry."

Well, at least he was sorry. Marsh managed to drink some of the tonic he'd brought, but she faded out of consciousness as he lifted the dressing. Aisha gasped in shock.

The rock mage was gone, and the camp was quiet when Marsh drifted back into consciousness to the feel of small hands fidgeting at the bandages.

"Hey," she said, only to be abruptly shushed.

"Sleep," Aisha told her. "I fix."

She'd what?

"You—"

"Sshh!"

Marsh shushed, her eyelids almost too heavy to lift as she struggled to see what Aisha was doing. It didn't take the little girl long to fidget the bandages free—or Marsh to work out what she was going to try. Everyone had magic, right? They only had to believe; wasn't that what Tamlin had said? And who believed better than a child?

Where in all the Deep had the kid learned that stuff anyway? She'd like to take whoever had taught him that and give them a good shaking—and then she'd like to give Tams a good shaking for saying it somewhere his little sister could hear it.

"Aysh…"

"Sshh!" Aisha sounded even fiercer than before. "You'll wake them."

The little brat had made short work of the bandages and was now looking down at the wound, her nose wrinkled in disgust.

"I have to bring the light."

"Bring the light?"

"Like Lennie."

Sure, kid, Marsh thought. *You do that.*

Her eyes were getting too heavy to hold open, so she closed them for just a minute. For...

She woke to voices—quiet voices, Aisha talking to someone else. By the Deep, she hoped it was a grownup.

"You sleep," Lennie was saying. "It's my turn."

"Not finished." Aisha sounded torn between tiredness and determination.

"No, but—"

"You need a cookie."

Marsh was glad to hear Brigitte's voice, even if the mage's traditional solution made her want to laugh. A cookie... Like that would work.

"Cookie?"

Marsh felt the small warm patches that were Aisha's hands lift off her stomach.

Okaaay. Apparently, it would. She flinched as two much larger hands replaced Aisha's light touch.

"Sshh!" Lennie's voice was like a louder echo of Aisha's. "Kid made a start, but you need a bit more to pull clear."

Pull clear of what? Marsh felt fatigue dragging her down. Whatever the Shadows required, right? Even if she didn't want to join them just yet. Whatever they...

She gasped as fingers gently probed the edges of the wound.

"Shadow's Heart and Shadow's Queen," Lennie murmured, and Marsh wondered how the old stories could mean so much to the hardened warrior. After all, neither Shadow's Heart nor its Queen had protected her Jorj.

Warmth spread across her stomach and down her side, and some of the pain eased. Green light carried her back into the depths of sleep, and Marsh rested.

23

THE VAGARIES OF MAGIC

The next time Marsh woke, it was to the warmth of bodies curled around her. She lay still for a moment, registering the smell of animal musk and the weight of someone's arm across her chest and shoulder. Her sleeping companions effectively pinned her beneath the blankets, and she very much needed to get out of bed.

Marsh wriggled experimentally, and the arm over her drew her closer.

"Hey!"

She'd meant it to be a shout, but it came out as a hoarse whisper. A second arm snaked around her, pulling her into the curves of a woman's body. Marsh tried to disentangle herself, but the arms only pulled her closer.

"Dammit! Let me up!"

Just like that, the arms let her go.

"Sorry." Lennie sounded as shocked as Marsh felt.

"I... It's okay, I just need to..."

"Latrine is to the left of the trail. Make sure you pull the curtain closed. No one wants to watch."

Well, that was good to know. Marsh got to her feet and let her eyes adjust to the light levels. It wasn't as dark as she thought. Someone had ringed the campsite with glows, so the latrine was easy to spot. It consisted of a low stone wall with blanket partitions. Marsh moved stiffly toward it, wondering how long she'd slept as she scanned the cavern around her.

The tall calla shrooms shrouded the ground beneath them in shadow but did not hide the soft luminescence of the fungi growing around their feet. Fire beetles darted between the growths, and Marsh caught the sharp scent of ditch mint mingled with other less familiar smells. She did not stop to savor the night air, however, but went about her business as swiftly as her sore muscles would allow.

The hoshkat was waiting when she emerged, her kits sitting on either side of her and her eyes glittering in the dark. Marsh stretched a hand toward Mordan, and she swiped her head against it before tilting her head back toward the camp. It was a little embarrassing to see Gustav and Roeglin waiting at the end of the path, but it was better than if they had been waiting for her outside the latrine.

"Thanks for that," Marsh told the kat. "I needed my privacy."

"Hurry up," Lennie called, appearing behind the two men. "You're not the only one who wants to use the facilities."

Her face flushing with embarrassment, Marsh hurried back to camp. Everything felt creaky, but there was no pain...not like before. She ran a hand over her stomach and realized no one had taken off the tunic she'd been wearing when she'd fallen. Her armor was gone, but that only made sense. Just how sick had she been, anyway?

"Nice to see you on your feet," Gustav said, exchanging a quick glance with Roeglin as he gestured toward the fire. "There's someone there who wants to meet you."

"The Master of Stone?" Marsh asked, but he shook his head.

"Best you see for yourself. He'd like to speak with the girl too."

There was only one girl that Marsh could think of who shared enough in common with her that they'd draw the attention of a rock mage.

"Aisha?"

"She's still asleep, the scamp," Roeglin said, as he fell in step beside her. "I ought to wring her neck. Her and Lennie both, but Gustav says Lennie's his to deal with."

"Why? What did they do?"

Roeglin stopped and looked at her, disbelief written on his face.

"Are you telling me you don't remember?"

Marsh stopped beside him. Frowning, she vaguely recalled warmth and emerald light and glanced down at her midriff again. Pushing aside the bloodied edges of the tunic revealed unmarked skin beneath.

"Are you saying that wasn't a dream?" she asked, her voice growing clearer as shock raced through her. "But... but, are they okay?"

Roeglin pursed his lips and turned back toward the fire. Marsh followed him.

"Lennie caught Aisha in time. Brigitte was able to get

Lennie to stop before she pushed herself too far, but she was tired enough that she just covered her with a blanket where she sat."

That explained why Marsh had woken wrapped in the woman's arms.

"The hoshkat laid down on your other side, and that was that." He came to a stop at the edge of a circle of low stones that had been arranged to form seats around the fire, gesturing toward a small man tending a pot hung at its edge. "This is Master Dureau. He wishes to speak with you regarding the…"

The man cleared his throat.

"Merci, Roeglin, but I will take it from here. If you would tend our breakfast?"

He held up the spoon and Roeglin shrugged, reaching out to take it from him and leaving Marsh to face the man on her own.

"You are Marchant Leclerc?" the man said, looking her up and down as though he was inspecting a new recruit.

He pivoted slightly, turning until his gaze rested on the small bundle that was Aisha. As he paused, Scruffknuckle raised his head off his paws and growled softly in his throat. The master tutted.

"The pup has attitude," he murmured, turning back to Marsh. "Tell me, does the child have as much?"

His question brought a short bark of laughter to Marsh's lips.

"Are you kidding? Where do you think the pup gets it from?" She caught the Master's look, remembering she was a trainee, and her laughter died. "I apologize, Master, but yes, the child has as much attitude as the pup if not more."

"And has she always had the abilities she has now?"

Marsh stared at him.

"You mean has she always been able to speak with animals, talk to rocks, and call light to heal?"

He shrugged.

"If that is how you term it…"

It was Marsh's turn to shrug.

"I do not know. You would have to ask her brother. From what I recall, she has been able to talk to animals for some time, but her ability to speak with stone came as a surprise not long ago. As for the healing…" Marsh sighed. "That is something she only thought to try last night."

"Are you saying that these children are not yours?"

Marsh felt her cheeks color.

"They are mine *now*, but I am not their mother if that is what you are asking. They lost her when their caravan was ambushed not long before arriving in Ruins Hall from Kerrenin's Ledge."

His eyebrows rose.

"You are from that caravan? But I was led to believe there were no survivors."

"When did you last hear news from the Hall?"

"It would have been a number of cycles now," he said. "Tell me, when did you return to the city?"

City? Well, Ruins Hall *was* one of the bigger townships along the trade route, even if it was nowhere near the size of Kerrenin's Ledge or the stretch of ancient ruins that surrounded the hill on which the Ledge stood. Marsh decided to let it slide.

"A full cycle of days."

Marsh tried to remember just how many days had

passed. She thought it was around seven since she and the children had made it out of Leon's Deep with Fabrice and her family, but she couldn't be sure.

"It could be a little bit more," she admitted, slightly put off by the intensity of his gray-eyed gaze.

"You can't be sure?" he wanted to know, and Marsh's cheeks warmed beneath his stare.

"I'm sorry," she said. "I lost track."

"Not the best trait for a seeker," he grumbled. Marsh knew her face was blazing and wondered just how red it looked in the light of the glows. The master ignored her embarrassment but took a seat on one of the stones by the fire, gesturing that she should come and sit beside him.

Marsh obeyed but sat with one stone between them. He noticed the separation, grimaced, and moved closer.

"Do you know who I am?" he asked, and Marsh shook her head.

"Roeglin called you Master Dureau, but that is all I know. I'm sorry, but I haven't heard of you before."

His lips quirked into a brief semblance of a smile and then settled into solemnity.

"Amongst the rock mages, I am known as the Master of Beasts, although you will hear others refer to me as Speaker since speaking to the beasts is what I do. You, however, seem to have developed the ability on your own. Why?"

Marsh ducked her head, choosing to stare into the fire rather than meet his eyes as she answered his question. She waved a hand at the hoshkat.

"We came across her when we escaped the ambush. She

was hunting, and I didn't want to kill her. *Couldn't* have killed her, but I wasn't going to let her attack the children either. I was ready for her attack when our eyes met, and she stopped. I don't know how I did it, or she did it, but we came to an understanding: we wouldn't die together. She would continue her hunt and go on to feed her kits unharmed, and I would leave her caverns with *my* kits to find our own people."

He nodded.

"That makes sense. You found your magic in a time of need. It often happens that way."

"Now tell him how you found your ability to speak with shadows," Roeglin prompted, and Marsh sighed.

"Tamlin told me that we all had magic, and that he couldn't call on the shadows because he was too tired from what he'd already done to hide us. He said I would have to do it or we would have to travel blind. Given we'd just narrowly missed the raiders, I didn't think we could afford that, so I tried."

"And you succeeded."

"Tamlin said everyone had the ability…" Marsh stopped; something in the look on the Master's face making her uncertain. "Is he wrong?"

The Master gave her a shadowed look.

"Once," he said, "quite some time ago, now, there was a visitor to these caverns, a traveler who brought the cure for the Madness and helped those of us hiding in the shadows to understand our magic. He said much the same thing, but we found that magic wasn't as easy for one person as it was for another. The ability to tap into it varies from person to person, much like athletic ability or intellect. Your Tamlin is both right and not. Everyone has magic, but not all of us learn how to use it...and not all of us can use the different kinds."

Marsh was confused and felt as though a part of her world had grown shaky beneath her feet.

"I don't understand. How can both ways be right?"

"To wield magic, you need three things: you have to *believe* you can, you have to want it and really feel that you *need* it. And then you have to discover how to call the ability within reach. You discovered the magic of the shadows and that of the beasts because you needed it. In the first instance, you also had a great desire to live and a need to protect the children. The same could also be said of the second instance."

"So, with respect, Master, why did you wish to see me?"

This time he did smile.

"Is it not clear?" he asked, although Marsh knew he was aware it very much was not. "Both you and the child need to learn to control your abilities—and in spite of that, you have both teamed up with some of the powerful creatures that stalk these caverns."

They had?

A large warm body came alongside her. The hoshkat sat to one side, her kits positioned behind them. The master's eyes widened as he took in the big cat.

Oh, but that didn't explain what he meant about Aisha.

"The child mastered a krypthund. Even if she'd spoken with beasts before, that is still a feat."

Marsh understood that he was referring to Scrufknuckle.

"He *was* a puppy at the time, and very frightened."

"And yet, he has chosen to stay." The master lifted his chin to draw Marsh's attention to where Scruffknuckle was sitting upright beside his tiny mistress. "He is of an age where he could hunt for himself if he had to. I have to ask myself why he stays."

Marsh followed his gaze and got an inkling of what he meant. Scruffknuckle was very much on guard, but she knew that the minute Aisha woke, the girl would be in charge—and Scruff didn't *have* to listen to the child if he didn't want to. Studying the pup, Marsh realized he'd put on weight and height.

How long had it really been? One week? Two?

"Do they always grow that fast?" she asked, and the man nodded.

"Krypthunds reach their adult size and weight faster than other beasts, although some argue they remain puppies in their heads for much longer. I'm not so sure. I think it is more that they take on an apprenticeship with the pack, learning the business of being what they were born into, so to speak. Not everyone agrees."

He paused, staring out into the cavern past the flames.

"Can you feel the life around you?" he asked.

Marsh frowned. "I...don't understand."

"I want you to listen to the cavern around you and tell me what beasts walk there."

Oh, he did, did he?

Marsh took a deep breath and let it out. If she was to do this using the shadows, she would know exactly what he meant, but she didn't think he wanted her to do it that way. Sense the life in the cavern? She had no idea where to begin, so she followed his gaze into the dark beyond the glows.

Now that she thought about it, she'd be better off trying to sense what the life she knew felt like. Without looking at it, Marsh tried to seek out the hoshkat. Once she knew what the kat looked like, so to speak, she could try to find other types of life in the cavern. Staring into the dark, Marsh tried to 'see' the kat without taking her eyes off the shadows and shapes of the shrooms and toadstools at the camp's edge.

If she wanted to, she could pull on the shadow threads connecting them all.

Connecting...

Oh. She didn't need to; she was connected to the lives around her. They shared the air of the cavern, touched its shadows, and filled a space inside it. They were all connected. She didn't need to find their minds or tweak the cavern threads. All she had to do was learn what shared the space around her...

Marsh took another breath, feeling her connection with the air around her, sensing the stillness of the tall callas standing in groves, the vibrant pushiness of the clustered blue buttons, the glistening surety of the golden gleams, and the purple darkness of the lurking shadow wraith.

Marsh was on her feet and reaching for her sword, spinning to face the danger even as she registered that she was unarmed. Without waiting, she stooped to scoop a stone from the ground, only to be knocked from her feet before she could throw it, the hoshkat placing both paws firmly on her torso as she screamed into the cavern dark.

A low growl rumbled out of the dark, and the kat screamed again. Marsh lay under her paws, stunned by the swiftness of her movement and bruised by the fall.

That's nothing to how you'd be feeling if you'd thrown that rock.

Marsh gave a wheezing chuckle.

Thanks, she thought. *Thanks a Shadowed lot, Roeglin.*

Shouts of alarm sounded around her as the camp woke, men and women lurching out of their bedrolls in response to the hoshkat's scream and that bone-chilling rumble.

"How many d'you think are out there?" Gustav asked as Lennie ran to join them, drawing her belt tight as she raced down the path.

They came to a stop near Marsh's head, but no one tried to move the beasts off her. Maybe Roeglin...

He laughed.

Not a hope in all the Deeps, he told her. *I think you're much safer right where you are.*

Marsh groaned as she felt two more sets of paws settle alongside the hoshkat's and heard the kits challenge the shadows in far less impressive versions of their mother's call. She might have laughed, except the Deeps-be-cursed things were heavy, and nowhere near as polite about sheathing their claws as their dam.

The guards were quiet as the kats' screams died to silence, and Marsh held her breath. Everyone stood perfectly still as if they had been frozen in time...

...and then the bone-throbbing growl seeped out of the dark, softer and farther away.

The guards drew weapons, shifting position to face the sound, and Marsh saw more booted feet join them and felt the faint wash of energy as mages called magic to their hands. She pushed against the kat, trying to get her to move, but Mordan merely lifted her paw and put it in the middle of her face.

"Hey…" Her protest was muffled, and Marsh twisted her head, trying to get her face clear.

Being hushed wasn't what she'd had in mind, but Mordan shifted her foot, and Marsh found she could breathe again. She roared at the darkness, and both guards and mages froze. This time the answering growl was barely audible, and the gathered force breathed a sigh of relief.

They waited for a few more heartbeats, then Marsh felt the gathered energy dissipate as spells were canceled and their power returned to its source. The quiet remained until a dragonfly took flight from the nearest shroom.

The shadow guards and rock mages slowly dispersed as Marsh watched it fly over her head and into the cavern's heights. She was still lying there when she heard a familiar scrabble of claws, followed by a child's treble shriek.

"Scruffy!"

The pup didn't listen, but he didn't go bounding off into the dark either. Marsh might have been happier about that if the pup hadn't stopped to wash her face.

"Get off, you furry menace!" Marsh sputtered, batting at the pup's face with her hands. "Get! Off!"

The same went for the kat.

She really needed her to get off her. It was getting hard to breathe.

Marsh looked up at the great creature, hoping to catch her eyes, but the kat had lifted her head and was staring defiantly into the dark. Marsh rested her head on the rocky floor and tried to work out how to get the monster to shift. This would have been easy if she'd been able to share her need.

Marsh closed her eyes, thinking of what it was like to communicate with the big beast and wishing she could. She recalled what it was like to fall through her eyes and felt the same brief sensation, landing on her feet in the kat's domain. The kat turned its attention to her, even though she kept her eyes fixed firmly on the cavern beyond.

Why was she here?

To ask you to get off me. I need to breathe, Marsh told the kat, sharing the difficulty she was having pulling air into her lungs.

Recognition of her difficulty was swiftly followed by the sudden absence of pressure on her chest and a growl that resulted in instant relief from the other two weights bearing down on her as the kits removed their paws. She wasn't quite ready to find herself rolled beneath the arch of their bodies and then behind them, and her concentration broke as she was pushed closer to the fire.

Coming back to her own mind happened in much the same way as before—with the sensation of having dropped from a small height. This time, though, Marsh landed on her feet. She gasped and sat up, suddenly aware of the fatigue making her limbs heavy and weak. Surely she wasn't still sick?

No, but you are still recovering from shadow fever, and you have just expended a lot of energy. Not the timing I would have chosen for your first lesson.

Her first lesson? What in the Deep did Roeglin mean?

With Master Dureau.

"I thought I was to have lessons with the Master of Stone?" Marsh took a sharp breath and covered her mouth with her hands. She looked at the Master of Beasts. "No offense."

"None taken," the mage replied, "but what made you think you would need tuition from the Master of Stone? Have you ever spoken with the rocks?"

Now that she thought about it...

Marsh shook her head, but fortunately, the master was in the mood to explain. It was pretty much what the Master of Shadows had said.

"They call us rock mages because that is what they call on us to assist with—working with stone—but we encompass so much more." He gestured to the fungal forest around them. "In other lands, we would be called druids and our stoneworkers would not be welcome among them. Down here, though, where the stone is as much a part of our environment as the shrooms and mosses..."

He paused, staring out into the cavern, his gaze following the blue-sparked flight of a dragonfly pack, and then expanded on what he'd said.

"It is only natural for all of those working with the environment to come together. We have masters who work with plants and animals as well as those who work with stone, but those skills have been overshadowed during the time of building. It is something that is starting to change as more mages emerge."

He nodded to where Aisha had kicked her blankets aside and was crossing the campsite toward them. Marsh followed his gaze, not complaining when the little girl sidled over to them and wormed her way onto Marsh's lap. The master studied the child as she settled and then spoke.

"Why are you here?"

"I was cold," Aisha told him, snuggling closer to Marsh.

"And what is your magic?"

Aisha frowned.

"I don't do magic. I just talk to the rocks."

He managed a smile for her.

"That's magic," he said, "and you talk to the animals, too. Just like me."

"Like you?" Aisha was all interest. "Are you a rock mage?"

And Master Dureau's smile grew wider.

"I am a rock mage *and* a beast speaker," he told her. "Are you going to have lessons with me?"

Aisha twisted around in Marsh's lap so she could look up into her face.

"Am I?"

Marsh looked down at the girl's expectant little face.

"Maybe," she said. "The Master of Shadow wanted you to have lessons from a rock mage so you can learn how to do more magic with rocks *and* with animals."

"What kind of magic?" Aisha's face took on a suspicious look.

"Whatever kind of magic you could dream up."

The little girl's eyes went wide.

"Really?" she asked, her voice breathless with excitement. "Because I had a dream...."

Marsh caught Master Dureau's eye and smiled.

"Time I helped with breakfast," she said, standing up, and placing the avidly chattering Aisha on the rock in her place. "No doubt we'll meet again."

24

MEETING THE MASTER OF STONE

Roeglin had breakfast well in hand, but he sat Marsh down on a stone beside him and handed her a cup of chocolate.

"You *trying* to fall over again?"

Marsh didn't bother answering. She knew what he was referring to. Magic took energy from the user, and it had to be replenished—and she was still feeling shaky from reaching out into the cavern to see if she could find what lived there. She let her mind play with that for a bit, surprised because she'd succeeded and surprised because she didn't feel as tired as she thought she should. She'd have to ask him about that later. After all, he was supposed to be one of her teachers.

As she sipped the strong, sweet beverage he'd given her, Marsh wondered how long it would take to get the trade routes back up and running—because this kind of chocolate, like kaffee, came from the Grotto and supplies wouldn't last forever.

So you'd better learn fast, Roeglin's voice said in her mind, *starting with how to recover quickly from using your gift.*

Roeglin handed her a cookie.

Brigitte, he added when he saw the look on her face. *She keeps me well supplied.*

Oh, she did, did she? Marsh said nothing, biting into her cookie before Aisha realized there were any to be had. The cookie and the breakfast that followed went a long way toward restoring her energy, but she was still tired when they broke camp and began the final short leg to the rock mages' stronghold.

To her surprise, the hoshkat and her kits walked beside her, apparently not bothered by being surrounded by a group of humans and one bouncy krypthund pup. Mordanlenoowar also had no objection to one of the kits walking with Aisha, and Marsh rolled her eyes.

As if the puppy wasn't more than enough!

Roeglin caught her thought and looked at the little girl. "You are kidding me…"

"Nope. Her master had better be able to cope."

"At least her big brother has his head around it."

Marsh took another look in time to see Tamlin reach down and ruffle Scruffknuckle's fur. The boy didn't seem at all bothered by the pup walking between them, and Aisha gave her brother a happy smile, indicating the kit.

"Scruffknuckle has a friend!" she exclaimed happily, and Marsh suppressed a groan.

The pup wasn't the only one to have a friend. She glanced back to where Master Dureau trailed them. The man didn't seem at all perturbed by having so many predators among them. When she thought about it, Marsh wasn't too bothered by it either. At least these predators had morals, something the raiders seemed to lack.

They arrived at a side tunnel and walked down the short passage to another cavern. This one wasn't as large as the one they'd just left and consisted mostly of bare stone from which large rock formations ascended to the ceiling. Glows were interspersed by clusters of luminescent mosses and shrooms, and Marsh blinked at the brightness.

"Our gardens need the light," one of the rock mages explained and Marsh looked around, trying to see the gardens he referred to.

It wasn't until they'd rounded a particularly large outcropping of rock that it became clear.

The light brightened and Marsh gasped, stunned by the sight of small trees growing around a communal square. Blockish mushrooms spread out just beyond them, hedged by grey-leaved shrubs crowned by spikes of purple flowers. Ditch mint trailed between them, forming a bright green carpet, and smaller lighter-leaved plants peered shyly from between the plantings.

"Come, the Master of Stone is waiting," Dureau said. Marsh realized they'd all come to a halt just inside the square, the rock mages watching them with amusement as she, the children, Brigitte, and the caravan guards stared in wonder.

"Are those oranges?" the apprentice journeyman asked. She swallowed. "And lemons? *Real* lemons?"

"Why?" Roeglin teased, touching her lightly on the shoulder. "You going to bake us some orange and lemon snaps?"

Brigitte glared at him.

"I might," she countered, and her glare melted into a grin, "but only if you ask nicely!"

"Pretty, pretty please?" came Aisha's childish plea that had more than one of them laughing.

Master Dureau's stern voice ended the laughter.

"When you're quite ready!"

Marsh turned to make sure Aisha and Tamlin were behaving. When she turned back, an imposing figure was making its way down the center of the square. Marsh couldn't recall ever seeing a woman so tall and still so graceful. All her people were lightly built, the tallest of them not topping five and a half feet.

Some said it was because they were blessed by shadow, others that it was years of living beneath the ground and hiding in the dark from the Madness of the surface world. Marsh didn't care. Tall was rare in her world, and this woman was at least six feet. Dureau hurried over to her.

"Master of Stone!"

He glanced nervously past her to where the square opened into a short passage leading back into the rest of the cavern, relaxing only when he saw a silent squad of guards armored in bronze and green standing before it. Marsh followed his gaze and frowned; she should have heard some sound of their passage. Beside her, the hoshkat tilted her head to look at her, grumbling softly.

Apparently, she hadn't been the only one caught off-guard. Marsh rested a hand on the kat's shoulder, switching her attention back to the Master of Stone—who was clearly female and misnamed in her office. Roeglin and Brigitte approached her, each giving a shallow bow as they came to a halt.

Her height and shimmering bronze robes were a strong contrast to their builds and dark garb.

"Master of Stone," Roeglin began, "the Master of Shadows sends his greetings."

The woman cast her gaze over the gathered guards as well as Marsh and the children.

"What is it he requests?"

"Please, Master, he asks that you meet with him in the name of the Guardians, and for your assistance in training."

Roeglin stopped, and Marsh could not blame him. The Master of Stone's face had gone from curious to solemn at the mention of the Guardians.

"How urgent is his business?"

Roeglin cast a swift glance toward Marsh and then answered.

"It is urgent, Master."

She snorted.

"Of course it is. He has sent you." Her eyes turned toward the kat and the Master of Beasts. "I take it there is a good explanation for *that* being with you?"

Roeglin shifted uncomfortably, answering in the Beast Master's place.

"If we could adjourn inside, I will explain."

The Master of Stone cast him a dubious look.

"I doubt it. If the Master's business is urgent enough to both send you and invoke the name of the Guardians, there is no time for pleasantries. Perhaps you could explain while my people gather what we need for the journey."

At this, several of the bronze-garbed mages behind her hurried into nearby buildings.

Marsh stepped forward. "I will explain," she said, trying not to quail under the Master's fierce gaze.

"And you are?"

"I am Marchant Marie Leclerc."

The woman arched her brows.

"Oh? And what makes you think your explanation will suffice?"

"Because the kat came to me for help," she said, moving forward, all too aware of the kat moving forward at her side, one of her kits coming with her, the other standing beside Aisha.

Marsh glanced at Roeglin, and he gestured for her to continue.

"She came to me looking for help in retrieving her kits from the raiders." She glanced toward the kat and back at the master. "I promised I would help, and she is staying with me until that happens."

What would happen afterward, Marsh did not know, but she would cross that bridge when they reached it. Up until that time nothing was more important than her promise to the kat, her promise to Tamlin, and her promise to Fabrice—that she would find out if their loved ones still lived and bring them back if she could.

"After you have secured the Ruins Hall cavern complex and restored the trade routes," the Master of Stone added, and Marsh stared.

It was as though the woman was reading her mind!

Roeglin snickered, and Marsh saw the white fading from his eyes. Okay, so maybe the Mistress of Stone *had* been reading her mind since it looked like she'd had the help she needed to do so. Marsh shrugged.

"At least you know why the kat is here."

"And she's staying with you, I take it?" the master asked, and Marsh felt herself tense.

Surely the woman wasn't going to suggest she try leaving the kat behind?

"Yes, Master."

The master turned to Roeglin and Brigitte.

"What are the Master of Shadows' training requirements?"

Roeglin indicated Aisha and Marsh.

"Both speak with animals, and Aisha speaks to rock. These are skills outside the shadow monastery's expertise."

"Just as raiders are outside ours. I trust the Master of Shadows has news on that?"

"Yes, Master." Roeglin glanced around. "But perhaps that is a discussion for later."

She pursed her lips.

"Indeed."

As she answered, the mages that had obeyed her instruction to pack for a journey returned and a second wave headed into the buildings.

Well, one thing's for sure, Marsh thought. *They're not very friendly.*

The Master of Stone accepted a pack from one of the mages.

"We can make the mid-point if we leave now," she said, sliding the pack over her shoulders. "We'll eat as we move. You *do* have trail rations, I take it?"

Again that arched eyebrow, but the master didn't wait for an answer; she started walking toward them, and the guards and mages stepped to one side as she approached.

Marsh watched as she passed, holding her breath as the mage dropped a hand to the hoshkat's head. She was surprised to see the master's eyes burn green and the kat lean into her palm.

They exchanged nothing more and the master continued, leaving the kat beside Marsh before coming to a stop in front of the rock mages they had rescued on the way in.

"Make your report to Master Voclain. She will lead while I am away."

"Yes, Master."

She turned to Roeglin, her gaze falling on him and then on the Master of Beasts.

"You will accompany me," she said, then added, "You did not tell me there was an attack."

For a moment Marsh held her breath waiting for Roeglin to tell her that she hadn't asked, but the shadow mage was more diplomatic than that.

"We have only just arrived."

"True, and now you are just leaving. You will brief me on the way. Master of Beasts, I take it you are coming?"

It was more an instruction than a question, but Master Dureau answered it anyway.

"You have already gathered my people, and I am thankful."

Whether it was thanks or reproach, Marsh couldn't be sure, but the master was already accepting a pack from one of the green-garbed guards and coming to stand alongside the kat. They did not stand still for long. Once the rock mages they had rescued vanished into one of the buildings to make their report and the others returned with supplies for the journey, the Master of Stone led them back the way they had come.

Marsh sighed and turned, and the children followed her example. She waited for one or the other of them to say that they were tired but neither uttered a word, even though Tamlin cast an anxious glance toward his sister. Aisha ignored him, glowering after the Master of Stone with the intensity of a thunderstorm.

Looks like trouble. Roeglin murmured in her mind, and Marsh saw him nod toward the child.

Could be interesting, Marsh thought back, but she watched the youngster as they moved out of the rock mages' home cavern and back onto the trail.

None of them said much after that, not even when they passed the camp they'd broken that morning and the Master of Stone pushed them forward. She did not stop for the evening meal and did not rest. Marsh had thought the plan was for them to overnight between the two mage settlements, but if it had been, the Master of Stone gave no sign.

Marsh nudged Roeglin.

Can't you see what's on her mind? she thought and gasped as Roeglin nudged her in the ribs in return—a good deal harder than she'd done to him. He answered her out loud.

"No."

She wanted to ask him why, but he was clearly not in the mood.

The master was setting a hard pace, her long legs eating up the distance as the rest of them stepped double-time to keep up. They walked in silence, the caravan guards forming the corners of a rough square around Marsh, the children, and the two shadow mages. Beyond them, the green-and-bronze-armored mages kept a tight perimeter.

What's going on? Marsh wondered and plucked at the shadow threads around her, thinking one of them had the answer. Were there others in the cavern around them? Did the threads touching her touch them, too? She got no answer, the threads sliding through her fingers as though they didn't want her to handle them.

Marsh wanted to ask what that was about but she couldn't. Roeglin and Brigitte were moving slightly ahead of her, and the mages wouldn't have a clue what she was asking. Marsh looked at Tamlin, but the boy seemed to be focused solely on staying on his feet and not falling behind. That, and making sure his sister was all right.

For her part, Aisha had a firm grip on both the kit and Scruffknuckle. Her small face was pale and she occasionally stumbled, but she was still glaring at the Master of Stone. Marsh had to wonder what the child was going to do when the woman finally called a halt. Something told her she should worry, or better yet, make sure she had the girl well in hand when they did finally stop.

In the meantime, there was only one other thing she could think of to do: she tried to sense the life in the cavern. It was a good deal harder to do while walking than it had been when she'd been sitting at the fire that morning. At first, she sensed nothing more than her own harsh breathing, and then all she could feel were the hoshkat and her kits, and Scruffknuckle's fierce joy of life.

It was the pup who alerted her to the rest. His energy changed from happy vibrancy to darker shades of tension. Marsh snapped out of her magic and into her own head as the first mage fell to a spear of shadow twisting out from between a tall boulder and a calla shroom. The next spear shattered against a suddenly gleaming chest plate and the mages were facing outward, shields of stone forming on one forearm while blades of iron and rock materialized in their opposite hands.

Battle was joined less than a heartbeat later, but it was a fight against humans and not the shadow monsters Marsh had expected.

"Take them down!" came the Master of Stone's command, and the mages roared in response.

"Protect the children," Brigitte ordered, her eyes turning shadow-dark as she pulled a sword and dagger from darkness and stepped to the back, helping Gustav and Lennie guard the rear.

Marsh wanted to argue, but she could see that there were enough blades around them that hers would be better suited to catching anything that made it through the gap—especially as those blades were being wielded far more competently than she was able. Circling to put herself between the children and the mage guard, Marsh kept watch for any incoming threats.

Roeglin had placed himself firmly on the other side of them, the hoshkat coming to stand beside him.

"What makes you think I need your help?" he asked the kat as a spear blade slid between the two mages in front of him and buried itself in the armor he wore.

The kat didn't bother gracing that with an answer, just rammed her way between the mages and pounced into the dark. A scream rose from where she'd landed. It ended in a gurgling crunch and a snarl. Marsh dropped back beside

Roeglin in time to see him dispel the spear. She was also in time to see the blood that trickled from his side.

He stumbled and Marsh caught him, lowering him to the ground.

"Aisha! Tamlin!" she called, wanting the children close by so she didn't have to worry about them as she tried to stop the bleeding.

She hadn't counted on Aisha thinking she'd been called to help. Instead of crowding close to Marsh, the little girl dropped to her knees beside her, pulling on Roeglin's tunic and trying to part the dark leather beneath it. When she wasn't strong enough to pull it apart to get at the wound, she turned tear-filled eyes to Marsh.

"Help."

It wasn't a plea or a request; it was a directive. Marsh hesitated, not sure what to do, and Aisha set about solving her own problem. She seized the hilt of Marsh's dagger and pulled the blade from its sheath.

"I cut," she said, angling the blade toward the hole.

Roeglin drew a breath of alarm and Marsh wrapped her hand around Aisha's small hilt-filled grip.

"*I'll* cut," Marsh insisted, taking the dagger from Aisha's hand and carefully slipping it beneath the leather.

It took a bit of effort to cut a slit in the armor, but she succeeded despite the grip becoming slippery from the blood flowing from the wound. Around them, the battle raged. Metal rang and screams echoed through the cavern. Beside her, Tamlin grunted as he hung onto Scruffknuckle's neck.

"No!" he argued when the pup tried to yank himself free. "Stay!"

Aisha ignored the struggle, focusing instead on the wound. Marsh watched as the child used one hand to pinch the rent together and stroked her finger over the join. Nothing happened the first time, although she heard Roeglin bite back a cry of pain.

Aisha wasn't dismayed. She stared down at the wound, and her eyes took on a slightly green glow. Again she moved her finger across the wound, but Marsh didn't have time to see what she was doing. A shout from the mages on her right drew her attention and she looked toward them.

She was in time to see a raider pulling his bloodied sword from the mage he'd just killed, and then the man was coming toward them. Marsh saw him pull his arm back, ready to swing the heavy blade forward, and wished she had a shield. In her mind's eye, she saw the shadow engulfing Lennie's fist back in the eatery. She wanted something bigger, something rounder; something that would cover her and Roeglin and the children and the kits and the pup. She wanted the shadows to form a barrier between them and stop the sword before it hit.

As smooth as thought, Marsh pulled the darkness from between the surrounding shrooms and dragged it down from the ceiling arcing overhead. This time it was not like grasping a thread, but more like taking hold of the edge of a cloak or moving a shutter. Marsh grabbed it and pulled it in between her and the blade.

She pictured it forming an oval shield large enough to stop the blade and raised her forearm above her to hold it. Shadow fell over her, darkening where she and the children crouched. Pressure slammed into the shield, and then slammed into it, again—and again. And—

It stopped.

Marsh opened her eyes.

All around them, the sounds of battle had ceased, and relative silence descended.

It was broken by a drawn-out yowl and the sudden shuffle of footsteps as people moved to make way, and then Marsh caught the sound of something large snuffling around the edges of the shield she had created. She sat there for a moment, and then the Master of Stone's voice rang around them.

"You can drop the shield now."

25

SPEAK NICELY TO THE DARK

Dropping the shield was easier said than done, especially once the hoshkat started clawing at the edges trying to reach her kits. In the end, the mages reached in and pulled Roeglin clear. Aisha and Tamlin crawled out after him, followed by Scruff and the two kits.

"Are you coming out too, Marsh?" called the Master of Stone, and Marsh realized she had a problem.

When she'd conjured the shield, she'd thought of it as strapped to her arm so she could hold it above her head... and now she couldn't unstrap it.

"*Merde*," she whispered, and the Master of Stone's head appeared around the edge.

"Trouble?"

Marsh felt her face glow red. She pulled on the straps, but the shield didn't move.

Huh. Maybe she hadn't had to hold it up after all.

"Give me a bit."

"Trainee, we do not have a bit. I want to reach the monastery by nightfall."

"I am sorry, Master."

And she was. She truly was, but not because she couldn't obey the master's order; more because she didn't want to be trapped under a shield of shadow no matter how handy it had turned out to be. She jerked against it once more.

"Let. Me. Go," she growled and repeated the action.

The straps bit into her arm, and the shield didn't budge. It was as though it was jammed into solid air and wrapped tightly around her arm. She tried worming her arm out of the straps, but that didn't work, and then she tried pushing the shield up and out of the way, but it stayed stubbornly in place. As she bounced off it and hit the ground, Marsh wished the children were somewhere much farther away, because *merde* was not the word she wanted to use right now.

"Aagh!" she shouted, and three curious faces peered under the rim of the shield. "What!"

Roeglin started smirking, and Tamlin was grinning. Aisha stared at her in wide-eyed wonder.

"You stuck?" the little girl wanted to know, and Marsh wanted to scream.

Some of that must have shown in her expression because Roeglin chose to intervene.

"Aysh, why don't you go see if Brigitte has any spare cookies? I'm sure she'll share…"

Aisha shot Marsh one more worried look and disappeared. Roeglin crouched to get a better look at her. The smirk was back, and it wasn't an improvement. From the look on his face, there was plenty he wanted to say and just wasn't. Tamlin didn't have the same sense of decorum.

"Lennie would find this hilarious," he said, and it was as if he'd summoned the guard.

She stuck her head under the rim of the shield, took in Marsh's situation, and disappeared with a bark of laughter. Given the noises that followed, she was in danger of literally pissing herself from mirth. Roeglin snorted, and Tamlin started snickering.

"I'm going to murder you all when I get out of here."

Roeglin tried to look offended.

"That's not an incentive for me to help you, you know."

"I could send Scruffy in," Tamlin said, laughter leaking around the words. "He'd cheer you up in no time."

And then the boy was gone, rolling out of sight as he cackled like a hen that had just laid an egg.

"*Very* funny," Marsh muttered, but her tone said it was anything but.

She rested her head on her forearm, glad the boy hadn't followed up on his threat. She didn't need a face-washing on top of everything else. Roeglin chuckled and moved closer, and Marsh eyed him with disgust. He didn't even have the decency to come in on the side that wasn't trapped.

Smarter than he looked, that man—because she really wanted to hit something right now and he was looking good.

"I *can* read your mind, you know," Roeglin told her. "And I'm not stupid."

Marsh wanted to argue that, but the evidence was against her. She sighed, biting back the urge to ask him to help her all over again. She was not going to beg.

"Never said you had to," he said, his voice suddenly

serious. "Besides, I'm your instructor; I'm supposed to help you get out of things like this."

He edged closer until she felt his warmth against her side, and Marsh tried telling him that as her instructor, it was his job to not let her get into situations like this to start with.

"Not true," he said, "and, even if it was, I was indisposed."

Oh. *Indisposed.* Is that what he called it? Because to her, it had looked like he was in danger of bleeding to death.

"That, and I had to stop Aisha from overdoing it."

He had? To be honest, Marsh had lost track of what was happening when she'd tried to pull the shield up in time to stop the sword from falling.

"Yeah, so let's figure this out quickly because I'm gonna need Lennie's help." He paused. "Unless you *want* to carry me?"

Marsh ignored the mock hope in his voice. Carry him? In a mule's eye, she would! She'd ask the hoshkat. Maybe Mordanlenoowar would eat him first.

"Do you *want* to get out of there?"

Oh. Right. Mind reader. Damn. Maybe it was time for her to rethink her policy on begging.

"No, don't do that. Just keep being your charming self. So, you called the shadow, right?"

Marsh nodded.

"And you asked it to be strong enough to stop the sword, right?"

"Mmmhmmm."

Marsh wondered how long it would take him to get to the point.

"You know, you could at least pretend to be grateful."

Well, double Deep damn!

"Don't you know anything stronger?"

Marsh groaned. Sure she knew stronger curses; she hadn't grown up in a waystation not to know all the good swear words. She just didn't want to say any of them where the kids could hear her.

"Fine, but when they're asleep, you're going to have to let some of that tension loose, okay?"

"Just tell me how to get out of here," Marsh said, but she couldn't help adding, "Please."

"I thought we agreed you weren't going to beg."

"I may have to kill you when this is over."

He snorted at that.

"Remind me never to let you talk in any negotiation we need a favor on."

"Well, pu—"Roeglin cut her off before she could finish.

"And I thought you were worried about the children..."

"*Merde!*"

Marsh sagged, her arm pulling her up short. When Roeglin next spoke, there was no hint of amusement in his voice.

"Did you ask the shadows to form a shield or did you make a shield out of the shadows?"

Marsh considered that.

"I pulled them between us and imagined what I wanted them to do."

He sighed.

"Asking them would have been easier. You could have just asked them to go back to where they came from."

"You mean I can't?"

"Have you tried?"

"Didn't you hear me shouting?"

"Shadows are like anything else. You have to ask nicely."

"Oh, fine. You mean like, 'pretty please, Mr. Shadow, will you let my arm go'?" Marsh hadn't meant for it to come out sounding quite so sarcastic.

"Well, you could try that, seeing as polite isn't really your forte."

Now she really *did* want to hit him, but she also wanted to try asking the shadows to let her go because, sarcastic or not, she'd thought she'd felt something give. Taking a breath, she straightened up and rested her head on her forearm.

Ask the shadows, right? Well, it was worth a try.

"Shadow's Heart and Shadow's Deep," she began and then stopped. "Thank you for your help. I return you to your homes to sleep."

She accompanied the words by thinking of the shadows returning to the hollows and crevices from which she'd called them.

"Sleep," she whispered. "Go home and sleep with my thanks."

She raised her eyes, willing the shadows to leave the shield and return to the cavern dark. To her surprise, it worked. The pressure on her arm eased, the dark bands that had bound the shield to her skin slowly letting go as the shield dissipated into mist and floated away. With a sigh of relief, Marsh collapsed over her knees and took a deep breath, then she straightened up.

"Thanks, Roeglin."

"You're welcome. Now, if you would call Lennie..."

Looking at him, Marsh realized he was a lot paler than before, and his eyes were dark with strain.

"Lennie!" she called. "Lennie!"

And the guard came running. Marsh remembered something the woman had said earlier.

"Not when you can stop it, right?" She looped her arm around Roeglin's waist and pushed herself to her feet, lifting the mage until his injury became visible.

Lennie had no problems swearing in front of the children, and she didn't waste any time asking Roeglin to sit down, either. She just pushed the cut flap of armor aside and swore again.

"Stand still," she ordered and did exactly what Aisha had done: pinching the two sides of the wound together and running her finger down the seam—except that Lennie called on the Mother of Shadows, Shadow's Heart, and Shadow's Queen, and the light that flowed from her hands was brighter than any Aisha had managed.

With a shout of alarm, Henri rushed over and pulled her away.

"What are you trying to do, girl? Lose the baby? Make me carry you the rest of the way? Are you insane? Jorj would kill me if I let anything happen to either of you!"

When Lennie tried to go back, the Master of Stone stooped to examine Roeglin's side. After probing the wound, she looked at the guard.

"You've done enough," she said. "He'll scar, but he'll be fine."

She paused, studying Lennie, Roeglin, Marsh, and Aisha

with a disgusted eye. With a huff of impatience, she turned to the Master of Beasts.

"We'll camp at the next rest point and march into the fortress in the morning. I'll need assistance in fortifying it." Her face took on a hint of mischief, and she looked at Brigitte. "I believe the journeyman has brought cookies."

From the look of dismay on Brigitte's face, Marsh guessed the girl's cookie supply was running low. Fortunately, Roeglin stepped up to help her out.

"I have some as well," he said. "Between us, we'll have enough."

It was roughly an hour's walk before they reached the waystation and they were all ready to stop well before they did. The Master of Stone was merciless, however. When Aisha stumbled, she strode back and swung the little girl onto her shoulders.

"Hold on," she said, ignoring Aisha's scowl as she continued down the path.

Scruffknuckle whined, but the kit picked up its pace until it trotted at the master's heels and the puppy had no choice but to hurry after. Marsh almost wished she was small enough to be carried, but then decided the indignity of it would far outweigh any advantages. She did her best to keep up but her footsteps dragged, and she was not alone.

Gustav, Henri, and Lennie walked with her and Roeglin, even though Tamlin joined Scruff and the kit on the master's heels. The mages and the fourth guard, Jakob, surrounded them, their eyes wary as they moved through the cavern. It was good when they arrived safely at the rest stop, although a bit unnerving to watch as two of the green-clad mages asked the moss and shrooms to reshape themselves into broad benches while the rock mages called stone from the cavern floor, their eyes turning as black as pitch as they asked it to form walls around the site.

Marsh pulled dried fungal bricks from her pack and built a fire in the existing pit. They might not be cooking, but at least they could heat water for kaffee or chocolate and enjoy their rations in the light and warmth of the flames. She unhooked the kettle from Roeglin's pack, trying to ignore the buzzing in her head. It had been a long journey, sure, but she had no reason to...

Tamlin took the kettle from her hand.

"You need to sit down," he told her. "I don't know how much magic you used when you called the shield for us, but that took some conjuring. You should have been feeling it ages ago."

He was right, and he was wrong.

Marsh knew that if she'd been the same person she'd been when they were fleeing the shadows, the magic she'd used would have seen her too tired to move, but she wasn't. She'd called the shadows since, talked to the hoshkat and to Roeglin, and she felt stronger than she'd been. She could do more and felt less tired than before.

The kid had a point, though. She did need to take a break.

"I'll make the chocolate and the kaffee. You grownups look beat."

He wasn't alone. Gustav, Henri, and Jakob were all on their feet. When the mages had completed their crafting and swayed with fatigue, the three guards guided them to a space around the fire and made them rest. The three men worked to finish setting up camp and then joined the rest of them.

The Master of Stone turned to Roeglin.

"Tell the Master of Shadow that we will join him for breakfast," she ordered, her voice filled with iron and command.

Marsh watched as Roeglin nodded, his eyes turning white as he did as she asked. He was still for a moment, staring into the dark without making a sound—and then he blinked. Across the fire, the Master of Stone saw the shadow mage's lips move as if he were having a conversation with someone they could not see. It was brief, and Roeglin nodded at its end.

"Yes, Master. I'll tell them. I won't forget. Thank you."

Both Marsh and the Master of Stone were waiting as his eyes returned to their usual color, but Roeglin blinked twice and slumped slowly onto his side. The Master of Stone frowned and then shrugged before turning to Marsh.

"I want that message from him as soon as he wakes." Before Marsh could reply, she had risen from near the fire and rolled herself in her blankets on one of the benches the druids had coaxed from the moss.

As if she'd given a signal, the rest of the rock mages rose from around the fire and retired, leaving Gustav snorting with disgust. The guard looked at Jakob and Henri.

"I'll take the first watch," he said and jerked his chin toward where Lennie was asleep. "She'll take the last. Jakob, you're up next, then Henri."

He settled himself a little way away from the fire and looked at Marsh.

"And you need to be sleeping."

Marsh raised her hands in mock surrender, but she checked that both Tamlin and Aisha were asleep before settling a blanket over Roeglin and looking for her own bed. It was almost logical that the hoshkat would be curled beside her pack.

26

THE ART OF BEING A TRAINEE

Marsh woke to the sound of cave crickets chirping and Scruffknuckle growling. When she looked, the pup had a corner of Aisha's blanket in his mouth and was trying to pull it out of the child's hands. At first, Marsh couldn't work out what had gotten into the pup, but then she noticed the tufted end of a hoshkat's tail sticking out from underneath the blanket and realized what was happening.

The kit had ousted the pup from his place at Aisha's side.

Marsh unwrapped herself and hurried over before the blanket could tear.

"Aisha! Time to get up. Make sure Scruff and the kit are ready. You don't want to make the master cross."

She reached over and took the blanket out of Aisha's hand, folding it quickly before handing it back.

"Put that in your pack before I decide you don't need it."

"You're mean."

"I can find you cookies."

The blanket was stowed in double-quick time, and Marsh could sense when Aisha joined her. She ignored the child, tipping Tamlin out of his bed, much to his sister's delight. The boy repeated one of Lennie's more colorful curses from the night before, and Marsh poked him.

"That will be enough of that," she said. "What's your mother going to say if I bring her back and you're using language like that?"

As soon as the words left her mouth, Marsh knew she'd made a mistake. Until then, the guards and druids had been slowly packing up. Now they stopped. Looking into Tamlin's face, Marsh knew she was in trouble. Across the camp, the hoshkat gave a rumbling growl and got to her feet.

Taking a long, slow breath, Marsh straightened up and turned around. It was exactly as bad as she'd thought it would be. Lennie, Henri, and Jakob were gazing at her. The rock mages, those in bronze as well as those in green, were staring in her direction, and the Masters of Stone and Beasts were stalking toward her looking angrier than she thought possible.

Marsh pretended she hadn't seen them and headed for where Roeglin was pushing back his blankets and looking like he'd just recovered from being hit by a rockslide. His gaze sharpened when he saw Marsh coming toward him, the two masters moving purposefully in her wake.

"What's my apprentice done this time?" he mumbled as Marsh stopped beside him.

"Didn't you get the message?" Marsh demanded,

tapping him with her foot. "I'm no one's apprentice. I'm a *trainee.*"

"Whatever you are, you're still mine, and I need to clean up your messes."

"No one cleans up my messes but me," Marsh told him, "and you can ask them yourself what beetle's crawled into their britches. I just came to get your lazy ass out of bed."

"That's the most undisciplined trainee I've ever seen," the Master of Stone snapped as Roeglin struggled to his feet.

Marsh didn't offer to help him. Thought she belonged to him, did he? Well, that was one notion she was going to dispel. She'd add it to the list.

You have a list? Roeglin sounded mortified, although his face didn't show it.

And I'm checking it twice.

He cleared his throat and took hold of her arm, turning her so she faced the two masters and four worried-looking guards. Marsh did a double-take when she saw Lennie's face. Well, worried wasn't quite the word she'd use for that look.

Angry, maybe. Furious, even. Kinda like the woman was thinking of another round of pounding on Marsh's ribs, almost definitely. Not that Marsh could blame her. She'd be mad too if someone was going after missing folk and had left her soulmate out of it...not that she had a soulmate.

You want to focus?

Marsh blinked and did just that. The Masters of Stone and Beasts had stopped in front of them, Lennie advancing to stand beside them.

"You want to explain what you just said?"

It was a challenge, and Marsh looked at Lennie.

"I promised Tamlin I'd go looking for his parents once the trade routes were restored."

It was difficult to keep her voice calm in the face of Lennie's anger, but Marsh managed it. She watched the guard's face and waited, but it wasn't Lennie who spoke next.

"And you promised the hoshkat you'd help her find her kits."

That was the Master of Beasts. The Master of Stone just watched the exchange with raised eyebrows, then she added her piece.

"Who else have you said you'll do this for?" she asked.

Marsh was aware of the mage moving in closer, of the children coming to stand beside her, and of the hoshkat moving in from the campsite's edge.

Marsh closed her eyes and took a long, slow breath.

"Fabrice."

She heard movement both in front of and beside her and opened her eyes, taking a step back and calling a shield of shadow to her arm. She stopped just short of drawing her sword, both relieved and annoyed when Roeglin moved between her and Lennie.

"Stop!"

The Master of Stone's voice rang clear around them and they all froze. Marsh flicked the woman a fast glance, but made sure to keep an eye on Lennie. The guard's hands were balled into fists and her face was contorted with fury, but she had stopped her advance. Henri made to lay a hand on her shoulder and she turned her head, her lip lifting in a warning snarl. It was Gustav who wrapped his hand around the guard's bicep and pulled her away.

With the immediate threat gone, Marsh relaxed a little.

"Tell me how you're going to do that," the Master of Stone ordered, and Marsh felt her face redden.

"I'm still working it out," she replied, then decided she wouldn't be intimidated.

She lifted her chin and looked the Master of Stone straight in the eye.

"I will find them through the shadow. It is why I am here—to learn what I can do with my magic so I can use it to help me in my search."

She caught movement beyond the master and recognized the face of one of the mages she'd helped rescue. A memory sparked, and she took a breath.

"I have seen portals made through the shadows. When I find where the raiders go, we can go to them and take back those they took from us."

"I'm coming." Lennie's voice carried clearly across the camp. "And you're going to promise to find Jorj for me."

"Done," Marsh said, "but your child comes first. I'm not facing him if either of you is harmed when I could have stopped it."

She had no desire to be explaining that one to a man fierce enough to have won Lennie's heart. Lennie did not hesitate.

"Witnessed and sealed."

The Master of Stone rolled her eyes.

"Oh, wonderful. Now I have two of you whose minds

won't be on the job. You can both take up your little side trip with the Master of Shadows when we get there. We leave in half a turn."

She tapped the hourglass hanging at her waist and the mages scattered. Marsh grabbed her arm when she went to walk away.

The master stopped mid-stride and looked pointedly down at the hand on her arm. Marsh ignored it and spoke her piece.

"It's not a side trip," Marsh told her, "and we won't be distracted. None of us can leave until we've secured the Four Settlements. If we do, there won't be a place to bring our families back to."

The master's eyes were cold as she looked Marsh up and down.

"You have no family." She tried to shake Marsh's hand loose, but Marsh wouldn't let go.

"My parents disappeared when I was four," Marsh said. "I thought they were long dead, but they might not be. I intend to find the truth."

She let the master go, but the woman didn't break eye contact.

"Your duty comes first," was all the master said before turning to Roeglin. "Your *trainee* needs some discipline. Good luck with that."

"Yes, Master."

Roeglin bobbed his head in agreement, his cheeks coloring as she left them. When she was several steps away, he turned to face Marsh.

"Do you—"He was interrupted before he got further.

"I'm certain she does not," the Master of Beasts said,

"and since she is to be my trainee as well as yours, we need to talk."

As he drew Roeglin away, the shadow mage shook his finger at Marsh, his lips set in an angry straight line. Marsh hung her head and sighed. *That* hadn't gone at all well. She'd planned to take a minute to gather her thoughts, but a small hand wound its way around one leg and a heavy weight leaned against the other.

"You okay?" Tamlin wanted to know, and Marsh drew a shaky breath.

"Yeah, sure, kid. I'm fine."

She was not undisciplined, but as she thought it, Marsh caught sight of the shadow shield still strapped to her arm. She sighed.

"Go back to where you came from—and thank you for your aid."

For a minute nothing happened, then the shield drifted apart, its component shadows floating away to join the others in the cavern. Watching them, Marsh breathed a sigh of relief and dropped a hand to the kat beside her. In response, she pulled her weight off Marsh's leg and swiped her face against it before wandering off to join her kits.

When she was gone, Marsh looked down at Aisha. The little girl's eyes were dark with distress, and she had the hand not wrapped around Marsh's thigh buried in the soft fur of Scruffknuckle's neck.

"You want breakfast?"

"She's mean."

The little girl could only be talking about one person, so Marsh ignored the comment.

"Breakfast?"

"Cookie."

"Let's find Brigitte."

"Mum's gonna kill you," Tamlin interrupted.

"She doesn't have to know."

"She'll find out." Tamlin lowered his voice to a menacing whisper. "She always does…"

It made Marsh smile.

"Kaffee or chocolate?" she asked, her gaze drifting to where the Master of Beasts and Roeglin were sitting to one side of the camp, their heads close together.

As she watched, Roeglin lifted his head and glanced in her direction. His lips moved, and the Master of Beasts also looked toward her.

"What I wouldn't give to know what they were saying," Marsh murmured, and felt threads of shadow stir around her.

Before she could do anything to investigate them, Tamlin poked her in the ribs.

"Breakfast," he said. "Whatever they're planning, you probably don't want to know. It's not like you can do anything about it anyway."

The boy was right, and Marsh set about making sure he and Aisha were looked after. Brigitte rolled her eyes when Marsh gave her a cup of kaffee and asked her for a cookie.

"You do know that I'm not made of cookies, right?" The woman huffed, but she pulled one out of a bag hanging from her waist and handed it to Aisha.

She handed another to Tamlin before he could ask, and he took it with a sheepish grin. Marsh got the impression he'd been going for grown up and hadn't been about to ask, even though he'd clearly wanted one.

"Thanks," she said and was about to head back to the fire when Brigitte caught at her tunic.

"I want to come," the apprentice-journeyman said when she turned back, and she clarified, "When you go to try to get the families back, I want to come."

Marsh cast a glance in Roeglin's direction.

"I'll ask," she promised, then frowned. "Although it would be easier if you were *his* apprentice journeyman."

She blushed as soon as she'd said it, stumbling over her words as she tried to mend it.

"Not that that would even be possible, but if it was..."

Brigitte frowned.

"I can ask." She caught Marsh's second glance at the mage. "Not him. The Master of Shadows. I can ask the Master of Shadows. It's not common, but if the circumstances demand..."

Marsh caught what she was saying.

"And your master *is* cut off from here, isn't he?"

"*She*, and yes, she is."

There was a wealth of story behind Brigitte's tone and words, but she didn't look like she was going to share any of it. Marsh figured the woman was a little higher in the pecking order than a new trainee and decided not to pry. She turned back to the fire.

"Apprentices are usually tasked with looking after their master's gear and making sure their masters are fed," Brigitte said, her voice just loud enough to reach Marsh. "He probably wouldn't insist on it, but you need to know."

She gestured to the mages working around the camp.

"There are others watching."

Yes, there were—and Roeglin had already been reprimanded on his trainee's lack of discipline. This, at least, was easy to fix.

"Thank you," she said, shooting Brigitte a grateful smile. "That's good to know."

27

NEW MASTERS AND ISOLATION

R oeglin and the Master of Beasts were still deep in discussion when Marsh came to a halt in front of them.

"I brought you kaffee," she said when they stopped talking long enough to look up at her.

Roeglin raised his eyebrows but took the mug she offered. Marsh blushed at his look but decided she wasn't going to explain. He could work things out for himself.

Or I could just look for the answers inside your head, came his quiet comment where only she could hear it.

"*Merde!*" Marsh muttered as the Master of Beasts took his cup.

"I'm sorry?"

"Sorry, Master. I... I forgot something. Here's breakfast," Marsh managed, and, passed over the two compact shroom loaves that she'd been juggling with the kaffee.

She tried to ignore Roeglin's half-suppressed smirk at her discomfort. If the Master of Beasts didn't buy her comment, he was at least polite enough not to say so.

He took his mug.

"Thank you."

He turned back to Roeglin.

Marsh left them to their plotting and made for Roeglin's blankets. She wasn't on her own for long.

"I found a grackle vine," Tamlin whispered, coming alongside her as she rolled Roeglin's blanket and slid it into the shadow mage's pack.

He held up a handful of long reddish stems studded with the sharp, round spurs of the grackle vine's prickly seeds.

"We could add these to his bedding…"

Marsh glared at him.

"Are you *trying* to get me into trouble?"

Tamlin looked offended.

"No, but it would be pretty funny."

"Right up until he had us both mucking out the stables or lifting rocks," Marsh retorted, snatching the grackle stems from his hand and pitching them to one side. "Now, go and do something useful—like watching your sister."

"Grouchy."

"And make sure you're both packed before the Stone Master wants to leave. You know, *useful.*"

"Sure, sure. Have it your way."

Watching him walk away, Marsh made a note to check her own bedding for the foreseeable future. She didn't want grackle scratches when she was trying to sleep. Securing Roeglin's pack, she looked for the one belonging to the Master of Beasts.

It didn't take her long to find it. The man had slept on the edge of the camp hard up against one of the walls, and his bedding was still untouched. With a sigh, Marsh stuffed it into the pack waiting nearby and then hauled both packs over to the two mages.

The Master of Beasts grunted an acknowledgment, looking over to where he'd slept. For a second, Marsh felt her heart plummet. What had she forgotten? She followed his gaze, scouring the area with her eyes but not seeing anything amiss.

"Thank you," Roeglin said, drawing her attention back to them. "Don't forget your own gear. It looks like we'll be leaving soon."

Marsh followed his glance and saw the Master of Stone reaching for her pack. She looked at the fire as one of the rock mages lifted the kettle clear and covered the coals and ashes with a slab of stone. Glancing around the camp, she saw that her blanket was the only one not packed.

"*Merde.*"

She was pretty sure she could hear Roeglin laughing as she rushed away. Another time. She could deal with him another time, master or not, she was starting to regret not keeping the grackle vines. Marsh had rolled her blanket and was just stowing it into her pack when the Master of Stone called them together.

"We'll make the monastery by mid-morning," she announced, and Marsh assumed the woman knew that because she'd made the journey before. Personally, she remembered this leg of the trip as being longer.

The reason for the Master of Stone's announcement became clear the minute they stepped through the gates to the waystation. The woman broke into a slow jog, and the rock mages matched her step for step. The caravan guards caught on fast and were soon trotting with the rest of them.

Marsh swore softly under her breath.

How Aisha was supposed to keep up the pace, she didn't know. Tamlin was going to find it hard enough. Marsh moved over to where the little girl had broken into a trot.

"I can do it," the child assured her, ducking Marsh's first attempt to pick her up.

Marsh decided not to argue with her but ran alongside her until the girl began to flag. This time when she reached down, Aisha didn't shy away. Marsh hauled the little girl into her arms and lifted her onto her pack. Of course, she had to stop to do it and the rest of the group did not, although Gustav and Lennie circled back to keep her company.

"We'll take turns," the founder's guards said as they fast-trotted to catch up.

Marsh snuck a look over at Lennie, wondering how the woman was taking it. If Lennie saw her checking, she didn't show it. They jogged on, Gustav taking Aisha as the first hourglass was flipped. Roeglin came alongside.

"I'm next."

Gustav didn't argue, and the four of them kept on. After the first hour, the Master of Stone dropped into a walk. That lasted for twenty paces, then she broke into a jog, again. Marsh suppressed a groan but was ready when the pace went from jog to walk after another twenty paces. She wondered where the woman had learned it and added it to the list of questions she wanted to ask.

The jolting pace continued until the monastery walls

came into view. When they were within a half mile, the Master of Stone slowed them to a walk and let them slowly regain their breath, so they arrived at the gates looking as though they hadn't done any running at all.

Marsh watched as Aisha slid from Henri's shoulders and wrapped her arms around Scruffknuckle and the kit. The pup had had no trouble keeping up, trotting briskly at the heels of whoever was carrying his little mistress, the hoshkat kit running by his side. Somewhere over the journey, the two of them had worked out a truce and now ran easily together.

Aisha pulled both critters close.

"Good puppy. Good kit."

"We have an audience with the Master of Shadows," the Master of Stone announced when asked her business.

As she did so, the hoshkat grumbled from behind the group and Marsh walked back to where it hovered uncertainly at the edge of the path. She looked into Marsh's eyes, and she met the kat's mind without hesitation.

That she was afraid to enter the humans' stone lair was understandable. Hoshkats and humans had a long history of not getting along. The kats hunted the humans' livestock and anyone foolish enough to enter their territory, and humans had long prized the hoshkats' teeth, claws, and pelts as trophies.

It's time to make a pact, Marsh told her, picturing the Master of Shadows in her mind and making his position in her hierarchy clear.

He was the most powerful beast in the cavern. He was the one who could keep her in the fortress or let her hunt for those who had stolen the hoshkat's kits. It would be better if the two of them faced him together. Marsh pictured the kat and her kits by her side, not minding that Aisha appeared there as well, with one kit closer to her than either Marsh or its mother.

That was just the way it was going to be.

The hoshkat stepped closer and Marsh knelt before her, registering an alarmed shout from the walls. She ignored it, pressing her forehead against the kat's, and rested there as the kat agreed to trust her, then their minds separated. As she pushed herself to her feet, Marsh became aware of the hush that had fallen over the group and her heart skipped a beat. What had she missed?

Looking toward the gates, she noticed that the Masters of Stone and Beasts had returned to the group and that they were not alone. The Master of Shadows stood between them, his head cocked to one side as he observed her and the kat. Slightly to one side of the trio stood Roeglin, his hands on Aisha's and Tamlin's shoulders and a look of concern on his face.

"I beg your pardon, Masters," Marsh began. "I did not mean to delay you."

The Master of Shadows stepped forward.

"You did not delay us," he said. "You frightened the guards on the walls, who were sure you were about to be eaten."

Marsh looked down at the hoshkat, and laid a hand on her shoulders, stroking her fur as she stared at this chief of humans. The kat glanced up at her in response and the contact between them flared. This time Marsh did not need to hold her gaze as she turned back to the head of the shadow mages.

"She will not eat me. We have a pact."

"What about the rest of us?"

Again Marsh glanced at the kat.

"Her pact is with all who would help her retrieve her kits."

"Her kits?"

"The raiders took them."

The cat hissed softly, and the mages drew back.

"Indeed," the Shadow Master said, stepping toward them—and causing a flurry of movement as six armored mages ran forward to array themselves alongside him.

Marsh sensed the kat's sudden apprehension and sent her soothing thoughts, reassuring Mordanlenoowar that she was safe and promising she would summon a shield and defend her if it came to battle.

"This is the Master of Shadows. Making a pact with him makes a pact with this pride of shadow wielders," she whispered, and the cat's head came up, her ears cocked forward.

Before Marsh could say anything, the big beast stalked forward, her eyes fixed firmly on the Shadow Master's face. As she drew closer, she uttered the strange chirping call she used to summon her kits, and both of them bounded to her side.

"Kitty!" Aisha's cry of distress bounced off the cavern's ceiling.

It was swiftly followed by Roeglin's shout of frustration as the child ducked beneath his hand and ran after her kit. She hit one of the shadow guards hard behind the knees, knocking him off balance as she pushed past, and there was a flurry of alarm.

The Master of Shadows stilled it with an upraised hand and knelt before the kat.

"Roeglin, if you would focus once more."

Marsh now understood how he could be so calm. Roeglin had been mindwalking again.

"Marchant, if you would pass this on?" the master added.

Pass what… Oh…

Roeglin had connected them all, pulling the Master of Shadows' promise of alliance and protection through to Marsh's connection with the kat. Marsh stilled, letting the Master of Shadows and Mordanlenoowar get a sense of each other. When they were done, the kat walked back to her, one kit by her side as the other retreated with Aisha to where Tamlin was waiting.

"Let's go in."

It was more a command than an invitation, and the Master of Shadows didn't wait for a reply. He merely turned and walked back through the assembled mages and guards, not even glancing over to where Roeglin had returned to the children. Marsh cast the mage an anxious look, knowing he must be tired after linking them all together.

She angled toward him, both to make sure he was okay and to rejoin the children, this time with the hoshkat in tow. Roeglin waited until she'd reached him and offered her his arm, murmuring an explanation as he did so.

"If you don't take it, I'm going to fall over."

Marsh contemplated letting him fall on his ass for all of a second, then smiled and slipped her arm through his, taking some of his weight as he leaned on her.

"Thank you," he whispered.

"Where are we going?" Marsh wanted to know.

"To see the Masters."

Marsh wondered if he'd make it up the stairs.

"I'm not that far gone!"

Marsh decided not to argue, but she was grateful when Gustav came alongside them and lifted Roeglin's arm across his shoulders. Between them, they got the mind mage up the stairs and along the corridor in time to join the Masters of Stone and Beasts as they entered the Master of Shadow's office. Other shadow mages ushered the rock mage guards away, showing them to their quarters and where the dining hall was, but the mages gave the hoshkats and the children a wide berth.

In the end, only two of the green-clad and one of the bronze-clad mages remained alongside the children, the kats, and the pup. Marsh guessed the mages were assigned to the Masters' protection and maneuvered Roeglin to one side to let them pass. She wasn't entirely surprised when Gustav and Lennie followed them in, both guards keeping a close eye on the children. It looked like they were taking their promise to the cavern founder seriously.

They joined the other guards standing around the edges of the room, and Marsh wondered how Lennie was handling the journey. It seemed a lot to ask someone who was also carrying a child. If it was, the surreptitious glance she shot the woman didn't show it.

Fortunately, Lennie didn't notice. Marsh was sure that if she had, the two of them would be having words. Lennie didn't take too well to being coddled. She turned her attention to what the Masters were discussing.

They had started by acknowledging their duty to the Guardians for the safekeeping of the caverns, and now they turned to Roeglin, Marsh, and the two children.

"We need to formalize your training," began the Master of Shadows. He turned to the Master of Stone. "I believe you will agree that both the child and Marchant are in need of instruction from one of your beast speakers."

The Master of Stone gave a single dip of her chin.

"I do."

"And the child is in need of instruction in stone."

This time the Master of Stone met the Shadow Master's eye.

"She showed no sign of stone speaking…" she began but stopped when Aisha interrupted.

"Can so."

"Hush, Aysh," Tamlin said, looping an arm around her shoulders. "Don't be rude."

The Master of Stone didn't seem to be worried about her rudeness.

"Can not," she taunted. "You didn't speak to a single stone where I could see, not even a little one."

"Rude!" Aisha said and slipped out of her brother's hold.

Tamlin made to grab her, but Roeglin stopped him, and the boy subsided with a groan.

"See?" Aisha said, moving to stand beside the wall and promptly disappearing into it.

"See? Can so!" she said, reappearing and flouncing back to take her place beside her brother.

Tamlin was staring at her in open-mouthed surprise. When he caught the smug look on her face, he closed his mouth with a snap and leaned close to her.

"You little cheater," he grumbled, wrapping his arm around her shoulders.

"*You* talk to the shadows!" she snapped back. "Dat's cheating, too."

"Is not!"

"Is too!"

"Is—"

"If you *don't* mind!"

The Master of Shadows was not impressed with their bickering. Judging from the look on her face, the Master of Stone was *very* impressed.

"I'll be her teacher," she said, but Aisha was having none of it.

"Will not!"

The Master of Stone leaned back in her chair and eyed the little girl.

"Why is that?"

"You're mean!"

The master's face colored but she didn't argue, and even Marsh had to admit the girl had a point. After a moment, the master stood and moved to an open space just beyond the chairs.

"I might be mean," she said, "but I can show you how to do this."

She moved her hand, pulling stone from the wall and reshaping it into a rocking horse. Aisha eyed it carefully and then folded her arms across her chest.

"So?" she asked, doing her best to sound unimpressed.

The Master of Stone frowned.

"And this..."

Aisha refused to turn around, but Marsh watched in

wide-eyed amazement. She had to admit, the woman deserved the title of master. Stone clicked and clattered as small squares of it detached from the walls and floor, stacking one on top of the other to create the shape of a bird, its huge tail spread behind it. Aisha resisted the clacking for several heartbeats before she peeked cautiously under her arm and saw the bird.

Once she knew the little girl was looking, the Stone Master waggled her fingers, making the bird shake from side to side. Marsh saw a sly grin cross Aisha's face.

Uh oh.

At her thought, Roeglin turned his head to watch the child, and they were both in time to see when she raised her small hands and focused. Darkness engulfed the blue of her eyes, and she curled her fingers. Across the room, the bird's tail started to curl as well, the stone tiles clattering down the length of each feather to rearrange themselves.

From the look on the Stone Master's face, this was unexpected. She frowned, flicking her fingers to return a tile to the wall, and Aisha made a snatching motion with her hand, stopping the piece in mid-air. The girl bounced excitedly.

"Yes!" She skittered the piece back to where she'd placed it.

"Oh, really?" the master challenged, and let all the tiles collapse to the floor.

"No fair!" The girl picking them all up and continued building her picture.

"Oh, no you don't," the stone master told her and made a sweeping motion with her hand.

Aisha wailed as the pieces scattered to their points of

origin and blended back into the stone. She glared at the master.

"Dat was mean!"

"Want to play tomorrow?"

The kid considered the offer and finally managed a nonchalant shrug.

"Sure," she said. "If I'm not busy."

"You bring the cookies, and I'll bring the milk," the stone master said, but Aisha shook her head.

"Nope. *You* bring the cookies."

The stone master shook her head.

"Nope. It's your turn."

"But..." Aisha glanced over at Brigitte, who gave the child a nod. "Fine."

The Master of Stone returned to her seat.

"Now that that's settled," she said and looked at Marsh, "you might want to—"

Tamlin had already moved to catch his sister as she slid sideways, and Roeglin was at his side to scoop the little girl into his arms. The Master of Stone turned to the Master of Shadows.

"I'll instruct her. That much power is...impressive."

"But she doesn't like you," Tamlin protested. "She's going to make things difficult."

"We'll come to an understanding," the master reassured him and turned away. She glanced at one of the shadow guards standing behind the Master of Shadows. "I have some experience with difficult students."

The man's face flushed and his jaw worked, but he said nothing. Marsh figured that was a story she'd have to discover at another time. With Aisha's training settled, the

Master of Shadows turned to Marsh. He indicated Roeglin.

"Master Roeglin will be your instructor for shadow magic," he told her and turned back to the Master of Stone. "I need an instructor in beast magic."

"That will be me," the Master of Beasts replied before his fellow master could utter a word. "With the masters' permission, I will stay at the fortress and begin in the morning."

He glanced at Marsh.

"I think there is much we can teach each other." He glanced over at where Aisha was sleeping in Roeglin's arms. "I'll teach the little one as well."

The Master of Shadows nodded and looked at Marsh.

"Are we agreed?"

"And Tamlin?"

"Brigitte and Roeglin will share the responsibility. I think the boy will need the extra challenge."

"The *boy* is right here, you know," Tamlin muttered, glowering at the master.

"Then he knows who his first teachers are, doesn't he?" the Master of Shadows retorted. "Your first round of testing will happen seven cycles from now. Do either of you have any questions?"

Stunned beyond words at the early testing date, Marsh shook her head. The master studied her for a moment and then nodded.

"Now there is the matter of the attacks." He raised his head and looked at the Master of Stone. "How many have you suffered in the last month?"

"One a week, two in the week just gone," she answered,

glancing at Roeglin and Marsh. "We'd have lost a patrol if your envoys hadn't intervened."

"Do we know where they're coming from?"

"We've identified two points of entry and closed both. There is at least one more."

"They use portals," Marsh said. "I saw them open one to let the shadow monsters in. They escaped through it too."

"But we can't tell if they use those to enter or open them once they've arrived," Roeglin added, and Marsh knew he was right.

From the looks on the masters' faces, it was not welcome news.

"We need to find the source."

That comment came from the Master of Beasts, and the Master of Shadows sighed.

"And to do that we need to hold the caverns long enough to discover where they're taking the people they steal."

All eyes turned to Marsh as they realized this was exactly the plan she'd mentioned before.

"How did you know?"

At the Shadow Master's question, her skin turned cold and the color drained from her face.

"I didn't," she said, then repeated herself in the face of the disbelief in their expressions. "It was the only thing I could think of in order to get our people back."

"And you really think that's possible?"

"I have to try." Even Marsh could hear the stubbornness in her voice.

She wasn't going to consider what would happen if she discovered there was no way to follow the raiders back to their source. She wasn't even going to consider that it was an impossibility. After all, the ones they'd already encountered had seemed human enough—and if they were human, they had to have somewhere to call home. All they had to do was discover where that was.

She was just about to say as much when she heard the sound of running footsteps from outside the Shadow Master's office. Seconds later, someone was pounding on the door.

"*Entré!*"

The soldier who stepped into the room spared a startled glance for the Shadow Master's company before focusing on the monastery's head.

"The road..." he said, breathing hard. "The glows..."

The Master of Shadows was out of his seat and moving toward the messenger.

"Show us," he ordered. "Quickly, now!"

And the man gave him one startled look and then ran out the door. To Marsh's surprise, the master didn't protest the pace but broke into a run to keep up, the other masters racing in his wake as they took the stairs at the end of the corridor. Marsh followed, and before long they had reached the top of a tower overlooking the road leading to the trade route that passed the cavern's entrance.

It was marked by a long line of glows, the trail branch barely visible at its end. The soldier stopped and pointed to the road.

"We had a rider," he gasped, indicating the trail before turning to face the Master of Shadows. "Man said the trail started going dark. Said he heard screams from the back of his caravan and then everyone ran. He was riding point.

When he went back, the caravan master told him to bring word. Master, we have to help them."

To Marsh's surprise, the Master of Shadows shook his head, his eyes turning dark gray streaked with flashes of silver.

"It's too late."

"Master?"

The head of the monastery indicated the trail, gazing in the direction.

"Ring the bells and bar the gates. Gather the shadow guard in the main hall. They have taken the road. Send me Masters Herenvel and Kaspar. I need shadow speakers on the walls."

His eyes were still a swirling mix of black and silver when he turned away from the cavern and moved for the stairs, touching the Master of Stone on the shoulder as he passed.

"I must apologize, but I think you might be staying longer than planned. I trust you left your best in charge?"

"Master Voclain," she replied, and Marsh saw some of the tension leave the Shadow Master's shoulders.

"Very good. Will you join our council of war?"

He included the Master of Beasts in his invitation, and the man nodded.

"It would be our pleasure."

Marsh barely noticed when they left the tower, although she was aware when the space around her grew less crowded. She had looked beyond the Master of Shadows and out into the cavern, noting the long line of glows and the few that indicated the trade route, but that wasn't why she kept staring into the dark.

No. She knew why the Master of Shadows had called for the bells to be rung and the shadow guard gathered. The glows indicating the main trail were going out one at a time until the shadows bled over where the trade route had once been clearly marked. She saw that it was worse than that. Far worse.

As she looked out across the cavern, Marsh saw the trail of lights growing shorter as shadows swallowed the road leading to the fortress. On one side of her, Tamlin took her hand. On the other side, Roeglin drew a sharp breath. Marsh knew they were watching the same thing she was—the glows being extinguished one by one.

Tamlin's grip tightened, and she took her eyes from the vanishing trail long enough to meet his gaze.

"We're going to have to learn really fast, aren't we?"

Marsh lifted her eyes to the trail and nodded.

"Yeah, Tams. You up for it?"

"Brigitte's going to teach me how to use shadow blades," he said, "and you're going to show me shields."

It was news to her, but Marsh didn't argue. Roeglin didn't sound impressed.

"And what am I going to teach you?"

But Tamlin had no doubts.

"Everything," the boy said. "We're gonna need to learn all the things."

"Yeah. *All* the things," Marsh said, breathing a sigh of relief when the shadow stopped its inward creep. "We need to know *all* the things, and then we need to stop them."

Of that, she had no doubt. They had to learn to master their magic, and they had to learn fast. Then they had to find the raiders and stop them, or the Four Settlements were finished. Looking into the encroaching dark, she couldn't stop a shiver from running through her.

The trail of glows leading toward the cavern's edge was shorter, but it was still there. All Marsh could hope for was that it would shrink no farther and they could restore it. She also had to hope Ruins Hall still stood and Kerrenin's Ledge had not fallen by the time they reached them.

No pressure, right?

Footsteps sounded on the stairs, and she turned away from the view in time to see two mages in black robes trimmed with silver emerge into the tower. They were followed by four mages in black leather armor.

"You need to clear the tower."

"We're leaving now," Roeglin told them. "May the threads be kind."

"And your sleep be deep."

It was as close to an order as Marsh had ever heard, and Marsh did not argue when Roeglin signaled for her and the children to follow him from the tower. Up until that moment, she hadn't noticed the silent presence of her four guards. Now she did.

"What are you going to do?" she asked, and Lennie gave her a fierce grin.

"Exactly what the cavern founder wanted," she said. "I'm going to hole up here until the baby's born, and then I'm going to go and kick some raider ass."

"And the rest of us will be guarding you and Master Roeglin, as Monsieur Gravine hired us to do. You have yet to give him the Shadow Master's answer."

Marsh took a deep breath and followed Roeglin down the stairs, aware of Tamlin walking at her side. Aware too that her future was not going to be what she'd thought it would. Gone were her plans to be a seeker of ancient artifacts, but she didn't regret their loss. What she was planning now was so much bigger than searching for clues to the past.

Now she had to find a way to preserve both the present and future, and looking at those descending the stairs with her, Marsh knew she was in good company. Together they would drive the raiders back and find the ones they'd taken, but first, they needed to master the skills they had and take back the cavern they were in—and they had to do it fast.

All she could hope was that they'd be fast enough and the four settlements would still be there when they reached them.

AUTHOR NOTES - CM SIMPSON

Firstly, THANK YOU. For picking up this book, and for reading to the author notes... which, by the way, are really, really hard to write. I am currently tempted to sneak a short, short story in here, because it would be fun, but I'm pretty sure Michael would notice.

However, if any of you would LIKE to see... er, no?

Wow. The man can yell....

Kidding – he hasn't seen these yet, and I'm nervous so I'm poking the bear... Not... that Michael is a bear, okay? Soooo...perhaps I'd better change feet, and maybe talk a bit about the book and the characters, and what a blast it's been to write it—because it has been; it really has.

I love stories. I love creating them, writing them, and discovering the worlds and people hiding out in my head. Okay, I admit it—most of the time it's me hiding out in my head, and the characters and stories just happen to be there when I arrive—and, sometimes, just occasionally, I like to take a walk in someone else's universe and discover the amazing people and places that exist there.

It's always a privilege when I am invited or allowed to do this, and I'm always honoured when someone is kind enough to let me. Thank you, Michael. It's quite a universe you have here—and I have loved the time I've so far spent in this small corner of it. And thank you Amy, L.E. and C.M.

Who knew there were so many mushrooms beneath Paris? Or creatures?

And the people... well... I hope they've kicked a sufficient amount of ass. Trust me, they're planning on kicking a whole lot more.

The last week has been a bit of a whirlwind, as I've been writing Book 4 for this series, but also balancing editing for Books 1-3 with homeschooling my youngest and working out covers and all the rest of the things that go with being a writer. Today, for instance, was spent editing this book, and putting the next to last pieces together for its release. Tomorrow, I get to head out to spend some time with my family, who, for some reason are still talking to me...

Actually, they're a funny bunch; the busier I get, the more they invade the writing corner and hug me. There are days I think I need a box I can stuff them all into so I can have fifteen minutes' peace, but then it would be too quiet, and I'd get nothing done, anyway. They keep me sane, while driving me absolutely crazy.

And they're not the only ones, I've met some of the very nicest people while putting these stories together, both in the KGU and Age of Magic Facebook groups, and in the amazing teams that support the creation of these books. I have the best editors in the world, and the most scary-awesome Beta and JIT teams... and a cover artist whose work I love. *And* I get to write stories set in the Age of Magic? Hell, yes! Sign me up.

Oh, wait... you did already... and you what?

When's the next book coming out?

Soon, I promise. Soon.

Now, go bug Michael, while I get it done.

Thanks for having me, for reading this far, and for enjoying this universe as much as I do.

I look forward to catching youall on the flip.

If you want to catch me sooner, you can find me on my blog, or on Twitter, Facebook, or Pinterest, or you can sign up for my newsletter.

Whatever you decide, thank you for sharing this part of my journey.

AUTHOR NOTES - MICHAEL ANDERLE

FEBRUARY 24, 2019

THANK YOU for not only reading this story but these *Author Notes* as well.

(I think I've been good with always opening with "thank you." If not, I need to edit the other *Author Notes*!)

RANDOM (*sometimes*) THOUGHTS?

I'm going to riff on what C.M. Simpson talks about (well, part of what she talks about), and that is the voices and characters in our heads.

Especially when we are growing up.

For a long time in my life, I assumed everyone had these episodes of activity in their heads. So, imagine my surprise (and new understanding) when I realized I was the one listening to the story in my head, and others had no comprehension why I wasn't listening to them speak to me.

Didn't others have these troubles? Didn't others have characters talk to them when their father was displeased, and they couldn't focus on their father because two tiny elves just started a fight on his shoulders while they were trying to look meek and mild?

Apparently not.

He didn't appreciate my smirk that slipped out, I don't think.

"But I *was* listening!" I would argue. Then my eyes would look at his shoulder to see if the elves would peek out.

I think I got grounded three extra days for those damned elves.

AROUND THE WORLD IN 80 DAYS

One of the interesting (at least to me) aspects of my life is the ability to work from anywhere and at any time. In the future, I hope to re-read my own *Author Notes* and remember my life as a diary entry.

Las Vegas, NV USA

Right now, my wife is watching the Oscars as I type these *Author Notes*. The Divine Miss M just performed a song, and I'm fighting a splitting headache.

I'm reminded, as I'm staring at the tv in the other room, that one year ago we did not have that tv in my household, and my wife was watching the Oscars on YouTube TV.

On an iPad.

She missed the last ten minutes because of a screw up on YouTube TV, and it killed the Oscars feed to the iPad. My nice world, at that moment, *ended* in our household.

Thanks a lot, Google. YouTube TV cost me over a thousand dollars to make sure she never missed ten minutes of the Oscars again.

Happy wife, happy life.

It seems money can *buy happiness.*

FAN PRICING

$0.99 Saturdays (new LMBPN stuff) and $0.99 Wednesday (both LMBPN books and friends of LMBPN books.) Get great stuff from us and others at tantalizing prices.

Go ahead. I bet you can't read just one.

Sign up here: http://lmbpn.com/email/.

HOW TO MARKET FOR BOOKS YOU LOVE

Review them so others have your thoughts, and tell friends and the dogs of your enemies (because who wants to talk to enemies?)... *Enough said ;-)*

Ad Aeternitatem,

Michael Anderle

https://www.facebook.com/OriceranUniverse/
https://www.facebook.com/TheKurtherianGambitBooks/

BOOKS BY MICHAEL ANDERLE

For a complete list of books by Michael Anderle, please visit:

www.lmbpn.com/ma-books/

All LMBPN Audiobooks are Available at Audible.com and iTunes

To see all LMBPN audiobooks, including those written by
Michael Anderle please visit:

www.lmbpn.com/audible